PENGUIN BOOKS
THE OTHER CHILD

Susi Fox is also the author of bestselling psychological thriller *Mine*, which was shortlisted for the 2019 Davitt Award. Susi is a GP specialising in relationship and family therapy, with a focus on Internal Family Systems. She lives in the Macedon Ranges with her family.

THE OTHER CHILD

SUSI FOX

PENGUIN BOOKS

PENGUIN BOOKS

UK | USA | Canada | Ireland | Australia
India | New Zealand | South Africa

Penguin Books is part of the Penguin Random House group of companies
whose addresses can be found at global.penguinrandomhouse.com

Penguin Random House UK,
One Embassy Gardens, 8 Viaduct Gardens, London SW11 7BW

penguin.co.uk

First published in Australia by Penguin Books 2026
First published in Great Britain by Penguin Books 2026
001

Copyright © Susi Fox, 2026

The moral right of the author has been asserted

Penguin Random House values and supports copyright.
Copyright fuels creativity, encourages diverse voices, promotes freedom
of expression and supports a vibrant culture. Thank you for purchasing
an authorized edition of this book and for respecting intellectual property
laws by not reproducing, scanning or distributing any part of it by any
means without permission. You are supporting authors and enabling
Penguin Random House to continue to publish books for everyone.
No part of this book may be used or reproduced in any manner for the
purpose of training artificial intelligence technologies or systems. In accordance
with Article 4(3) of the DSM Directive 2019/790, Penguin Random House
expressly reserves this work from the text and data mining exception

Printed and bound in Great Britain by Clays Ltd, Elcograf S.p.A.

The authorized representative in the EEA is Penguin Random House Ireland,
Morrison Chambers, 32 Nassau Street, Dublin D02 YH68

A CIP catalogue record for this book is available from the British Library

ISBN: 978–1–405–93556–2

Penguin Random House is committed to a sustainable future
for our business, our readers and our planet. This book is made from
Forest Stewardship Council® certified paper.

For Dad

Your task is not to seek for love, but merely
to seek and find all the barriers within yourself
that you have built against it, and embrace them.
—Rumi

1

THREE AND A HALF YEARS EARLIER

FINDINGS INTO DEATH WITHOUT INQUEST [cont.]

Deceased: Baby BD

Cause of death: 1a: DROWNING

CIRCUMSTANCES IN WHICH THE DEATH OCCURRED (cont.)

11. Both LD and AD were aware that the pool gate had been faulty for some years. The gate had been earmarked for repair; however, this had not occurred prior to the time of BD's death. LD recalls securing the pool gate closed with a heavy pot plant upon exiting the pool enclosure on the morning of BD's death, as was their common practice. LD believed she had closed the back sliding door upon returning inside the house.

12. LD had been experiencing difficulty with insomnia leading up to the day of BD's death. LD was unable to definitively confirm that she had taken mirtazapine the morning of BD's death; however,

she confirmed that she had previously taken a mirtazapine tablet on several mornings when she had been unable to sleep the night prior and that it was possible she had done so on this occasion. A mirtazapine blister pack was noted by police on the kitchen bench beside a glass of water, and a blood test subsequently confirmed the presence of mirtazapine in LD's and BD's bloodstreams.

13. LD gave BD lunch followed by a breastfeed at approximately 12 noon, then placed BD in his cot in his bedroom at the front of the house for his lunchtime nap at about 12.30 p.m. LD lay down on the couch and fell asleep. BD's lunchtime naps were usually of 1–2 hours duration.

14. On waking at 3.30 p.m., LD entered BD's bedroom and noted that he was no longer in his cot. LD reported that BD had been able to self-extricate from his cot for a period of approximately four weeks prior to his death.

15. LD checked through the house and noted that the back sliding door was open, offering direct access from the house to the pool enclosure. AD reported that he and LD were in the habit of leaving the back door open on hot days for the breeze; however, they were always careful to supervise BD at these times as there is direct access to the street via the side of the house.

16. LD reported that she found the pool gate wide open when she entered the pool enclosure. It was subsequently noted by police attending the scene that the gate had been propped ajar with a pot plant. Both AD and LD were unaware of how the pot plant came to be in the position of propping the gate open, rather than its usual position of securing the gate closed.

THE OTHER CHILD

17. When LD entered the pool enclosure, she saw a shape at the bottom of the pool and jumped into the water, retrieving a body and identifying it as her son BD. She subsequently commenced CPR, calling emergency services at 3.45 p.m.

2

SIX DAYS EARLIER

'Hey, Alex, seen my work badge?' I call to my husband as I fumble in vain through the oversized handbag that doubles as my work bag.

'Try the nursery.' His voice echoes down the hall. 'I'll check the car.'

My mobile vibrates in my pocket. *Caesarean, category 3*. Not an emergency, but the sooner I get to work, the sooner we can get the operation started.

I hurry into Charlotte's room. The décor is minimalist in style, with sparse beige furniture and few decorative features, so it only takes a moment to scan all the surfaces. No sign of my badge. I rush through our bedroom, the living room and the kitchen to the back of the house. My study, in contrast to the nursery, is cluttered with an eclectic mix of objects stretching far into my past: the wooden knick-knack box from travels in Thailand, my trophy from Under 10s athletics, a leadlight candleholder that was a 21st birthday present from a friend. There's no sign of my work badge in here, either. Dammit.

I rush to the front door, then pause as I see Alex speaking to our next-door neighbour. He's at the chest-high hedge separating our houses, his arms gesticulating wildly. My throat tightens. I do not want to engage with her right now.

Instead, I step back into the nursery beside the front door. On the floor, spread out on a cot mattress, Charlotte is playing with her hands. Her wide baby-blue eyes, framed by her silky brown hair, meet mine, and I melt.

The front door closes with a clang. From behind, Alex taps my shoulder. I turn, and he's holding my work badge up to my face.

'Where was it?'

'Passenger seat.'

'Thanks,' I reply. 'What's with the neighbour?'

'Karla?' He shakes his head. 'She was trying to give me parenting advice. I couldn't believe it.'

'What did you tell her?'

'I told her where to go, of course.' He kisses my forehead. 'First week back is always rough. Anything else I can do to help?'

My eyes fix on Charlotte. 'Do you think she knows when I'm not here?'

'She sleeps most of the day,' he says, 'and then, by the time she wakes for her evening feed, you're home again. Try not to worry. I've got this.'

My mind flicks back through the past twelve weeks – his adoration of Charlotte, his diligent care of her. Yes, he's got this.

My phone vibrates again in my pocket. I tug it out. *Caesarean, category 2.* Is this a second operation, or has the previous one just been upgraded? Either way, I can't justify being late.

'Gotta go.' I give Alex a swift peck on the lips, then kneel down beside Charlotte and kiss her forehead. 'Be good for your daddy, baby girl.'

I survey the familiar scene: the neatly placed designer nursery furniture, Alex with a reassuring smile on his face as he stands tall beside the doorframe that still bears the faint notchings of his childhood growth, Charlotte cooing excitedly on the mattress at my feet. Everything is as it should be. So how, then, am I to make sense of the trepidation I'm feeling?

Alex places a soothing hand on my shoulder. 'I totally get it, babe. It was always going to be hard for you going back to work and leaving her with me. Separation anxiety is a real thing. But, please, trust me. I promise everything will be all right.'

My mouth clamps shut. It's hard not to imagine the million ways things could go wrong.

My phone beeps with another message from my registrar, Devan. *How far away are you?*

I look down to text him back. *Be there in 15, okay?*

Perfect, he replies almost immediately. *The category 3's been upgraded.*

I grab my bag. 'You'll call me straight away if there are any issues at all?'

His eyes crease with concern. 'Of course I will.'

The words are a balm to the ache inside me. I step back and kneel beside Charlotte, rub her baby-soft hair.

'Bye, darling girl. Mummy's going to work.' Charlotte's eyes are bright as they meet mine. I turn to Alex. 'I trust you. Really I do.'

'I'm glad,' he says. 'You know you can always count on me.'

3

After a brief lull, the ward is chaos. Devan and I have only just completed the emergency caesar that was escalated to a category 2, but another – category 1 this time – has just been called. Standing at the nurses station, I check the baby's heart trace on the monitor, almost a flat line with deep, wide dips after each contraction. It's not looking good. We need to get this second baby delivered, and fast.

An emergency code booms from the loudspeakers as the orderlies push the mother to the lifts on a trolley. At this point, for me, it's faster to take the stairs. My breast pads are soggy, pressing against my sore nipples, but there's no time to change them as I scale the stairs two at a time back down to the operating theatres. Pulling a fistful of tissues from my pocket, I shove a few into each side of my bra, hoping that will do for now; it'll soak up some of the dampness at least.

Scrubbing up outside the theatre, I glance at my distorted

reflection in the mirror above the metal sink: chin and neck elongated, making me appear taller than I actually am, limp blonde hair with dark roots I haven't had time to remedy, large black circles under my eyes extending down to my jutting cheekbones. I switch my focus to the Betadine as I smear its golden-brown foam up my arms to my elbows, then over my wrists, the back of my hands, the webs of my fingers, the jut of my thumbs. It's soothing, this ritual; I've known it for years now. The calm before the storm. Inspecting myself in the mirror again, I meet my own gaze and try to curl my chapped lips into a smile. The words of Natalia, my good friend and colleague, come to mind. *You are the obstetrician in charge. You can do this, Laur.* I smile wider. There. Convincing.

In the operating theatre, the scrub nurse is meticulously laying out the surgical instruments. I dry my hands, then tug on the sterile gown and gloves. My mask is fogging up, hardly unexpected given the urgency of the situation; the mother is already on the operating table, her husband clutching her hand beside her. The anaesthetist has done her job efficiently.

I introduce myself to the couple. 'We'll be as quick as we can,' I say. 'Any questions?' Devan has already talked them through the procedure and I can see they are desperate to get on with it. They shake their heads, their faces tense and white. They've used an egg donor. This child is very much wanted.

The anaesthetist is at the mother's head. Devan is prepping the mother's belly. I nod to the consulting paediatrician waiting in the corner, Elspeth. I've known her for some years, initially from work and later from my mothers group. She is competent and diligent – someone I would trust with the care of my own child.

Everyone is in their places. Except me.

A quiver runs through my body. Although I'm here to support more than supervise – Devan is highly competent – I'm not brimming with personal confidence. My meeting with the medical director earlier this week, on my first day back, hadn't been particularly encouraging. 'You have our full backing,' he'd said. But behind his words, his meaning was clear: *We'll be keeping a close eye on you.*

Drapes cover the woman's belly, exposing only a small area of skin. A hint of stress-induced body odour rises from Devan as he makes his first incision. A thin line of blood pools. I dab it with a white cloth, soaking up the red liquid, aware of the tense silence in the room.

Devan cuts down through the layers: skin, fat, peritoneum. Within a few minutes, we're down to the uterus. It's shiny, rubbery almost, and pinky mauve.

Another incision, and there is the baby, its skin whiter than I would like. Devan reaches his hand in, inserts his cupped fingers beneath the baby's head, and lifts the crown into the hole he has created in the uterus. Within moments, the head is delivered, the baby's body slipping out after. It's only taken three or four minutes of surgery, and she is born. The scrub nurse clamps and cuts the cord while Devan hands the baby to Elspeth, who begins the resuscitation.

Confident in Elspeth's skill, I turn my focus back to the mother. I inspect her soggy womb as Devan delves his hand into its depths, attempting to shear the placenta from its wall. He succeeds and slops it into a silver metal dish where it lies like a chunk of liver. Then he checks the uterine cavity with a white cloth. No bleeding. The uterus is responding to the removal of baby and placenta, contracting spontaneously just as nature designed.

Devan is head down, pressing gauze against the inside of the uterus. I observe him quietly, his thick yet deft hands, his sharp eyes behind his thin-rimmed glasses, his solid, reassuring presence. He'll make a good obstetrician.

'It's going again,' Devan says and something in his tone catches me. When he lifts his hand away, I notice the uterine wall, rough like the outside of a rockmelon, blood pooling fast. Another glance at Devan and I note a furrow between his brows.

'Ergotamine and tranexamic acid. Let's get two units of blood,' I say to the anaesthetist, then to the nurse, 'And a Bakri balloon please.'

People begin to scurry even as a heavy hush settles in the room. The next steps form a flow chart in my mind: the list of procedures to arrest the bleeding, the final intervention being a hysterectomy when bleeding simply cannot be stemmed by any other means.

Devan is still pressing gauze against the uterine wall, a slight fog misting his face shield.

'You've got this,' I say, and his shoulders relax a little.

He lifts the gauze away and inspects the uterus. 'It's easing.' His eyebrows relax as the bleeding begins to settle.

'Great work.' Even though his face is largely concealed by the mask, I can sense his flush of pride at my words. It seems only a fragment of time ago that I was in his position, desperately vying for affirmation, anything to know that my bosses approved of me, that they believed I was good enough to progress in the training program. Now, I am the one in charge, the final stop in the chain of responsibility.

Devan takes the suture from the nurse as I turn my attention to the corner of the room. Elspeth is still immersed in the paediatric resuscitation, placing a tube down the baby's throat. To me, it's not looking good.

'What's the pH?' I ask.

'6.9,' says the nurse assisting Elspeth in a neutral voice. 'We're taking her to the nursery now.'

I head for the parents and crouch down beside them. 'Hello, Mr and Mrs Parnos. I'm Doctor De Vale – Lauren. Your baby is needing a bit of help. The paediatrician will take her up to the special care nursery shortly.'

'She's not crying,' the mother says in a panicked voice.

'They're doing everything they can.'

'Can I see her?'

'They'll try and show her to you on the way to the nursery,' I say, even though I'm not sure that will be possible, but it's clearly what she needs to hear.

The mother presses the fingertips of one hand against her eyes. The father turns his attention to her, lays a palm on her forehead. A flash of memory: Alex, on the day Charlotte was born, being similarly tender with me.

I bring my husband to mind. His beach-blue eyes. His sandy hair. His soft lips that know how to melt me. No wonder I fell in love with him. After the run of unreliable and irresponsible men I had dated, Alex was a dream catch. He was supportive, encouraging. He always texted back promptly with witty responses that made me laugh. He was willing to meet up often, and discussed commitment from early on. He made me feel like I mattered to him. And though I had a sense that things were progressing rather quickly, there were no red flags evident.

The newborn's father is staring up at me. 'Is she going to be okay?' His voice cracks on the last syllable.

'I absolutely hope so. I can't say anything for sure right now. But I'll come up to see you on the ward later today and we can have more of a chat then.'

The baby's health is now the paediatric team's responsibility, but I know that in the days to come, this couple will have questions. I'm not sure of the sequence of events that preceded this caesarean and I will need to check with Devan how this labour progressed, how the baby had been allowed to get to this state before we intervened. Had I been here earlier – if I hadn't misplaced my work badge and spent time bidding Charlotte farewell – could we have started the operation any sooner?

The parents might blame themselves. Or they might blame the hospital, or Devan, or me. Because, as I know all too well, everyone needs someone to blame when things go so very wrong.

Devan enters the tearoom, holding my mobile. 'Call for you,' he says.

It's my mother-in-law, Magdala. 'Lauren. How lovely to finally speak with you.'

We have an interesting relationship, Magdala and me. Sometimes I wonder whether it's related to my own mother walking out on me when I was ten, and sometimes I'm able to appreciate that the challenges most decidedly spring from Magdala herself. Thank god that when it comes to his mother, Alex always has my back.

I step into the empty corridor beside the tearoom and begin to pace the hall. Magdala is still speaking, her voice shrill down the line.

'I've been saying to myself, I haven't spoken with Lauren for so long.'

It doesn't seem to occur to Magdala that she could have rung me before now, that it would be the normal mother-in-law thing to do, particularly after the birth of a grandchild.

She clears her throat, then continues: 'It makes me worry, is something going on?'

I don't know what she's referring to. Alex being a stay-at-home dad while I return to work? My postnatal depression after our first child's birth? Or the fact I took her son away from her? I have a sense she will never forgive me for that.

'I'm sorry, Magdala, I'm not following.'

Her voice has a distinct edge to it. 'I've just spoken with Alex. He has *so much* on his plate. I worry about him. Taking care of a baby is a full-time job. It leaves no time for him to do his work, does it?'

'He and I discussed it. It makes more sense this way around.'

She gives a stifled laugh. 'I'm sure you can imagine how hard it is for him.'

My jaw tightens. 'I don't need to imagine it. I was a full-time mother with Billy, remember?' Magdala doesn't have to speak for me to read her thoughts. She retired from her job in child services five years ago, ostensibly to help out with Billy after he was born. In reality, following her move interstate, we barely saw her or her proffered 'help'.

'I just think my Alex deserves an easier life,' she humphs.

My Alex?

'Yes, Magdala.' I stop in my tracks and give a brief nod to a colleague striding into the tearoom, trying to pretend I'm engaging in a work-related discussion, rather than placating my mother-in-law.

'I told him settling down with a career woman would be a challenge,' Magdala continues. 'All work, no time for family. The job takes priority.'

'What if Alex were a doctor too?'

'Oh, well then . . .' and she's off: how Alex could have done anything at all, but he chose not to do medicine because . . . I cease listening. Deference and respect, I remind myself. It's the only way to deal with my mother-in-law, the rottweiler that threatens to latch onto my ankles before I've even taken a step.

She is still talking. 'So, I can see that me providing extra help is the solution. As long as one of us is with the baby, I'm sure nothing can go wrong.'

I don't take the bait. 'I'd better go.' I head towards the theatre reception and press the green exit button on the wall beside the door.

'I do worry about you, Lauren. Please look after yourself. You must keep yourself right; it's the best thing you can do for Charlotte.'

I exit the theatre, facing a sea of lifts. The doors open on the centre one, and Elspeth steps out, a worried expression on her face.

'Just a minute please, Magdala.' I press the mute button and hold up my hand to stop Elspeth. 'How is she?'

'Alive,' Elspeth says with a frown, 'but sheesh, advanced-maternal-age births give me a heart attack. Makes me wonder if I might have to rethink my pro-stance on egg donation.'

I nod, recalling Elspeth's willingness to speak with me about using an egg donor to get pregnant, and the measured encouragement she'd given me when I was looking to get pregnant with Charlotte. And she'd been so thoughtful after Billy's death. It seems a shame I've hardly caught up with her properly since.

'Let me know how she goes?' I say.

'Will do.' Elspeth nods.

Before I can ask her anymore, Magdala pipes up in my ear. 'Any more concerns, you call me first, you hear? Don't disturb Alex. You can reach out to me anytime. I'm here to help.'

I bet you are. I swivel around. The hall is empty. Elspeth is gone.

Magdala, sadly, is not. 'After all,' she concludes, 'I know my Alex. I know just what he needs.'

4

18 MONTHS EARLIER

Advance Fertility
186 Victoria Street
Mooradon

Dear Ms Walker,

We are writing to inform you that your donated eggs have been placed back on our egg donor waiting list following confirmation that your acute medical issues are now resolved. As discussed during counselling sessions, you will receive a letter from our clinic notifying you if any children are born from your donation, and any donor conceived people born from your donated eggs will be eligible to request access to your identity when they reach eighteen years of age. Also, just a reminder that you are able to withdraw your donation at any time.

Thank you again for your generosity and commitment in donating your eggs, and don't hesitate to reach out to our team at any time in future if required.

Yours sincerely,
Elie Alzein
Donor Recruitment Team
Advance Fertility

5

It's nearing the end of the afternoon's gynaecology clinic when I head for the expressing room, a tiny makeshift office crammed with boxes and files at the back of the ward. I pull out the breast pump and lock the door behind me. Placing the cups over my swollen breasts, an image of Billy's limp body flashes before me. My firstborn, gone far too soon. The bruises on his chest from CPR. The broken ribs I traced with my fingers in the morgue as I dressed him one last time. A tiny suit, for his funeral. I hadn't known they made suits that small. Coffins, either. I'd felt like I was dressing a doll, not saying goodbye to my baby boy. None of it seemed real.

My heart is beating hard in time with the mechanical sucking of the pump and I shake myself, reminding myself that this is not the past. This is the present. This is about Charlotte. The foreboding I felt this morning has only grown stronger throughout the day. I know I should trust that Alex is keeping a close eye on our baby, but I need some reassurance that Charlotte is completely fine. I haven't heard how she is since this morning.

I flick through the slew of texts I have sent Alex in the last thirty minutes.

Babe, call me. How's Charlotte going?
Could we do a videocall? Let me see her just for a minute, Alex?
Please write back. I need to know she's okay.

I dial his number. No answer. I try again. Nothing. I leave a voicemail this time. 'Just checking everything's okay. I had this feeling . . .' I stop myself. 'I just want to make sure Charlotte is fine.' My voice trails off and I hang up.

The breast pump whines, tugging at my nipple. Rough. Painful. But nothing is coming out. Just like when I was on the mother–baby unit struggling to bond with Billy. I would sit in the leather armchair in my hospital room, huddled over one of these wretched, whirring machines, trying to generate enough maternal feeling to pump oxytocin into my bloodstream, to help release the breastmilk. Even as I wept, the staff reassured me. 'It's okay,' they'd say. 'You do love him. It's just hard to feel it right now.'

Muted voices echo along the corridor. I'm at work, not in the psych ward. Billy is gone. But my daughter, so easy to love, needs me to focus on the task at hand.

I pull out my phone and flick to the photos. Sometimes when I look at pictures of Charlotte it helps with my milk let-down. I scroll through recent videos of her giggling, lying on the grass, rolling on the mattress. The mattress. She was lying on a cot mattress when I said goodbye to her this morning. Could she have rolled off and hurt herself in some way? No, I remind myself – it was a thin mattress. But I can't explain the lack of a reply from Alex. Could he at this very moment be whisking her to the emergency department?

No response from him on my mobile. I try again, texting, then emailing. The pump is emitting a high-pitched squeal as it sucks at my breast, thrusting back and forth, trying desperately to extract milk.

I switch off the pump and call Devan. He picks up straight away. 'Everything okay?'

'I've got to go. I'm worried something's not right at home.' It won't make a difference, me leaving clinic a little early. Devan is more than capable of mopping up the remaining workload. Though I'm well aware this is likely me catastrophising – and perhaps the postnatal anxiety I had with Billy resurfacing – in this moment I can't seem to hold myself back from acting on the impulse to check on Charlotte.

'Course. I've got this,' he says. 'Go.'

6

The harsh December sun beats through the windscreen, outpacing my car's struggling aircon. It can never keep up in summer. And then there's the peak hour traffic. I reach to honk the driver in front of me, too slow to cross the intersection. *Breathe, Lauren* – I catch myself. No need to project my fear onto anyone else.

I pass familiar landmarks: our favourite bakery, the homewares store, the petrol station up the road. As I turn into our cul-de-sac, I heave a sigh of relief. Trees line the street, their canopies casting cooling shadows over the bitumen. Manicured lawns slide up to well-kept houses. The street is empty, save for Karla's sedan outside her stately Edwardian.

As I pull into our driveway behind Alex's car, I regard our place. His childhood home, a Californian bungalow, was gifted to us by his mother soon after we moved in, when she heard we were pregnant. It's neither the style of house nor the type of suburb, if I'm being honest, that I would have chosen, but I'm nonetheless deeply appreciative of his mother's generosity.

As I stumble out of the car, I breathe humid air into my lungs.

'Everything okay?'

I startle at the voice, then turn to see Karla, our next-door neighbour, peering at me from over the low hedge between our properties. Her shiny lipstick glints in the late afternoon sun, offsetting her loose linen blouse. It's rare to see her outside. She's usually perched before her laptop at her front window. I envy her ability to work from home. I've had almost nothing to do with her since we moved into the house a few months before Billy's birth. Then after he was born . . . I don't want to think about that.

I flash her the politest smile I can muster. 'Busy day.'

She leans over the hedge. 'I was hoping to catch you. I heard a lot of crying today.'

'Oh, sorry. Charlotte is getting used to the new routine.'

'You've gone back full-time?'

I picture Alex's plaintive face as he pleaded with me a month or so ago. *Babe, going back to work will be the best thing for your mental health. You know what happened last time around. This is optimal – for all of us.*

'This week,' I confirm. I pull my over-full handbag from the back seat and wipe my forehead. 'My husband is taking care of her.' Why do I feel the need to say this?

Karla raises her eyebrows above her sunglasses. 'It must have been quite a day for both of them. Your baby sounded quite distressed. I was going to reach out, but I got waylaid with work.'

I'd love to brush her off, but I feel a tinge of guilt about the disturbance she's experienced – moreover, that I had once vaguely contemplated taking out an AVO on her. In the height of my paranoia, after Billy was born, I'd felt everyone and anyone was out to get me, and poor Karla, living so close by, had borne the brunt of my suspicions. Since then, I have remained distant. Conscious that my own problems are hardly her fault, I sigh and try to make amends. 'I'm sorry my daughter was bothering you.'

She takes off her sunglasses and tucks them into the front of her blouse so I can see her piercing blue eyes. 'It's not that. I'm relieved to hear she's all right. Colic, I imagine. I was only concerned because she sounded quite distressed, and the screaming seemed to go on for so long. It made me wonder if anyone was with her. Or if they were, why they weren't attending to her.'

I squint. Alex would have contacted me if she'd truly been distressed. And yet, my breath catches as I contemplate the possibility that my return to work might be impacting Charlotte harder than I thought.

'I'd better go check on her,' I say, 'but please let me know if her crying bothers you again.'

Karla's voice is soothing. 'Of course, I'll leave you to it. And take care. Your baby – all the babies – need you.' She gives me a dazzling smile, then waves as she heads to her front door.

Hurrying along the stone path to our verandah, I check my phone. I'm rostered on call for the night, but there's no word from the hospital. No messages from Alex. No reply to my calls, either. A trill of terror flutters at the back of my throat.

I push open the front door – it's unlocked – and nearly trip over the Christmas tree box in the entry way. I right myself. Since we lost Billy, we've avoided decorating the house for

Christmas. I don't have the mental space to contemplate why Alex has made the decision to pull out the decorations this year.

The house is cool, the air less dense in here than outside. It is also silent. Where is Alex? Where is Charlotte?

I dump my bag by the door and rush into Charlotte's room, struck by an unfamiliar citrus scent filling the air. There she is, fast asleep in her cot by the window. I'm instantly relieved; she is okay. I approach her cot, avoiding the floorboards that creak, and lean over the railings. She is alive, and beautiful. She looks content, her sleeping bag clean and correctly fitted, her face peachy in the glimmering light of the night lamp. I watch her for a while, her chest rising and falling, her eyelids fluttering. My heart expands and I know this feeling is love, the kind I'd longed to feel for Billy when he was alive. It had come too late . . .

The nursery door swings further open and there stands Alex with an encouraging grin. 'She's fine.'

I squeeze the wooden rail on her cot. 'I was so worried when you didn't respond to my messages.' This anxiety is different from what I had felt on my first day as a doctor, and different again from the muted panic that came with transitioning from a registrar to a newly qualified obstetrician, just prior to meeting Alex. I know the fear is misguided, but it feels so real and somehow so much worse.

Alex runs a hand over the back of my neck to soothe me. 'I'm sorry I haven't got back to you this afternoon – it's been a bit . . . messy. Projectile vomit. All over her, and me. Look, I'm sorry I worried you, but please don't stress if I don't get back to you straight away. I promise I'll text back as soon as I can. Maybe, if the times when I'm caught up and can't get back to you immediately are going to freak you out, it might be better not to contact me while you're at work. What do you think?'

He's right, of course. I remember his attentiveness to me throughout my pregnancies, his willingness to pop to the supermarket even late at night to satisfy my cravings: smoked oysters, ginger tea, absolutely anything I wanted. And then, Karla's beaming face springs to mind. 'The neighbour next door was just saying she heard Charlotte crying a lot today.'

'What? That's ridiculous.' His eyes widen. 'I was here the whole day. Charlotte was asleep for most of it.' His eyebrows crease. 'Wait. This is Karla we're talking about, right? The neighbour who has nothing better to do but spy on us all?'

I give a small smile. 'The very one.'

He rolls his eyes. 'She's an interfering busybody. Bailing me up this morning, and you this afternoon.' He looks down at Charlotte, a serene expression on her face. He gently caresses her cheek. 'She doesn't look like a baby who's cried all day, right?'

'No.' I stare at her gorgeous, placid face. 'To be honest, I did find it a little hard to believe. Karla must have been exaggerating.'

He shakes his head and places a hand on one of my cheeks. 'Shall I go over and have a word to her?'

'Let's leave it for now,' I say.

'Of course,' he says, pulling me into a warm hug. 'And, oh my god, I have to say, babies can be a lot of work.'

'They sure can.' I relax into his embrace. 'Delivering them can be too.'

He kisses my neck, his lips wet on my skin. 'I can't begin to imagine,' he says. 'You do amazing work, babe. And I'd really love to show you how admiring I am, later.' He smooths my hair away from my ear and nibbles at the lobe. 'I have a lasagne in the oven. It's almost ready. Let's eat soon.'

'Amazing.' My belly rumbles. 'I haven't eaten all day.'

'Oh, god. I hope you aren't forgetting to look after yourself.' His eyes crinkle.

'It was too hectic to think about lunch today. But I'll make sure to find time tomorrow.'

'Okay.' The concern in his eyes settles. 'Then, no wonder you're so tense. Is there anything extra I can do?'

'No,' I say, 'I'm fine. Thank you. Really, I am.'

7

FIVE DAYS EARLIER

Entering the outpatient clinic, I try not to focus on the tinsel strung up on the walls. The silly season and the memories it triggers are all too much given everything else going on. I channel thoughts of Christmas into a far corner of my brain. The ability to divert triggers – Magdala's harsh judgements, my father's angry voice, the challenges of the past – into containers and seal the lids has always served me well, allowing me to focus on what needs to be attended to in the moment. It's a form of suppression, I suppose.

I used the same technique the first week of medical school. After the horror of seeing the rows and rows of bodies laid out on stainless steel trays in the dissection room, I began hyperventilating so intensely that black spots formed in my peripheral vision. I fled to the changeroom, slumped onto a bench, and dropped my head between my knees. I shoved the knowledge that those motionless forms had once been living humans into one of the boxes in my brain. From then on, cutting into the formalin-soaked flesh of the cadavers each week no longer made me feel like passing out.

I refocus on the clinic room, the desk, the papers before me, the pen in my hand.

The first file on my desk is for Lethabo Matuto, twenty weeks pregnant with her first child. She and her husband greet me with a smile and I'm instantly reminded of why I chose to specialise in obstetrics. Most patients are healthy, well and happy to be pregnant. Seeing them regularly, building a therapeutic relationship with them, and caring for them through their pregnancies as they grow healthy babies is deeply rewarding and often humbling. It's the most joyful work I can imagine. In some small way, it feels like I'm making a difference to the lives of the next generation. Lethabo's pregnancy is going smoothly, her baby growing well. I bid her and her husband farewell with an encouraging smile and check the next file.

Jody Gregor, thirty weeks pregnant. Anxiety. Antidepressants. Four children under the age of six at home. No wonder she's anxious. I call her name in the waiting room.

A small, thin woman, wearing a long skirt and baggy long-sleeved shirt draped over her pregnant belly, gingerly rises to standing. Beside her, a man with a thick neck and ruddy skin hauls himself to his feet. I usher them into my room.

Ignoring the plastic stool by the door, he plonks himself into the padded chair beside the desk and I'm assaulted by the stench of cigarette smoke. Jody eases herself onto the far stool, as if in pain. There could be multiple reasons for this; pregnancy can be uncomfortable. I know that from personal experience. But something in the room feels wrong.

Before I've sat down, the man launches in. 'I'm Mike, her partner. And I'm concerned,' he says, sounding irritated.

'What exactly are you concerned about?'

'The baby is not getting much nutrition. Jody is hardly eating anything. How can my baby grow when her mother's not eating right?' His eyes are hooded as he stares at me.

'And you?' I direct my question to his partner. 'Do you have any concerns?'

Her gaze is downcast and she doesn't look at me when answering. 'I'm really trying to eat.'

'She needs to see someone about eating more,' Mike says. 'She doesn't try hard enough.'

The skin prickles on my forearms. Funny, it's the same involuntary response I've had every time I've thought about returning to work these past few months.

'Let's check the baby,' I say. 'I'll need to do an examination. I'm going to ask you, sir, to wait outside.'

Mike glances over at Jody, then back to me. 'Fine.' He heads for the door.

The catch in my breath releases. At least I've bought a little time. I direct Jody to the examination couch and help her climb onto it.

'So, how are things at home?'

'Okay.' Lying on her back on the couch, staring at the ceiling, she presses her lips together.

'Sometimes when we're under stress, it can be hard to eat.' Her baby is already measuring small for its age. But that isn't my main concern. 'Just to let you know, I'm not here to judge. And I'm not going to force you to eat. It would be helpful to know how stressful things are at home, so I can help you get the support you deserve.'

From the pillow, her foal-like eyes meet mine, brown and forlorn.

'I know I should be eating more,' she says. 'It's just so busy at home with the other kids. I really didn't need any more. I didn't plan this one . . .' Her voice trails off.

'How did you make the decision to go ahead?' I try to keep my voice casual, curious, as I listen to the galloping of her baby's heart with the fetal doppler.

She covers her eyes with one forearm, and I see them, the faint tan fingerprint bruises across the thin line of her bone.

'Mike doesn't believe in abortion.'

'How about contraception after this baby?'

'He doesn't agree with that, either.'

My insides are heavy. Counselling is beyond my scope of practice, but I know what I need to say. 'I'm not allowed to tell your husband anything without your express permission.' I assist her into a sitting position. 'I'm wondering if you ever feel scared at home?'

She stares at her belly, now concealed by her loose top. 'Yes.' Her thin hands are shaking on the couch. 'A fair bit.'

'It's okay,' I say. 'I'm here to help.'

She shakes her head. 'No one can help.'

I close my eyes ever so briefly. I had thought that too, when I had been struggling to bond with Billy. *No one can help.* After all, my thinking went, it was *me* who was failing, who wasn't feeling for her baby what a normal mother should. *I* was the problem, so the only person who could help me bond with Billy was myself. I simply couldn't fathom the point of discussing my difficulties with anyone else.

After weeks of Alex begging me to explain what was wrong, I finally disclosed my shameful secret. His face sank. 'I just knew there was something bothering you,' he'd said. 'We'll tell your GP. She'll know what to do.'

I'd begged him not to, but he'd insisted. And of course he was right; it did help a little, to open up. But even my GP's reassurances that difficulties bonding with your baby were common, that there was nothing wrong with me, weren't enough to stop my brain from freefalling into anxiety. Is that what is happening to me now? Are my excessive concerns about Charlotte's wellbeing a recurrence of my mental illness? But I'm not making them up – my neighbour's words from yesterday: Charlotte, crying, for several hours . . .

Jody is staring wide-eyed up at me. I steel myself, pushing my fears to the far corners of my mind, then open my mouth, confident in my words. 'I know someone brilliant who sees women in your situation regularly. How would you feel about meeting her now?'

Jody swivels towards the door, concern etched across her face.

'I can have her here in a jiffy, and she'll come in via the back. As far as Mike is concerned, you're in here being examined by me.'

Jody nods a cautious consent. As she rises from the couch, I text Natalia, my closest confidant in the hospital, and, as it happens, the obstetric unit social worker. Natalia knows everything about my life, including everything that has gone wrong. If a woman can trust anyone, it's her.

Family violence. Patient's partner is in the waiting room. Any chance you could see her quickly now?

Course – be right there. How's your first week back been btw?
Could've been worse. Time for a coffee later?
Sounds good. Rose garden 2 p.m.?
Yep. See you soon x
Hugs, she writes, and warmth floods me.

Jody takes a seat beside my desk, her hands folded over her belly.

'Our obstetric social worker is on her way. Her name is Natalia. She'll ask you a few quick questions, discuss options with you,' I say. 'Your partner won't know you've seen her and anything you tell her will be confidential. I'll see you straight after, then I'll bring Mike back in here to discuss the pregnancy. I won't tell him anything you've told me, either. How does that sound?'

The lines in her forehead smooth a fraction as she gives a nod. I shift slightly in my chair to loosen the guilt I carry inside about Billy.

'Everything is going to be all right,' I say to Jody in my calmest voice, even as I find it hard to fully believe myself.

Natalia and I both like the rose garden; its heady scent is always a relief after the antiseptic sterility of the hospital. We often meet in its walled garden, or at least we used to, before my leave of absence. Natalia has been one of my biggest supporters over the years, right through my training and into consultancy. I know I can rely on her for anything, and I trust she'll always be there for me, no matter what.

By the time I stumble under the archway, Natalia is already seated beside a tray holding two coffees. She's chosen our favourite park bench beside the climbing rose. Framed by short-cropped cinnamon-coloured hair, her elfin face seems thinner than I remember. But as soon as I settle myself beside her, the tension in my core dissipates.

'Must be something serious if you're taking time out of clinic for a coffee.' She elbows me gently as she passes me a cup. 'That woman. Poor thing.'

'I know.' I shake my head. 'What was the outcome?'

'She's coming back to see both of us next week.' She sighs. 'She's left him twice already. Each time he beat her so badly, she ended up in emergency. The last time, he told her she deserved it because she'd had lunch with a male friend.'

I roll my eyes. 'Some men. Geez.'

'Ever wonder why I'm a lesbian?' Her eyes twinkle with laughter.

'Ha. There are *some* good ones, you know.'

'I know.' She grins. 'You're lucky you bagged yourself one of them.'

I crinkle my nose. 'That's what I wanted to talk to you about.'

'Alex? What's up?'

Feeling uncomfortable, I clear my throat. 'I don't think Alex is telling me the full truth about how Charlotte has been coping with me going to work. He's trying to protect me, I suppose.'

'What do you mean?'

'Apparently Charlotte was crying a lot yesterday. The next-door neighbour stopped me when I got home after work.' I repeat Karla's words.

'What did Alex say?'

'He said Charlotte hardly cried at all.' My guts curl in on themselves. 'I was on call last night. I was exhausted, and

Charlotte seemed fine when I checked on her, so . . . I didn't see the point in making a fuss. But I hate being away from her.' I reach for one of the flesh-coloured roses beside me, running my fingertips across its soft petals. 'Flashbacks of Billy, I guess. I've been leaving clinic early to race home every day this week, just to make sure Charlotte's okay.'

'Do you feel better when you see her?'

'I mean, yes. But I can't keep doing it forever.'

'And she's always okay when you get home, right?'

Heat sears my face. 'Well, yes.'

'What does Alex say about how she's been getting on when you're not there?'

'He says she's fine. She sleeps most of the day.'

Natalia rubs a smudge of coffee froth from her upper lip. 'It sounds like Charlotte is more than all right. You know it's only natural to be anxious about going back to work.'

My body softens at her assurances. Natalia knows babies and she has a good radar. If she trusts Charlotte is okay, she must be. 'So, you think I should just ignore what the neighbour said?'

She takes another swig of her coffee. 'This neighbour – is she the same one you were talking about applying for an AVO on a few years ago?'

I clutch the warm cup between my palms. I know I was overly anxious back then, verging on delusional. Every time I had taken Billy out for a walk in the pram, I believed I could feel Karla's eyes watching me from her front window. Although in reality I'd rarely caught sight of her, I had persuaded myself I could see her permanent outline behind the blinds. After a while, I had refused to leave the house during the daytime, only taking Billy for walks in the darkness of night. And even then, I had imagined her observing me.

I cringe at the memory of Alex's and Magdala's unsettled expressions as they had listened to me venting my fears about our neighbour. After a time, they had insisted I see a psychiatrist, who had strongly suggested hospitalisation and antidepressants. Even though I'd initially been horrified at the suggestion, and ashamed to have become so unwell without being aware of my own mental state, I'd felt I had little choice but to agree.

Thank god I began to feel better during the admission. By the time I returned home, my hypervigilance about Karla had evaporated. I could see how desperately paranoid I had become – how, by focusing all my energy on the next-door neighbour, I had been avoiding the very thing that terrified me most: that I had failed to bond with my baby boy.

'Yes, same neighbour.'

Natalia tips her head. 'Remind me, she's how old?'

'Maybe mid-thirties? Single, no kids.'

'So, she probably doesn't have much experience with how much babies cry or how upset they can sound. As opposed to Alex. I don't think you need to worry about what she is saying.'

'I guess not.'

'Do you think it would be a good idea for you to talk to someone?'

'I'm okay,' I say quickly.

When I was finally discharged from the psych ward, the psychiatrist wanted me to continue taking the antidepressants she'd prescribed, to help me sleep, among other things, as she believed my anxiety and difficulty bonding with Billy were in part related to sleep deprivation. I hated the way the medication made me feel, but I played along, took the tablets for another week or so and went to several follow-up appointments. After a few months, the psychiatrist seemed happy with my progress and was willing to lengthen our time between sessions. I never told her I'd stopped taking the meds and, as I felt fine, I never went back.

Alex was concerned initially, but I told him that the medication had made me too drowsy, so I'd stopped it. I reassured him that the psychiatrist was happy with my progress and didn't want to see me again. At that point, we both believed I was okay, so it was a shock when I became so unwell again after Billy's death. But that time, the stay in the psych ward definitely helped and I was able to get better without needing medication. Now I know that my grief was normal – there was nothing wrong with feeling so overwhelmingly sad after losing my son. So, although I'm aware I need to keep a close eye on my mental health, particularly now, by the same token I'd prefer to manage it without medication where possible. And preferably without interference from other professionals.

Natalia clears her throat. 'Has your obstetrician arranged any psychiatric follow-ups for you?'

'Mmm.' I chug mouthfuls of coffee, paying attention to the sensation of the warm milky froth sliding down my throat. 'At this time of year, it feels especially tough to go to an appointment. You know I find opening up hard enough at the best of times. I just can't put myself through that at the moment.'

She clasps her hand over her mouth. 'God, I'm so sorry. I forgot to reach out for Billy's birthday the other week. How was it?'

'Just like any other day,' I say, as the memory of the first and only birthday he'd had – a celebration full of laughter, balloons and chocolate cake – resurfaces. Four years now. I long for it to get easier, even as I know the awfulness of it will never fully go away.

Natalia swirls her coffee cup in her palm. 'It would be normal for grief to flare again, at this point.'

I squeeze my eyes tightly closed, Charlotte's cherubic face floating to mind. 'I don't think this is grief. It's just – I feel scared.'

'Of course you're worried about Charlotte. That's to be expected. You lost a child. Now you have a new baby. You've gone back to work, and it's just gone Billy's birthday. What you're feeling is completely normal, Laur. You're bound to feel super protective.'

It must be I'm not explaining it properly. Me, developing postnatal depression after failing to bond with Billy. Me, responsible – albeit unintentionally – for his death. And now me, returning to work so soon after my second baby's birth. I am the common denominator here, so what does that mean for my new baby? I desperately don't want to screw it up this time.

'It's more than that, Natalia. I'm scared going back to work this early will harm Charlotte . . . impact our bonding. I'm worried that maybe it already has. She's asleep when I get home. I hardly get to spend any time with her. I don't know if, maybe, there's already a slight disconnection forming between us.' I dip my head. 'Oh, god. I thought I was doing the right thing coming back to work. But, in reality . . .'

'Laur.' She puts her arm around my shoulders, squeezing me tight. 'Of course it's harder to feel as connected now you're not home as much. But your relationship goes beyond how many hours you spend with her. Remember how worried you were initially about using an egg donor – thinking that somehow you wouldn't bond with her as much? No matter how much or how little time you spend with Charlotte, you'll always be her mother. It's a unique bond. No one can take that away from you.'

'I worry she won't be okay if I'm not around as often.' I sniff back the tears threatening to erupt. 'That it'll somehow badly impact her.'

Natalia nods. 'Of course you're concerned about her wellbeing. Because you love her and care about her. And she knows that. But don't forget, she's not alone. Alex is with her. And he's equally as capable of providing her with nurturing and care.'

She's right, of course. Alex is a great parent. Charlotte will be absolutely fine with him. Yet I can't help the tingling fear that courses over my skin like electricity. As Charlotte's mother, the one who birthed her just three months ago, I feel I should be staying home with her. Holding her. Feeding her. Surely, she needs me.

I picture Alex's gleaming smile as he waved me goodbye from the front verandah this morning. Did he head inside straight away? Or did he stay outside and water the garden, make some phone calls?

'He wouldn't leave her to cry, would he?'

'What are you saying, Laur?' she says.

I take a gulp of air. 'Maybe he thought he should teach her to self-soothe now that I'm back at work? That could be why she was crying so much.'

'Wait a sec, Laur. Slow down. I think you're jumping to worst-case scenarios.'

No, I think as I hold my breath, willing the tightness in my muscles to soften. Worst-case scenario would be Charlotte dying too.

Natalia gives my arm another gentle squeeze. 'I think you should speak to Alex. Tell him your fears.'

I fiddle with the lid of the coffee cup. 'I don't want to worry him.' I recall Alex's face each time he'd come to visit me in the white-walled psych ward: his forced smile, his concerned eyes. I didn't blame him for having found it so hard; how could he have understood what it was like for me, attempting to mother a child I felt so disconnected from?

Natalia frowns as she glances at her watch. 'I have to head back. But Alex would want you to share your concerns with him. I know it's hard, but he'd want you to open up.'

'You're right.' I try to smile. 'I'll speak with him tonight. Tell him I'm worried about not having enough bonding time with Charlotte. I'm sure he'll be supportive.'

Natalia holds out her hand for my empty coffee cup, and I pass it to her.

'I know you've got this, Laur,' she says. 'You love Alex. He loves you. You both love Charlotte. He can help you understand that Charlotte will be safe with him. And that it's safe for you to love her.'

What is she implying? That I don't love Charlotte? I shake my head. Geez, I'm overthinking things again. I need to remember that Natalia always has my back.

'You're brave. I know you are,' she says. 'After all you went through with Billy, it's not surprising you're anxious. But trust yourself.'

8

Email to Patrizia Safi, relationship therapist

Friday 14 December

Dear Patrizia,

I apologise for emailing you out of the blue. I know it's been a few years since Lauren and I attended an appointment with you. We both found your session helpful, especially your suggestion about grief rituals. Playing with Billy's train set on a regular basis since then has certainly been helpful, and Lauren and I have been closer now we're able to talk about Billy more.

I'm writing because I've become quite concerned about Lauren and I don't know where else to turn. We ended up having another baby, Charlotte, twelve weeks ago. Lauren has just gone back to work this week. She's been contacting me frequently, convinced something is wrong with Charlotte. And yesterday she mentioned something about our neighbour, the same one she got fixated on last time. I think her postnatal depression might be kicking in again. Would it be possible to book in another session with you as soon as possible?

Regards,
Alex

Dear Alex,

Thanks for your email. I'm glad the appointment was helpful last time. Congratulations on your new baby and I'm sorry to hear what you and Lauren are going through.

I would suggest Lauren see a mental health clinician individually first for assessment and treatment. I'd encourage her to start with her GP, then either a psychiatrist or the mother–baby unit. I'd be happy to see the two of you once Lauren is more stable. Please reach out then and wishing you all the best.

With warm regards,
Patrizia

9

'Don't forget to lock the car.' As I step out into the sweltering early evening heat, the high-pitched voice calling from behind me makes me jump. It's Karla, at the gate of our driveway. 'You never know who might be nearby.'

'You startled me,' I say.

'Everything all right?' She peers at me through her sunglasses.

'Fine.' I give a cursory smile as I haul the esky storing my breastmilk from the boot.

'Are you sure?'

'Absolutely,' I say with all the fervour I can muster. 'My baby didn't bother you today, I hope?'

'She wasn't bothering me yesterday,' she says. 'But, may I ask, if there were things happening that could hurt Charlotte, you'd want to know, right?

'What on earth do you mean?' My shoulders stiffen. 'Is Charlotte okay?'

'Yes, she is. But her wailing went on for hours today as well. It started about the same time as a woman showed up at your house.'

My face burns, and not only from the heat. 'Alex wouldn't leave her crying.'

She raises her eyebrows. 'I keep a pretty close watch on all the comings and goings in this court. And I can promise you, your baby sounded quite distressed. The crying lasted the whole time the woman was there.'

Incredulity thrums through me as I recall both Natalia's and Alex's dismissals of her comments. Even so, I'm driven to sate my curiosity. Trying to conceal my disbelief, I step closer to Karla. 'How long are you saying she was crying for?'

'It went on for several hours. But I can tell you exactly. Let me see. I write *everything* down.'

She pulls an electronic notebook with a maroon cover from the pocket of her jacket and swipes through a few pages.

'*Blue Peugeot arrives De Vale residence, 1.32 p.m. Unknown female driver approaches front door, is let into house.*'

Geez. Maybe Karla *was* watching me with Billy back then.

'*Departs 4.07 p.m.* So, she was there for over two and a half hours.' She looks up at me. 'I heard your baby crying the whole time.'

This all sounds ludicrous. A woman showing up at our front door, staying for hours, and Charlotte crying for the duration? I simply can't believe it. I draw a breath of sticky air into my lungs and try to shut down the anxiety surging within me. I recall Natalia's counsel and remind myself that Alex has never done anything to cause me to doubt his loyalty or his judgement. There must be some simple explanation for this, something that makes sense. The validity of Karla's notes is a good place to start.

'Those are very precise.' I nod at the notebook.

'Indeed. Maybe, I'm a bit obsessive.' Her mouth twists. 'One of the downsides of being a private investigator, I'm afraid. Attention to detail is vital.'

I try to suppress a smirk. Don't tell me Alex and I have been right all these years. I clear my throat. 'I thought you were in marketing.'

'I am now – have been for the last few years. We PIs have a high burnout rate – all those anti-social hours spent watching dodgy characters.' She shakes her head. 'But some habits are hard to break.'

Sweat trickles down my back as I recall my paranoid beliefs about how Karla had been tracking me with Billy. A feeling of grace washes over me. So, I hadn't imagined things after all . . . yet, there'd been nothing malicious in it. Just as my practice of keeping observation charts had spilled into my personal life (the detail in my breastfeeding diaries), so had Karla's work habits carried on.

My legs are heavy with heat. I reach for the top of the hedge to steady myself. Glancing up at Karla's house, I note the gauze curtains drawn across most of the glass and a sheer white blind on the window closest to our home. It's clear she has full view of our front door. So, on the off-chance Karla's observations are accurate, what the hell could Alex have been doing leaving our baby to cry while some unknown woman came to our house?

'I imagine it's hard,' Karla continues, 'going back to work when they're so young.' She has an almost motherly expression of concern. 'Please don't hesitate to reach out if you'd like a hand with anything. Meals, babysitting.'

'Thanks. That's very kind. I'll let you know,' I reply. Despite my new understanding of her background, I remain reluctant to get too close. I don't really know her, after all. It will take some time to shake my ingrained mistrust of her.

She smiles softly. 'Seriously. I know people often say it, but I'm more than happy to help out. Christmas tends to be a quiet time for me.'

'And for us.' I look down. Billy's death will always be tied to the festive season. My beautiful boy.

As Karla goes to replace her journal back in her pocket, it strikes me: there is a gap in my knowledge that her notes may be able to fill. What happened in the few hours before Billy's death as I slept on the couch? I just can't piece it all together.

'That day.' The words emerge from my dry mouth before I have a chance to think them through. 'Did you see anything unusual happen? Anything at all?' Perhaps Karla remembers witnessing something that will jog my memory, help me understand.

Karla looks at me enquiringly.

'Billy's—' I clear my throat.

She gives me a sympathetic smile. 'Let me check.' She begins to swipe back through the pages. Then suddenly, after glancing up at our house, she snaps the notebook cover shut. 'Smells like a summer storm is on its way. I'd better go.'

Confused, I reach out. 'Please – tell me.' As I turn to follow her gaze, our bedroom shutters twist open.

'I've said too much,' she says. 'I don't like to interfere.'

'But . . . I need to know more,' I stammer.

The front door opens. It's Alex.

'Babe, would you like a hand with the esky?'

'Er – yes please, hon,' I say, tripping over my words.

He makes his way down our verandah stairs, holding up his hand in a salute. 'Hello, Karla.'

'Hello, Alex.' Her voice is wary as she takes a step backwards.

'Are you okay, Lauren?' he says, grabbing the esky with one hand and taking my hand with his other.

I nod slowly.

He stares at Karla. 'I told you yesterday, we're not wanting parenting advice.'

'Got it. I'd best be getting home. See you both 'round,' she says with an unreadable expression on her face.

Alex shakes his head as she walks away, then ushers me along the stone steps to our front door. 'That woman,' he says. 'I'm sorry you got stuck talking to her. It looked like you wanted rescuing.'

'Thank you,' I say. Then, 'Is Charlotte okay?'

'She's absolutely fine. But we'd better not wake her. She's only just fallen asleep.'

'Didn't she nap today?'

'She wasn't tired earlier.'

I nod as I step into the cool of the house. Alex heads down the hall to the kitchen and I take the moment to slip into Charlotte's room. It's pitch black inside. How can it be so dark in here when it's still light outside? I head for her cot, bumping into it before I realise – the room has been shifted around.

Stumbling to the wall, I fumble for the light. I dim the setting, then flick the switch. As my eyes adjust to the semi-darkness, I note Charlotte's cot, now in the very centre of the room. Black material covers the glass of her windows. Lying peacefully in her baby sleeping bag, beneath the fish mobile, Charlotte wrinkles her nose and gives a small sneeze.

Alex appears in the doorway. His outlined body, backlit against the hall, is broad and tall in the half-light. He approaches me, his hand slinking round my waist as I stand rigid beside the cot.

I have so many questions for him, but I can't seem to muster the courage to ask them. Instead, I mutter: 'You've moved her room around.'

He steps away from me, adjusting Charlotte's covers ever so slightly. 'I noticed she was bothered by the noise of cars coming and going, so I thought she'd be better off away from the window.'

'But there isn't much traffic in our cul-de-sac.'

'When you're home all day, there's more than you'd think.' He gives me a knowing look.

'And the blinds – have you replaced them?'

He stares at me in apparent disbelief. 'Blackout blinds. We talked about them with Billy, remember?'

I can't recall discussing blackout blinds before.

'I figured they might help her sleep better,' he continues.

'You said she'd been sleeping well these last few days.'

'She has been.'

I pause. 'Did she cry much today?'

'Hardly at all.'

'What do you mean, hardly at all?'

His eyes are wide. 'I don't know – maybe a minute or two when I put her down for a nap just now, but then she fell straight asleep. Why do you ask?'

In an instant, I'm not sure who to believe. Karla had said Charlotte cried for hours. Yet Alex is my husband. I have no reason to doubt him. 'So, who came to the house today?'

He looks at me, confused. 'Do you mean the blind installer?'

Oh. I exhale. 'Were you with Charlotte while she installed the blinds?'

'I let *him* do his job. Charlotte and I hung out in the lounge.' His tone is of muted frustration. 'Are you feeling okay?'

I try to smile. Karla could easily have been mistaken about the gender of the person who came to our house – couldn't she?

'Did it take long?' I ask.

Alex stares at me, a flush creeping up his neck. 'A while, yeah. A couple of hours, I guess, maybe closer to three?' He shakes his head. 'How was your work?' he says then, more kindly.

A tingle of fear runs through my body. 'Fine.' I don't mention the baby with the unsurvivable heart malformations. Nor what Karla had said about there being a female visitor. Not yet. 'Tell me more about your day.'

'It's been wonderful.' He takes my hand and caresses it with his thumbs. 'Charlotte has been doing well.'

'How much did she drink?'

'Exactly the amount you instructed: the last of the expressed breastmilk and, when that ran out, formula top-ups.'

'How could we have run out? I froze bags and bags of it.'

He stares straight at me. 'Oh, god, I'm so sorry, Lauren. I forgot to mention it. There was a power outage yesterday. When I rang the power company, they said they'd sent a letter. It was addressed to you, apparently.'

'I didn't see it.'

'The power was out most of the day. Breastmilk has microbes, right?'

'Yes, but—' Something occurs to me. 'How did you make up the formula if there was no power?'

He gives a quick laugh. 'By chance, I'd boiled a full kettle right before it went out. For my coffee. So, I had cooled sterilised water ready to go.'

'That was lucky, I guess.'

'Very lucky,' he says. '*We're* very lucky, the two of us.' He leans towards me, kisses me on the forehead. 'So lucky to be together and to have this beautiful baby.'

He's talking about Charlotte. And yet, all I can picture is Billy's dead body. My baby. A wave of grief strikes like a tsunami and I stumble against the cot, grasping for the rail, for anything to hold onto.

'Darling,' he says. 'What is it?'

A tear rolls down my cheek and my throat is choked. I can't explain what the matter is. He places his arms around me and squeezes me tight.

'I've got you, babe,' he says. 'What you're doing, it's the right thing. For Charlotte. For our family.'

The words, when they emerge from me, are tiny. 'I didn't do the right thing for Billy.'

'Oh, Lauren.' He hugs me tighter. 'You tried to do the right thing. You tried—'

'And failed.' Owning it now, with him holding me, I lift my head. My vision clears and I can see Alex – my Alex – his eyes full of concern. He's not the villain of my imaginings only minutes earlier. He cares about me. He cares about our daughter. And I know he cared about our son. More than I did.

I take a deep breath. 'I've been very worried about Charlotte. That me going back to work might be affecting our bond. I spoke to Natalia about it today. She said I should talk to you. Then when Karla mentioned the crying yesterday, I got even more worried. And just now, she was saying some more strange things.'

'Oh?' He strokes my hair from the crown to the nape of my neck, just the way I like it.

'She says Charlotte was crying for a long time today as well. That no one was comforting her.'

'She said this just now?' He sounds incredulous.

I nod.

'What else did she say?'

I want to mention Karla's comments about the woman who came to our house today, but the words stick in my throat. Instead, I say, 'She said that the crying went on for hours.'

'Jesus. That's ludicrous. And it doesn't make any sense. Charlotte was awake the whole day and I was with her the entire time. I tried putting her down a few times, but she wasn't tired until just now.'

'Maybe she cried a little bit?'

His hand on the back of my neck tightens. 'Maybe in the first few minutes each time I tried to put her to sleep. But I always pick her up as soon as she starts, and she stops right away. Just like we talked about. Listen, Laur – you know Charlotte's not a crier. I don't know what the neighbour is playing at. I think she might be somewhat unhinged. It has me wondering if you *should* have pursued that AVO.'

I give a weak smile and glance down at Charlotte and am instantly calmed by the serene expression on her angelic face.

He's right – Karla must have been mistaken about the crying. For those unused to it, a baby's wails can really grate, as I recall only too well from Billy's first few months.

'I knew what she was saying couldn't be true. How could a baby cry for so long without you realising? I believe you.'

'I'm glad.' He tucks a few strands of my hair behind my ear. 'But, Lauren . . .' He hesitates. 'You do seem overly anxious. Maybe we should get in contact with someone – your psychiatrist?'

'No!' I say quickly. 'There's no need to call her.'

He raises his hands in surrender, smiling kindly. He gently takes hold of my cheeks, clasping them between his palms. 'Are you *really* okay?'

'Yes.' I try to appear calm, reasonable.

'It's just – well, you're sure the neighbour said this, are you? You couldn't have misunderstood her? You know that happens occasionally.'

A mist blurs my vision and floats me away – away from Charlotte, away from Alex, away from the room itself. I *could* have misinterpreted Karla's words, her intention, I suppose. I've done it before . . .

'Let me speak with the neighbour, babe?' he asks.

'No.' I'm sharper than perhaps I should be. 'I'll talk to her again. I'll let her know there's nothing wrong with Charlotte.'

He grasps my hand and squeezes it tight. 'It's not Charlotte I'm worried about.'

A terrible image flashes in my mind. The pool. Billy. His body still beneath the surface.

I'm a terrible mother.

'You think I'll let Charlotte come to harm?' I gasp.

'That's not what I was implying,' he continues in a softer tone. 'It's just that when you're like this, you're distracted. I mean to say, yes, occasionally I've been worried about leaving Charlotte alone with you.'

He gives me a sympathetic smile. 'I'm not saying it was on purpose, what you did. Any of us could fall asleep. It's just . . . well, we might not mean for bad things to occur. But they do. And when they've occurred once, it's not so hard to imagine that bad things could happen again, is it?'

His face is pale, his body rigid, as if he's not really talking to me anymore.

'When I was on the phone to Mum today, she kept saying that when she spoke to you, you seemed distant and didn't seem to care,' he continues. 'I kept trying to defend you, like I always do, arguing that you've been doing all you can. And then, after a while, I realised something about what she was saying felt right, somehow. I'm sorry to say it, Lauren. But I worry that maybe you *don't* care.'

'What on earth do you mean? Of *course* I care about Charlotte.'

'I know you care about *her*.' His jaw tightens. 'I worry you don't care about *me*. Our marriage. Sometimes it feels like you don't care about *us* at all.'

When I glance at him, there is disappointment in his eyes. A chill rises deep within my bones. I cast my gaze to the floor.

'I'm sorry. I know I've been distracted,' I say. 'I could show I care more.'

He puts a hand under my chin, lifts it so that my eyes meet his. 'I can trust you with her, right?'

I don't know how to respond, though something in me

wants to ask the same of him. I have equally as many things to worry about: Charlotte's crying. The woman who came to our house . . . But I don't say anything.

'Let me serve dinner,' he says finally.

'I'll feed her today's breastmilk,' I mumble.

'Don't. You shouldn't wake her. She's already had her formula, so she'll be asleep for hours now.' He kisses me hard on the top of my head, then leaves the room.

Formula. We'd both agreed that our baby – our babies – would be fed solely with breastmilk. It was important to me. Yet, despite my obstetrics training, I'd had no insight into the excruciating pain, the ripping bare of the nipples, the lumps in my breasts that would have to be massaged out. With Billy, it was a process more brutal than I could ever have envisaged.

Each time I'd seen Billy's wriggling, mewing body, something in me had curled up inside, wanting to pull away before he'd even latched on. Alex had encouraged me to continue trying, and so I did, even when the agony felt like it was more than I could bear, until eventually the milk itself began to dry up. It was only then that I gave up. One more way I had failed my son. And myself.

And now, Alex is asking if he can trust me with Charlotte. Does he really think what happened to Billy will happen again? Was he insinuating I intentionally contributed to Billy's death, albeit subconsciously? I've never heard him speak like this before.

How could he even think that?

I know I was a terrible mother to Billy. But I'm not a monster. Am I?

*

Alex is already seated at the dining table, the leftover lasagne from last night laid out on two plates, precisely cut with straight edges, not a drop of sauce visible on the white china. Between the plates sits a perfectly tossed salad, balsamic dressing glistening on the surface of the leaves.

'What were you doing in there?' He passes me my plate, a neutral expression on his face.

'What do you mean?' I try to keep my voice even, concealing my confusion.

'I heard the rocking chair.'

I recall the baby monitor beside the microwave. 'Thinking about work.'

Rain hammers against the glass of our sliding door and I glance up to the next-door neighbour's house. A warm glow is shimmering from a room on her upper floor.

'I've been wondering whether we should get a Peugeot,' I blurt out.

He seems confused by my abrupt change of subject. 'Why?' He stares, picks up his cutlery. 'Has this got something to do with what the neighbour said?'

Why can't I just say it? 'No, they were discussing cars today at work. Apparently, Peugeots are safe. I thought it might be good with a new baby. I thought, if you knew anyone who has one, we could ask them for advice?'

'Toyotas are safe too,' he says, slicing into his lasagne with surgical precision. 'Why do you think I chose them for our two cars?'

'Of course,' I say. Then, 'Your mum had a Peugeot, didn't she?'

'Yes,' he says. 'It had a mechanical fault that wasn't easy to fix, so she traded it in years ago.' He places his fork down. 'I don't rate Peugeots, actually. Mum's gave her nothing but trouble.'

I nod, aware it would be unwise to ask him about Peugeots again.

There's a faint cry on the baby monitor. I watch Alex. He cocks his head, waiting for Charlotte to settle. Within thirty seconds, there is silence and he resumes his meal.

'I told you, she's a great sleeper,' he says finally. 'If you're calm, they're calm. They feed off your energy.'

'You think it was *my* fault Billy was a bad sleeper?'

'I wasn't saying that. But now you mention it, maybe he was stressed.'

'He was stressed before he died?'

He tilts his head. 'You said it, not me.'

10

Voicemail message, office of Dr Mikaela Georgiou, psychiatrist

Friday 14 December, 21:00

Hi, I hope it's okay to leave a message after hours. I'm Lauren De Vale's husband. I was wondering about making an urgent appointment for my wife as soon as possible? I'm quite concerned about her. Recently she's been acting like she did just before she was admitted last time, and she's also saying things that aren't like her. I'm at a loss as to what to do. Could you let me know if an urgent appointment is available? If not, please get back to me and advise who I should contact. That would be great. Thank you, and apologies, again, for reaching out after hours.

11

FOUR DAYS EARLIER

It's a busy on-call Saturday morning, with two emergency deliveries. As I head for the clinic kitchen to refrigerate the small amount of milk I've managed to express, I see the light on in Natalia's office at the far end of the corridor.

I poke my head through the gap of her open door. 'What are you doing here on a weekend?'

She looks up and shuffles the papers on her desk into a pile. 'Finishing off some damn paperwork before the holiday season. You know what it's like.' She inspects my face. 'You okay?' She gestures to one of the couches designated for patients. 'What is it?'

'You're not going to believe this.' I settle into the seat. 'That neighbour I mentioned – she has been recording data on the whole street *for years*, writing it all down in this weird electronic notebook.'

'Are you saying she *was* actually watching you all that time?'

I hold her gaze. 'Seems I wasn't paranoid after all.'

'And?'

'She said some woman in a Peugeot came to our house yesterday and stayed for over two hours. According to her, Charlotte was crying her head off the entire time.'

'Some woman?' Natalia looks quizzical. 'Did she give you any details?'

'No. And I didn't get a chance to ask more. But I can feel something isn't right.'

Her face creases. 'What does Alex say about all this?'

'He said *a guy* came over and installed blinds in Charlotte's room. That she wasn't crying at all.'

She shakes her head. 'This all sounds very peculiar. I mean, the neighbour must be confused. Or making things up?'

'I didn't get that impression.' I shrug. 'She told me she used to be a private investigator. It kind of makes sense of her odd behaviour to me. Then again, I guess it is a bit unusual to be recording so many details.' I bite my lip, remembering that with Billy I'd logged every aspect of my breastfeeding routine in inordinate detail. Over time, the documenting became more habit than obsession, something I didn't think too much about. I can imagine, though, that anyone reading my journal would find my detailed notes just as unusual as Karla's.

'Very odd, I'd say. Listen, you're not believing a nosy, interfering neighbour over your husband of what, seven years, are you?'

'Five,' I say. 'We got married right before Billy was born, and we'd only been together a year at that point, remember?'

Her eyebrows lift. 'It sounds like you don't trust him.'

There's an ache deep in my chest. 'I'm starting to wonder if I do.'

Natalia looks shocked. 'God, Laur.' She shuffles the papers on her desk. There's an awkward pause, then she looks me directly in the eyes, 'This all feels a bit much.' She shakes her head, turns off the computer. 'Look, I wasn't going to say anything . . . but you should know: Alex rang me this morning. He sounded really worried. He asked me if I had any concerns about you.'

Huh? Alex rang Natalia? He hardly knows her, has met her only once, at a work function years ago. Why the hell is he ringing my work colleague and closest confidant? And how did he even get her phone number?

'What did you say?' I finally manage.

'Nothing. I told him I had no concerns about you, obviously. But this is getting a bit messy. I don't want to get involved in things between the two of you. I hope you understand.' She shuts the file in front of her. 'There's a lot going on. I do have to say that I'm a *little* worried about you. You've only just returned to work. And with such a young baby . . . I'm guessing the hospital would be happy to let you have some time off if you need it. Do you want me to speak with medical administration on your behalf?'

'No.' I stare at the painting on the wall behind her. I'm sure its abstract blend of pastel pink and green stripes was chosen for its soothing qualities, but to me, now, the vertical bands remind me of jail cell bars. I hold out my hands, palms upwards, in a gesture of submission. 'You're right. I'm going to forget all this. I'll see my psych again to touch base.'

'Good.' She looks relieved, the furrow in her brow softening. 'I know you're just anxious about Charlotte. Like I said yesterday, it makes sense. But she's in excellent hands. Alex will be sure to keep her safe.'

12

'I'll head home as soon as we finish up,' I say to Devan, once the ward round is nearly done.

'No problem,' he says. 'I'll reach out if I need you. Is your baby okay?'

Karla's words are still humming in my head, but I simply nod. Better not to say too much.

He taps the phone in his shirt pocket. 'I just heard from my partner. She's pregnant.' He beams. 'Six weeks.'

'Congratulations.' I do the sums in my head. 'That'll be good timing. You can take the third rotation off in the new year.'

'I thought I might take a whole year off.' He flushes. 'You won't say anything to the other bosses just yet, will you?'

'Of course not.' A whole year off. It's what I'd planned to take after Billy's birth, but, of course, it ended up being much longer. By the time I wanted to return to work, after two psychiatric admissions and an extended break, I'd been required to complete further training and additional assessments to gain approval to return to my position. I'd have loved to have taken another year off with Charlotte, but with my history, despite any concerns I held about maintaining our bond, I felt I could only take three months. Though Natalia's suggestion to take more time off had been made with the best of intentions, I'm not prepared to risk everything I've worked so hard to regain.

I grab my expressed milk from the staffroom fridge before I depart. Only half a bottle today, less every time I try. I hadn't expected my volumes to reduce so fast. I suppose I haven't been expressing frequently enough at work to maintain my supply, but between emergency caesareans, ward rounds and clinics, there's only so much I can do. I take a deep breath. *Remember to be kind to yourself; practise self-compassion.* This mantra was the most helpful thing I'd learned from the psychiatrist, perhaps the only thing that has been of any use. *You're doing your best.* The clench in my heart eases off ever so slightly.

As I'm closing the refrigerator door, Elspeth strides into the deserted staff area then does a double take as she catches sight of me. 'Lauren!'

'Hi,' I say. 'You're not usually on this floor. Everything okay?'

'Just left something here.' She heads towards me, avoiding my gaze.

'How's baby Parnos?' I ask.

She removes a cold bag from the fridge. 'Improving each day. I think she'll be fine.'

'Great news.'

Despite Natalia's reassurances about Charlotte, I can't fully seem to shake my worries about leaving her while I'm at work. Perhaps I should run my concerns past Elspeth? Although our relationship has always been a little awkward, given she and Alex dated back in college, she's also one of the few people I know well enough, who truly understands what it's like to be a working mum in the hospital system. Back in our shared mothers group days, she was always willing to speak with me about my parenting anxieties. She is reliable in her knowledge of children, both hands-on and medically . . .

'Elspeth – would you have time for a quick chat?'

She gives a tight-lipped smile. 'It's a bit hectic today,' she says. 'I'll be at the mothers group Christmas barbecue tomorrow. Maybe we can chat there?'

My heart contracts. A barbecue, particularly with my old mothers group, is not exactly an occasion I feel like attending at present. But I suppose an opportunity to talk to Elspeth in an unpressured environment could be worth the discomfort. And perhaps hearing the experiences of other mothers might also help settle my anxieties about returning to work.

'I wasn't planning on going,' I say, 'but . . . maybe I'll see you there.'

At home, Alex's Toyota is nowhere in sight, but there's a bright blue car in the driveway blocking my space. Not a Peugeot, I note.

The front door is open, the wire door snibbed from the inside.

'Hello?'

'Hello, dear!'

Argh. It's Magdala. Her numerous beaded necklaces jangle over her floral dress as she trots down the hallway. She unlatches the wire door and ushers me inside. It feels unsettling, her letting me into my own house, though admittedly this place had been hers before we moved in – the blessings and curses of inheritance.

'Alex called me. I've come to mind Charlotte.'

'Is she okay?'

'She's absolutely fine.' She gestures towards the nursery.

I peer in. The cot is still in the centre of the room, the fish mobile dangling above it. Charlotte is fast asleep in one of her baby sleeping bags.

'Where's Alex?'

'He's just headed out to pick up some supplies.'

'What for?'

She looks down at me over the top of her glasses. 'What's with the twenty questions? Good god, you sound like the last one.'

'What last one?'

'The—' she grimaces, 'last girlfriend. Therese. The questions she asked . . . it was never-ending.'

I cast my mind back to when Alex and I had first met, when we'd exchanged details of our exes. He'd been in a serious relationship before me with a woman who had a daughter from a previous marriage. He had considered proposing to her, but ultimately decided to end things.

'She went off the rails after we broke up,' he told me. 'She became unhinged.'

When I said maybe he shouldn't speak about his ex like that, his face had darkened.

'You wouldn't say that if you knew her,' he'd replied.

Charlotte stirs, but as I approach the cot she settles back to stillness.

Magdala frowns. 'The things Therese used to say to Alex about me.' She tuts under her breath, while I'm reminded how close Alex is to his mother. I can't help wondering whether any of my own musings about my mother-in-law have been reported back to her.

'That's not good.'

'No, the things she said were awful actually. Shocking. When all I was doing was looking out for poor Alex.' She sweeps into the nursery and stands over the cot. 'After all, a mother can't help but be protective of her son.'

I try to smile, even as I'm aware she is probably having a jab at me.

'I'm sure Alex will be the same with Charlotte. Mindful of who she dates, you know.'

I nod, careful not to disagree, even though I have no intention of policing my child's choice of partners.

Charlotte wriggles, opening her eyes.

'She's such a delight, isn't she? Thank god you were willing to try again, Lauren. Unlike that Therese. She refused to consider a second child after the tragedy with her first . . . Zoe, that was her daughter's name. Zoe was beautiful. But not nearly as beautiful as our Charlotte.'

Wait – what is Magdala suggesting? That something happened to the daughter of Alex's ex? A solid lump hardens in the back of my throat. I try to recall the reasons Alex disclosed for ending his relationship with Therese, but nothing comes to mind. He has never told me anything about Zoe. How much more is there about Alex that I don't know? If there'd been some kind of trauma involving a child, why had he kept that hidden from me?

Charlotte lets out a weak cry. I place this new half-information into the far reaches of my mind and firmly shut off all connections to it for now, noting the coolness that flows through my body as I do so. I'm grateful for having mastered this skill in childhood, the ability to switch off things that are simply too hard to bear. There will be time to sort out the details about Therese and Zoe at a later date. I reach into the cot.

'Don't pick her up right away.' Magdala places her hand on my arm. 'You wouldn't want to spoil her.'

Charlotte begins to wail, louder now, and ignoring Magdala I scoop her out of the cot.

'It's *okay* not to be so soft,' Magdala says condescendingly. 'It's healthy for them to use their lungs a little.'

I cradle Charlotte and bring her to me, but she continues to whimper. 'There, there,' I say. 'I'm here. Everything is going to be all right.'

'You bet it is,' Magdala says, 'now that Grandma's here.' She coos at Charlotte, then turns to me. 'I'm *so* glad I came to help.'

I take a seat on the recliner, patting Charlotte lightly on her nappy. As I rock back and forth, I wonder whether Magdala had left Alex to cry as a baby rather than soothe him. That could explain a few things . . . Alex has never spoken much about his childhood. He tends to deflect my questions, particularly about his father. Perhaps Magdala will be more forthcoming.

'What was Alex like as a baby?'

'He was delightful.' A wistful expression crosses her face. 'He slept well, fed well. I couldn't ask for more.'

Like Charlotte. 'And what about Alex's dad? Did he help out much?'

'Doug? Ha! Piece of garbage, that man. Right from the start of our marriage he was too busy chasing skirt to attend to his family.'

'That must have been hard,' I say, trying not to show my surprise at her revelation.

'Frankly, it was a relief when he left. Even more of a relief when he had a massive heart attack – on top of his new wife, no less!' She scoffs, but I can identify a tinge of sadness beneath her disgust. 'Enough of the past. Now you're back, I might just retreat to my room for a lie down.'

'Your room?' The back of my neck prickles.

'Yes. Alex has made your study up for me. Didn't he tell you? I'll be staying for a few weeks to help out.'

What the hell? I can't remember Alex telling me his mother was coming to stay. Surely, he should have discussed this with me, particularly if she'll be sleeping in my study. I struggle to keep my voice even. 'Help out with what?'

'Help out my son and granddaughter. It's a lot to expect of a father – full-time parenting while trying to run a business on the side. The number of times I've told him – he needs stability, particularly with his new business venture.'

New business venture?

'I mean, he hardly has time for himself, does he? There's been almost no opportunity to get his new concept off the ground.'

I rifle through the fuzzy corners of my memory, but I can't recall Alex ever mentioning a new business to me. We'd negotiated that he would finish up in his last position – IT security for a pharmaceutical company – to care for Charlotte.

'Ye-ess . . . his new concept.' I try to sound assured. 'How much have you heard about it?'

'I don't know much at all.' She sniffs. 'I'll ask him when he gets home.'

Oh, crap. Triangulation – exactly what I try to avoid with Magdala. I can discuss this with Alex when it's just the two of us. 'No, it's okay. You don't want to stress him out. Like you say, he has enough on his plate.'

'I'll tell him you said that,' she says, overly sweet. 'It's nice to hear you care.'

I brace, sweat pooling in the armpits of my scrubs. Remember your usual strategy, Lauren, I tell myself. Never say anything *even remotely controversial* to this woman. Whatever you say can and will be used against you.

Magdala gives a tight smile. 'I can see that tonight is just what the two of you need. I'll be sure to excuse myself, of course.'

'Tonight? What's happening tonight?'

'Your anniversary, dear. Alex is out buying the ingredients to cook you a special dinner. He knew you wouldn't want to go to a restaurant if you're on call. Oh, don't tell me you forgot the date?'

I glance down at my phone: 15 December. Hardly surprising I hadn't remembered – it falls the week after Billy's birthday and four days before the anniversary of his death. A terrible time to celebrate anything, and it's not like we've ever made a big deal of our wedding anniversary.

Her mobile dings and she checks the message. 'Alex has just texted. He says he'll be at least another hour.' She continues wittering on. 'It's a busy time of year. I notice you haven't got the Christmas tree up yet. I told Alex I'd do it for you tonight, if that might help?'

It's the last thing I want, but I have no strength to argue. 'Thank you.' My breath is a wisp of air, barely audible.

Magdala begins to clatter around in the loungeroom, assembling the Christmas tree. I am finally alone with Charlotte in the nursery. I manage to push Magdala's revelations and my concerns about Alex from my mind, and refocus all my attention on my daughter. She's comfortable in my arms; her eyes meet mine, her mouth curling into a smile. The fear of losing connection with her since my return to work settles within me. She is beautiful, her soft hair falling over her forehead, her eyes bright. Is this how my mother had felt when she held me: wonderment, awe, overwhelming love?

There are only a few photos of my mother and me, most of them lost over our many moves from rental home to rental home. I love the one of Mum cradling her pregnant belly, seated on a patchwork-quilted bed, surrounded by soft toys. Was that the life she had hoped for me, one of comfort, of fun? Instead, my childhood was marred by my father's drinking and his harsh words, by Mum's whimpers echoing through the walls.

There's another photo of me at about three, seated on my mother's lap at a family barbecue. It's just possible to make out Dad in the background. The caution in my eyes is visible already, the awareness that being seated on my mother's lap wasn't quite protection enough.

Charlotte begins to mouth as if she is hungry. She is getting bigger and has been sucking at the teat of the bottle with significant strength. I can't help but wonder if she might be able to grasp my nipple more easily than she had in her first weeks of life. Without further thought, I lift my shirt, pull down the strap of my nursing bra and bring her to my breast as I'd been instructed. It wasn't my fault, the midwives had reassured me; sometimes babies just couldn't manage to latch on. But now, Charlotte takes my whole nipple into her mouth and sucks it deep into her throat, just like the books say. I almost cry in delight. If Charlotte can continue sucking this strongly, maybe it's not too late to re-establish breastfeeding. And I will be able to succeed where I had so dismally failed before.

I stroke Charlotte's head as she draws long, thirsty mouthfuls. She is hungry, despite Magdala's protests to the contrary. My maternal intuition is correct. I *do* know my baby, even if I doubt myself so much.

Watching Charlotte, I think of all I have lost. My mother, all her wisdom, gone. I can see now that she was just doing her best to survive. And, I remind myself, I *did* have a secure lap to rest upon, at least from time to time; Aunty Sal, my mother's only sibling, was my safe person, with her crushing hugs and afternoon teas. A pang in my throat. God, it has been so long since I saw Aunty Sal.

A memory comes to me. It must have been at some family gathering in our rambling backyard, right before Mum left us for good. The adults had retreated into the house, while I was left to my own devices outside. I climbed my favourite tree – a silver birch in the centre of the lawn – then settled myself on a lower branch and rested my back against the rough trunk.

'Yoo-hoo.' I knew that booming voice. Sal was loud and cheerful, the opposite of my quiet, withdrawn mother. 'What's little Lulu doing up in the tree? Does she need an Aunty Sal hug?'

'Sure,' I said and jumped down to the grass where Sal stood in her usual attire, a plain skivvy tucked into a corduroy skirt that stretched to her ankles, practical boots and a wide-brimmed hat. She drew me into her bosom and I was wrapped in the scent of her: freshly cut grass. As always, her hug squeezed the air out of me. And in that moment, I couldn't have felt more safe, more loved.

'You know you can always give me a call, Lulu,' she said. 'Don't ever hesitate to reach out.' Had she had some inkling, then, that my mother was planning to leave without saying goodbye?

Charlotte's sucking ceases. So soon. I bring her to my chest and pat her back gently.

'Time for a new nappy, my baby,' I say in a singsong voice, carrying her to the change table. I check the clock on the wall. It sounds like Alex will be a while. I briefly contemplate how to bring up my growing list of unspoken concerns: Zoe, his mother coming to stay, his new business. Not to mention the woman who came to our house for hours, causing him to ignore Charlotte's crying the whole time. Alex is keeping things to himself, making too many decisions without me. I need to know what the hell is going on.

Charlotte's nappy is full – and I wonder how long it has been since she was changed. But if she had a bottle an hour ago, perhaps that is explanation enough. I roll her over to make sure she is all clean there too. And there, on her lower back, is something I'm shocked to see.

A bruise.

It's approximately two centimetres in diameter. Round and purple, a few days old.

Quietly and carefully, I undress her, checking the rest of her body: her chest, her belly, her scalp. The tightness in my neck loosens ever so slightly as I note nothing else of concern.

I study the bruise more closely. It could be a Mongolian spot, a mark that resembles a bruise, a not uncommon finding on a baby's lower back. But no – it's the wrong colour, has brown and purple within it, and is irregularly shaped. It is most definitely a bruise. My god.

My mind ticks through possibilities. It's not from Magdala – the bruise is older than today. Could Charlotte have fallen off something? If so, why wasn't I told? If I ask Alex about it, will he accuse *me* of somehow hurting her? I scan my memory; is there a way *I* could have accidentally caused this, perhaps when changing her, or patting her to sleep, or . . .

No. This would have required some force. I'd have known if I'd hurt her. And at this age, babies can't roll, can't grasp objects to injure themselves. Any injury has to have been inflicted by someone else.

'What the heck it *that*?'

It's Magdala, behind me. I can't believe I didn't hear her come in.

'I don't know.'

'What happened?'

'Nothing.' I can barely speak. Why did I have to be lumped with a mother-in-law who used to work in child services?

'We'll have to show Alex.'

'Of course, I'm going to tell him.' I try to keep the defensiveness from my voice.

And then, I recall Zoe. Magdala may well know something about Alex that I don't. A small part of me is almost afraid to ask. 'Alex couldn't have been responsible for this, could he? By accident?'

'Don't be ridiculous! He'll be as appalled as me when he finds out.' She frowns at me. 'I can see *you* don't seem particularly surprised.'

My feet are frozen to the floor. 'I think I'm in shock, Magdala. Please, let me get my baby dressed.'

She clears her throat and strides from the room. I hear loud bangs and crashes as she continues erecting the Christmas tree in the lounge room.

Could Alex have caused this bruise? It doesn't seem like something he could have done. And Magdala seems certain . . . But I'm starting to wonder how well I truly know my husband.

I dress Charlotte, careful not to press on her lower back. No wonder she has been whimpering each time I lift her from her cot. My poor baby. I smooth her hair back from her forehead and run my palm over her soft scalp to soothe her. But my hands are trembling as I realise that if child services somehow become involved, with my past history I am likely to be the presumed perpetrator – the person who has inflicted this bruise. I can only pray Alex will believe me when I say I had nothing to do with this.

I shake my head, trying to clear my thoughts.

Another memory comes to me, a bruise I once saw on Mum. I had entered the bathroom to wash my hands just as she was stepping out of the shower. She raised a towel over herself just a little too late and I caught a fleeting glimpse of a monstrous violet mark on her hip.

'What's that?'

Mum lifted the corners of her lips into a smile. 'Nothing.'

She bustled out of the bathroom before I could ask anymore. She always kept the bathroom door locked after that.

I recall her face, the main image I have of her: auburn hair curled by rollers, large-framed glasses covering her owl-grey eyes, a solemn but thoughtful expression. If only she were here for me still.

Charlotte coos and I look deeply into her eyes, a summer-sky blue. I sense it now, the preciousness of this time with her. I curl a lock of her satiny hair behind one ear and press her against my chest.

'I love you, my baby,' I say, calmness flowing through me as I feel her soften into my arms. No matter what, I will always have her in my heart. My love will shield her from harm. Maybe that was the reason Billy died: I had failed to recognise the warning signs – I had simply not loved him enough.

13

FOUR YEARS EARLIER

Extract from Lauren De Vale's diary

Billy is coming up to his first birthday. The time has gone so fast. It's been so difficult. I didn't realise how hard it would be to love him. I should have predicted that, I suppose. Even before he was born, I hadn't wanted him. I knew I wasn't ready. Alex managed to convince me. And now look what's come of all that.

But maybe Billy will be okay – lots of babies are, even when a parent doesn't really love them. I guess I'm testament to that. It's just that I know that when I'm in my most dangerous mood, I'm not a very nice person to be around. I'm my father's daughter, after all. I don't know how far I could go, what I'm capable of.

13

FOUR YEARS EARLIER

14

Charlotte is still sleeping as I slip out of the front door, tiptoeing down the porch steps to avoid the creaks. Across the driveway and into Karla's yard, past the neatly clipped hedge separating our properties. The late afternoon sun illuminates the cast-iron lacework of her verandah. There's no sign of her silhouette at the window. Is she even home?

I give a sharp tap at the front door. No answer. I look back to check my house. From here, I can make out the empty roadway. I knock on Karla's door again.

Nothing.

'Karla,' I call. 'Are you there?'

I've never been in her house; our only interactions have been at the front of our respective properties. I peek through the frosted glass beside the front door, but I can't see any movement inside. It looks like I will have to come back another time.

I'm starting back down her patio steps when the door swings open behind me.

'Did you want to come in?'

'Oh, Karla! Yes, thank you,' I say, glancing back at the quiet street. I should have at least half an hour before Alex is home from the shops. 'I just wondered if I could ask you a few questions about what we spoke about yesterday.'

'Sure. Good timing for me. I've been hoping you'd pop in.' She gestures me into her hall. A green carpet runner stretches along the floorboards to a steep flight of stairs at the back of the house. She directs me into the front lounge filled with dark wood furniture and leather couches. Elegant paintings with heavy wooden frames adorn the olive-coloured walls. It's not quite the décor I was expecting from Karla's svelte appearance, but the room does have a stately, elegant vibe.

'Please, have a seat.' She points me to an emerald-green leather armchair in front of a window dressed with a sheer white curtain. From here, I can see all the way down the cul-de-sac and into the front yards of the houses that line it. She could certainly take note of anyone coming or going. Golden sunlight streams through the window, glinting off the framed pictures on the mantelpiece above the fireplace. A few baby photographs surround a large photograph of a stern middle-aged man standing beside a solemn young woman.

'Me and my father,' she says, following my gaze. 'I lost him a few years ago now.' Her face has a serious expression. 'I just boiled the kettle. Would you like a tea or coffee?'

'Coffee would be perfect. Milk, no sugar.'

'Same as me. Back in a tic,' she says, her heels tapping on the floorboards as she leaves the room.

I cast my eyes over a small desk beside me, the electronic notebook upon it. It's open. I glance at the only notation on the page.

17:43 – L approaches front door.

That's me. I check my watch: 5.47 p.m. Hmm – so she is equally as pedantic with her observations as I'd been with my breastfeeding notes.

I pause. It's not like me to cross boundaries or be nosy. But given everything that has happened, and what Karla told me, I don't think it's unreasonable to look for evidence of what Alex was up to yesterday – if only to get details of the person who came to our house.

Holding my breath, I flip the notebook over. The cover is maroon – it's the right one. I listen for sounds of Karla returning, but all is quiet. With tight hands, I scroll back a few screens. Karla's handwriting is minuscule and precise, filling each line. Each household in Maremma Court is recorded in a different column; she has been documenting details about all the neighbours. The entries for Alex and me are in the first column.

Heels click in the hallway. Dammit. With haste, I flick back to today's date, and position the journal back on the desk just in time.

Karla returns and places a tray loaded with mugs of coffee and a plate of biscuits on the desk right alongside the notebook. She hands me one of the cups. 'I guess I should be providing something a little more substantial than packet biscuits,' she says, seating herself in the wooden chair beside me. 'Sorry for the meagre offerings.'

'Butternut Snaps are great,' I say, my mouth salivating as I recall their familiar buttery coconut flavour – one of the staples I used to enjoy with Aunty Sal.

'My favourites,' she says. 'I was looking forward to introducing my kids to them . . . but it wasn't to be.'

'Why not?'

'She didn't make it.' She looks towards the mantelpiece with the baby photographs.

'Oh, god, I'm so sorry.' So stupid of me to have blundered in like that. Her solemn face is masked with the blankness I've seen on so many women who have lost children. I hesitate. 'Would you like to talk about it?'

She shakes her head.

'I get it. Some things are too hard to discuss,' I say, relieved to change the topic. 'There was something I was hoping to ask you about. Would that be okay?'

'Of course,' she says, the interest in her eyes returning.

'It's about yesterday. I was wondering if it was definitely a woman who came to our house? Alex told me a man came to install the blinds. I wondered if maybe that was when you heard Charlotte crying?'

Karla purses her lips. 'The blind installer came in a marked van, early in the morning just after you left for work. The woman arrived later. I can give you the times if you'd like?'

I swallow. 'Have you seen that woman at our house before?'

She turns to me, her face still. 'Are you suspicious your husband is having an affair?'

I recoil at her directness. 'No . . . I . . . Should I be?'

She shrugs. 'I guess my antennae are always up. Cheating spouses were at least half my previous workload.' She tilts her head to one side. 'Plus, that would be him taking after his father, after all.' I squint ever so slightly, trying to recall Magdala's exact words just now. Karla clocks my confusion. 'Neighbourhood gossip,' she says, 'and growing up next door. I've been observant since childhood, I guess.' She smiles, somewhat sheepishly. I might be beginning to like this woman. Though if the whole neighbourhood knows about Alex's father's dalliances, presumably he does too. So, why has he never mentioned it to me?

Karla taps her hand on the armrest of her chair. 'There is something that occurred to me. That car yesterday – the Peugeot. I'm almost certain I've seen it outside your place several times over these last few years.'

My heart stops. 'What?'

'I haven't had a chance to go back through my notes and compare details across my records. Of course, a lot of cars come and go in our court. But that vivid shade of blue is quite striking. So, it makes sense I've remembered it.'

I place my palm on my chest and inhale into my diaphragm. If I am to believe Karla, then what else about Alex can't I trust? It seems he left our child crying for hours yesterday while being visited by an unknown woman. *And* our baby has a bruise of unknown cause. According to Karla's notes, this same car has visited our house more than once – numerous times over the last few years. What else has my husband neglected to tell me? My list of questions for him continues to pile up, and yet I'm certain that Alex will categorically deny anything I put to him.

'Would you be open to me bringing Alex here? It would be helpful if you could confirm what you saw,' I suggest.

'No.' Karla stiffens. 'I don't think that's a good idea.'

'It's just . . .' This is hard to say, even harder to admit to myself. I'm sure Alex won't want to talk about any of this. But it's bigger than him, now. 'My baby—' I hesitate, unsure how much to reveal. 'I'm a little concerned, especially given what you've told me. But it's not just that. It's other things too. I know it might be awkward for you. But you have proof of what happened.' I indicate towards the notebook on her desk.

Karla shakes her head. 'Please forget I said anything. I really don't want to get involved. And besides, notes aren't proof of anything.'

'They're *something*,' I say, placing the coffee mug back on the tray. 'Why did you tell me about my baby crying, if you don't like to get involved?'

Her eyes narrow. 'Children must be protected at all costs.'

'Yes,' I say, as my heart begins to thump.

Karla rises from her chair. 'Which reminds me . . . I ran into Magdala yesterday and noticed that she didn't seem as spritely as before. She told me she'd been diagnosed with Parkinson's.'

I refrain from interjecting – how, and more importantly why, have Alex and his mother not told me this? Yet one more thing he's kept from me.

'You might want to be a little cautious about letting her babysit,' Karla says.

I can only nod mutely as she picks up the tray.

Abruptly, she turns towards the kitchen. 'I'd better let you get home to her. I imagine your husband will be back soon.'

In the split second after she moves towards the hallway, I do something I would usually never consider. I grab the notebook from the desk, shove it under my top to conceal it and follow her to the front door. With a racing heart, I mutter my goodbyes and leave. She watches as I hurry down her driveway.

As I pull our front door closed behind me, I catch a glimpse of Alex's car turning into our driveway.

Just in time.

15

'I'm home!' Alex calls from the hall. I'm unsure who he's calling to – his mother, or me? He enters Charlotte's room brandishing a shopping bag. 'You forgot, didn't you?'

'I guess so,' I reply. I'd just managed to slip Karla's notebook into my handbag before he appeared.

'I was planning to make our favourite. Veal scaloppine.'

Our favourite? Does he mean his and his mother's? He knows I don't like veal.

He notes my baffled expression and raises his eyebrows. 'We ate it on our first date. Remember?'

I nod slowly, even though I could have sworn we went out for Japanese.

'You're home early.' He glances into the cot. 'Did anything happen today that I should know about?'

'It was quiet at work.' A shudder runs through me, even as

I know I need to start the difficult conversation. 'I didn't know your mother had been diagnosed with Parkinson's.'

He shrugs. 'I thought I'd let her update you on her personal medical information. I didn't see that it was my place.'

'You didn't think we should talk about something that could affect her ability to babysit?' I say, trying to keep my rising concern in check. In truth, I hadn't observed any signs of Parkinson's in Magdala – it would never have clicked except for Karla's comments, so at this point it's not technically a problem. But still, isn't this the kind of thing that families share?

He frowns. 'It's early stage. Her doctor specifically said it has no effect on her capacity to take care of Charlotte.'

'I guess, I wish you'd at least mentioned she was coming to stay.'

'Lauren.' He fixes me with an incredulous stare. 'We discussed this last week. You said she could sleep in your study.'

I have no memory of this at all. 'I don't recall saying that.'

'Are you implying I'm making it up?'

'No. I just . . . well, I'd remember, wouldn't I?'

He turns his head slightly. 'I don't blame you, darling. But there are many things you don't remember.'

A flush of confusion. 'When exactly did you tell me?' I want to test his memory, as well as my own.

'You were ironing,' he says with a scowl.

Ironing is a rare enough event for me to immediately place the conversation to the day before I went back to work. 'I remember we talked about what to do on Christmas Day,' I recount. 'And we decided on a restaurant, with the three of us and your mum. We talked about Easter, where we would go for the holidays. You asked me how I was feeling about going back to work.'

'Yes. And I told you Mum was coming to stay.'

'No, you didn't.' I'm certain now. I can recollect our exact conversation, his tone, his facial expressions, as I ploughed through my week's supply of work shirts.

'Keep your voice down,' he hisses. 'I'm not going to argue about this. She's here now, and she's staying.'

Keep *my* voice down, when he's speaking with such barely suppressed fury? 'So, I don't have a choice in the matter?'

He raises his eyes to the ceiling. 'You're at work all day, every day. If you're not at work, you're on call. There's no time to get anything done with a baby. Even if *you* don't think you need help, *I* certainly do.'

I fold my arms and hug them into my chest. 'Your mum told me you have a new business venture.'

'Did she? Well, I've been trying to tell you about it for weeks. There just hasn't been the time.'

But there has. There has been lots of time, oodles of it, both of us lost for words as we spun spaghetti on our forks at the dining table, as we slumped on the couch staring at the TV waiting for Charlotte to stir, as we lay silently side by side in bed until his breathing fell into a regular pattern.

'When *were* you going to tell me?'

He drops the shopping bag onto the floor. 'Tonight. Fuck, Lauren. I'm trying. I'm trying *so hard*. It's like I'm never good enough for you. Do my efforts mean nothing?'

From the cot, Charlotte gives a sharp cry.

'So, please, tell me now. What's the new business?'

His face flickers in the glow of the night light. 'IT security, all right? I'm setting it up with Arun. The plan is to provide for our family, do the right thing by all of us.'

My back stiffens. 'Just like you'd been planning to do for Therese?' He'd used that exact phrase when he'd described to me how she'd 'ruined everything'. How he'd had all these plans before she 'flipped out'.

'What the hell does my ex have to do with this?'

'You never told me exactly what happened with her. And her child.'

'Zoe?' He snatches up the shopping bag from the floor. 'That's none of your fucking business.' He storms from the room.

I take deep breaths, trying to calm myself. I turn to my beautiful daughter who's now facing the window. I pull down the new blackout blinds. The fish mobile casts eerie shadows on the walls as it spins and I run my finger over its wooden shapes. It had been Alex's. His dad had brought it back from a work trip to Fiji with promises to teach his son how to fish when he was older. But his business had kept him away from home a lot, Alex told me, and they never got to go on that fishing trip. By Alex's early teens, his dad had moved overseas with a new wife and Alex never saw his dad again. Next he heard, his father had died suddenly of a cardiac event. Alex vowed he would never be like his father – he would always be around for his children whenever they needed him.

I pull on one of the fish, then release it. The figurines bob up and down, as if on a seesaw. Shadows dance on the walls as I ruefully contemplate the roles parents play. Alex and I had so desperately wanted to avoid re-enacting our own parents' mistakes. And yet, Alex is more like both our fathers than I'd realised, just better at hiding it. So, does that mean I'm replaying my mother's dynamic – the woman who fails to take care of herself, and so, her own children?

The fish mobile settles to stillness. I must read Karla's notebook. Yet a part of me doesn't want to know the truth. What if Alex *is* having an affair – what then? And although I'm desperate to fill in the blanks of those missing hours around Billy's death, what if I find I'm incontrovertibly liable? I've been able to hide in the haze of not remembering every detail. Am I ready to potentially be confronted with the evidence of my own failings writ in black and white?

Billy. I contemplate what he would have been like had he lived. At one, he already had the audacity of a much older boy, a cheekiness of spirit that reminded me of myself as a child – before my family's trauma had begun to impact me. Billy had been outgoing, cheerful and rambunctious. He'd have made a wonderful brother for Charlotte. He'd have continued being a wonderful son.

It occurs to me that Billy's memory chest is in here somewhere. I'd last looked at it before I was pregnant with Charlotte and for some reason it calls to me now. I want to see Billy, his things at least, and connect with him as fully as I can. I spot a packing box labelled 'baby wear' on the top shelf. I'm almost certain the memory chest is in there, along with Billy's clothes. I hadn't been ready to throw them out, torn between preserving his memory and using them for another child one day.

As I pull the box down, a baby monitor tumbles to the ground. It's not one I recall buying, or even seeing before – it has a video monitor, whereas the one I'd purchased with Alex only has audio. Its screen is illuminated green, displaying 25°C, so it is clearly switched on. Odd – why is a baby camera tucked away here? Part of Alex's new business in IT security, most likely. Yet another thing he has failed to tell me about. I place the video monitor back on the shelf, facing the wall.

There is a thin layer of dust on the top of the box. I sweep it away with the back of my hand, then rip the packing tape off and open the flaps. Inside are layers of neatly folded jumpers, jumpsuits and t-shirts. I place the contents, one by one, in a pile on the change table. Billy hardly had a chance to wear these. They will be Charlotte's now.

Finally, at the bottom of the box, my hand hits the wooden panelling of Billy's memory chest. I hoist it out and admire the photographs of my beautiful boy lacquered onto every surface. Natalia crafted it for me – one of her most thoughtful gifts.

I lift the metal clasp and am hit by the scent of cinnamon: Billy's smell. I'd so loved the scent of a baby soap a woman from mothers group had given me that, from then on, it was all I'd bathed him with. Billy's hair always smelled of it, and his clothes: peppery, uplifting, full of energy – just like him. Yet, the last time I saw him, in the funeral home, he hadn't looked anything like that, and his hair had stunk of chlorine, and bleach, and formalin. I'd snipped off a lock anyway, and at home that night I'd gently washed it in his cinnamon soap, then sealed it in a ziplock bag and nestled it among his things.

Gently I take out more items from the chest. Billy's handprint, and footprint, in blue ink on white cardboard. His patchwork blanky with satin edging. His hospital wrist bands. His birth certificate. My favourite photo of him, beaming at the camera, seated on my lap by our pool wearing his beloved dinosaur-print bathers. He'd worn them constantly, well past summer, so of course we had kept them, despite the memories they held. Suddenly, I'm desperate to touch them, to bring him close.

I rifle through the remaining items in the box – his favourite book, a beloved soft toy. But there are no dinosaur bathers. Why aren't they in here? Where on earth could they be? I'm frantic now, rummaging through the chest. It's not just the bathers that are missing; the ziplock bag with his lock of hair is gone too. I turn the chest upside down to empty it, but nothing falls out. I scour the larger packing box, running my fingers under the flaps, but it's empty. There is no lock of hair. No bathers.

The tears rise then, hot in my eyes. They spill onto my cheeks then course down my neck. It's not just Billy I'm crying for, but the loss of memories, the times we could have spent together, the lack of love I felt for him right from the start, and the overwhelming love I feel for him now, too late. I have no idea what shielded my heart for so long. Now it aches with unending loss. I cannot stop the tears from falling.

After what seems like hours, I rise, determined. I cannot change the past; I can only attempt to atone for my mistake by giving Charlotte the love that Billy never had. As I wipe the streaks from my face, I desperately hope that in the short life he had, Billy felt some semblance of my love – sensed it – and if not from me, then from his father and grandmother. Because he *was* loved. By them *and* by me. Although I had difficulty accessing our connection, my love for him was always there, and it remains, stronger than ever.

I wipe dry the shiny lacquered photos of him, wet from my tears. I hold his memory chest to my nose, inhaling the precious scent of him once more.

16

Alex's voice is cold as I slide into my seat at the dining table. 'I wasn't going to invite Mum to eat with us, but it seems right in the circumstances.'

I don't ask what circumstances he means.

'Well done, darling,' Magdala says. Then to me, 'I taught him to cook.'

'Mmm,' I say. Even with my vision still blurry from tears, I can see the veal is dry, the coating slightly burnt. Hashtag fail, Magdala. I remind myself never to trust her.

'So, Lauren.' Magdala's face is grim as she stares at me. 'Are you going to bring it up, or am I?'

Alex lays his fork on his plate.

'I was just about to,' I say, then reach for Alex's hand.

He stares at me, his eyes tight.

'I'm not accusing you of anything,' I say.

'I should hope not,' his mother retorts.

Ignoring her comment, I give Alex's hand a squeeze. 'I was changing Charlotte and I saw a bruise on her lower back.'

'A bruise.' His voice is incredulous.

'I can show you. I just wanted to check, did something happen?'

He snatches his hand from mine and slides his chair back. 'What? Nothing has happened. I should ask you the same thing.'

'It had nothing to do with me,' I say. 'I just wanted to see if – I don't know – a tumble off a mattress? Something falling on her, maybe, when you were moving the furniture around?'

'*Something falling on her?* I can't believe this.' His eyes boggle.

Magdala stares pointedly at me, before turning to him with a sickly sweet smile. 'Oh, I can.'

Alex's knuckles are white where he is grasping the stem of his glass. 'Besides, moving the furniture around was *your* idea.'

I shake my head, pause, try to remember. 'You said something about the traffic noise . . .'

'Come on, Lauren.' He stares at me with contempt. 'It's important to admit if you did something to her.'

I close my eyes briefly. 'The bruise wasn't from me, I can assure you,' I say. 'I'm hardly ever with her. There are other possible explanations of course. She might have a bleeding disorder. Platelets, or clotting factors. Something genetic, perhaps.'

'Nothing in our family,' Magdala says.

'Look, I'm not accusing you, either,' Alex says, his eyes narrowed but his tone more conciliatory. 'Of course, I'd tell you if something had happened. But it hasn't. And you're saying nothing happened on your end, either?'

'That's right.' I'm relieved to hear Alex's denial and his acceptance of mine.

'Then I'll take her to the doctor on Monday,' he says. 'We'll make sure there's nothing wrong with her.'

I take a deep breath. 'There's something else Karla next door told me,' I say, watching him and Magdala closely.

He rolls his eyes to the ceiling. 'Karla, again! What is she insinuating now?'

'I'm not certain,' I reply. 'But she saw a woman come to our house the other day and said she stayed for quite a few hours. You never mentioned that.'

His mother scoffs.

'Don't be fucking ridiculous,' Alex says. 'It simply isn't true.'

His denial is so emphatic, it's hard not to believe him.

'Look, I've been thinking.' I keep my voice as even as I can. 'Given what happened with Billy, and now with the bruise, maybe we need to think about what might help keep Charlotte safe. Like, we could install some extra surveillance around the house. Cameras. A security system?'

A glance passes between mother and son. Confusion? Concern my paranoia is flaring up again? Or guilt they've been caught out . . .

'Lots of doctors at the hospital have security at home,' I continue. 'They're connected to a central system, so there's someone to reach out to if something goes wrong.' I can sense my pitch rising. I try to still my heart. This is not for me, I remind myself. My intention is to keep our daughter safe. 'I don't want to have to rely on Karla to be our personal private investigator.'

'If that chap was still living next door,' Magdala pipes up, 'I might share your concern, dear. Karla's father was a shocker. But he died before your time. Nothing that cameras would help with now.' She suppresses a laugh. 'Although I'm sure he would have installed cameras if they'd been a thing back in his day. He always had his eye on you, didn't he, Alex? Thought you were up to no good with his daughter, if I recall.'

Alex glares. 'That guy was way off the mark. If anything, Karla had a teenage crush on me. She's always been a little—' He circles his finger about his temple.

Before I can ask more, he continues, 'Babe, I'm sure you're trying to be helpful. But this is going too far. I don't think we need home security. This is how it started last time, remember? Paranoia about the neighbour that turned out to be nothing . . . Now you're talking about things that haven't happened, accusing me of things I haven't done. I'm concerned about you. When did you last see Dr Georgiou?'

Perhaps he is worried for me, or maybe he has another agenda. It's hard to centre myself enough to interrogate his motives when his accusations, as usual, are framed as concern for my wellbeing. But I'm not the only one who has unease about my baby and about Alex, I remind myself. Karla has documented similar concerns – I'm not alone in my worry. My heart almost leaps as I steel myself. I won't allow myself to be dismissed.

'I don't need to see Dr Georgiou, Alex. I found a new baby monitor on the shelf in Charlotte's room – a video monitor – which is not the one we bought together. So, it looks like you've already made a start on implementing extra security. Am I right?'

Alex stares at me, apparently aghast. 'Surely, you're kidding? Jesus fucking Christ. Mum – can you see if you can find this baby monitor?'

Magdala pushes back her chair with a frown and heads off down the hall towards Charlotte's room.

'And, Alex... Billy's lock of hair, and his bathers; they're gone from his memory chest. Do you know where they might be?'

'Lauren – are you for real? If I'm not being accused of abusing our daughter or concealing baby monitors, I'm being blamed for stealing our dead son's memories. Our *dead son*, who died because of *you*.'

My mouth gapes, even as my heart chills deep inside. Alex has insinuated this before, but never said it in so many words. I knew, felt it in me, that he has always held me at fault. It is agonising, yet somewhat of a relief, to finally hear him say it out loud.

Before I can respond, he continues, his voice hostile. 'As for the bruise – I wouldn't be surprised if you hurt her without knowing. You know, by forcing her onto your nipple. Or picking her up from the cot after a long day.'

Although I'm quaking with disbelief, I remain logical. I handle babies all day at work – pregnant women too. I know my own strength. I have never bruised anyone to my knowledge. Yet I am starting to see that, even if I speak up, Alex and his mother will refuse to believe what I say. Also, what the hell does he mean about 'forcing her onto my nipple'? I've only breastfed her again *once* recently, and there's no way he could know about that.

Magdala trundles back into the room, a stern expression on her face. 'No baby monitor that I could find.'

Alex looks at me pointedly, his lips pursed in accusation.

'I put it back on the shelf,' I say. My heart skips a beat.

'I checked there,' Magdala replies.

There's clearly no point in me going to look for it now. One – or both? – of them has obviously already hidden it elsewhere.

But why – what's their game? What is it, exactly, they are so determined to keep from me? I'll have to search for it later.

Magdala lays her hand flat on the table. 'Why don't you tell her, Alex – about the surprise you were planning. Maybe that will help her calm down.'

Calm me down? It takes everything in me not to scream with frustration.

Alex sighs and arranges his knife and fork together on his plate. 'I had thought to book us a weekend away, just the two of us, over New Year's – a circuit breaker, if you will, from the stress of you going back to work. I had thought perhaps a few days off to recharge, away from all the pressures of life, would help.'

'I see,' I say slowly. This isn't like Alex. He has never planned a trip during our whole relationship. My mind flicks back to the early days of our courtship, me happily booking several weekend sojourns to the countryside, and to the beach. When he'd had to cancel each one due to 'urgent work projects', I'd tried not to appear dismayed. He'd subsequently promised to take me on one of his interstate business trips, but somehow they had never eventuated, either. Then, before I knew it, I was pregnant.

'I had thought a hotel in the city might be nice,' he says now, a bitter smile on his face. 'A little adult adventure together. I had thought that if Mum hadn't been available, we may have found another babysitter. If there was someone you know with older kids – or if we had to, maybe Karla, at a push?'

My heart softens a little. Maybe he's right. Perhaps it is just the stress of work that's sending me a bit bonkers. I imagine a few days away from it all, sharing a bottle of bubbles to ring in the New Year. Sleeping off the hangover and not having to worry about waking early to feed Charlotte. My body almost shivers in delight.

Alex's voice interrupts my daydream. 'But now, it doesn't sound like the best idea. Maybe we should just take some time to let the dust settle.'

Dust, settle. Like the dirt settling over the site of Billy's death. Alex had arranged truckloads of dusty earth to be bulldozed into the pool only a few short months after we lost him. The area had resembled a gravesite until the new turf, a lurid green against the surrounding yellowing lawn, was finally laid over it.

'Okay. I thought you didn't trust the neighbour anyway.' My eyes fall on the Christmas tree Magdala has erected, strung with dusty ornaments that haven't seen the light of day for five years. There are no presents beneath it, but then, why would there be? I haven't had a chance to think about shopping for Charlotte yet and no one has sent presents for me – it has been so long since I have engaged with my previous sources of support. But maybe it doesn't have to be completely that way.

'I'm thinking of going to my mothers group Christmas barbecue tomorrow. It might be good for me and Charlotte to spend some time with them, and I could ask around for a sitter.' It won't just be an opportunity to speak with Elspeth, maybe hanging out with other mothers is exactly what I need.

'Good idea,' Alex says. 'I'll come with you.'

'It's just for mothers!' I snap. Even though partners *are* invited, I need a little time away from Alex.

'Surely I'd be welcome now, as a stay-at-home dad.' He reaches out and places his palm firmly over my wrist. 'It will be good to reconnect – maybe we can find someone who can help out with babysitting. And once you're feeling a little better, we'll revisit the idea of some nights away.'

The pressure from his hand is starting to hurt. Goosebumps shoot up the length of my arm. My ring finger, encircled by my wedding band, begins to throb.

'Then we can spend some quality time together. Just the two of us. It'll be like old times, Lauren. You just wait and see.'

17

Email draft

Saturday 15 December, 9.35 p.m.

Dear Natalia,

I hope it's okay to reach out again. I honestly don't know who else to contact.

We've just found a bruise on Charlotte. My mum (a retired social worker who used to work for child services) told me babies can't usually roll at this age. If that's true, how could Charlotte have got the bruise?

I just remembered Billy apparently fell off the change table one day when Lauren was tired. He had a scratch on his cheek for weeks. Does this mean he didn't actually roll off? I'm really worried and I can't stop thinking about it. This is my mother's wheelhouse, but I'm sure you know my mum and Lauren don't have the best relationship, so I thought it best to ask someone more objective. If you have any advice for me, I'd truly appreciate it.

Regards,
Alex

18

I'm lying alone in bed, a thin doona over me. I shiver as a stream of cold air from the air conditioner catches my face. Alex calls goodnight to his mother from the hall, then I hear his footsteps padding into Charlotte's room.

'Night, my sweet one,' he whispers. I can only just make out his words through the baby monitor on my bedside table. 'You look comfy. I've got your formula all ready. I suspect you won't be getting much breastmilk tonight.'

What the heck does he mean? I was hoping to try to breastfeed Charlotte again overnight. My supply, although it has been reducing, is still present. And there should be at least two bottles of expressed breastmilk in the fridge. But something about Alex's tone sends an icy wave through me.

He enters our bedroom in darkness. When he slides under the doona, I keep my body soft and my breath even. I clench my teeth to stop them chattering.

His arm stretches over me, grabs the baby monitor from my side of the bed and settles it on his bedside table. 'Just in case,' he says quietly.

Just in case of what, exactly? My brain grinds through everything I have heard in the last few days, trying to compute. There's been a lot, but the thing that keeps snagging is that woman who came to our home yesterday. Karla mentioned she hadn't crosschecked details of the various blue Peugeots in her notebook – which is what I know I need to do. Yet, I'm resisting. It crosses my mind that Karla hasn't come looking for her notebook. Surely, she knows I took it? I must take the opportunity to read it tonight, while I still have a chance.

There's a soft cry from the baby monitor. Alex's breathing has settled into a deep and regular pattern. I ease out of bed and take the monitor with me as I head out of the room.

The house is dark. Loud snores emanate from my study. Magdala is most clearly asleep.

Charlotte is awake when I enter her room. 'Darling,' I say, settling the baby monitor on the change table and taking her into my arms. She coos in delight and tugs at my hair. As I change her nappy, I note the faded bruise. There are no others over her torso or on her limbs as I examine her from head to toe. But I'm not naive; the absence of any further bruising by no means confirms she is safe.

She puckers her mouth and I can see she is hungry. I settle on the rocking chair, raise my shirt and lift her to my breast. To my delight, she launches for it, takes my nipple wide-mouthed in just the right way. The let-down reflex kicks in quickly, a flash this time, as jets of milk squirt into her hungry mouth. It is primal, this sensation, joining me to her in a way I wasn't able to experience early on with Billy. Yet my bond with Charlotte is beyond biological. After all, we ended up having to use a donated egg to finally have her. I've tried to figure it out, the ease of connection I feel for her. I've wondered if it's because she's a girl, making it easier for me to empathise with her, easier to imagine her growing into a mini-me. But that's too simplistic. Besides, Charlotte doesn't, and never will, resemble me. Billy, on the other hand, was almost my spitting image. So, why was bonding with him so hard?

With Charlotte at my breast, I cast my mind back to that time. Alex was supposed to be at work, yet it felt like he was always home, always around. It was as if he didn't trust me with Billy. There were constant questions: should I really be bathing him that way? Feeding him so much? Using that brand of nappy, or dressing him in so many layers? It felt like no matter what I did, I was always falling short. I started to believe his implications that I wasn't a good enough parent.

The difference is, I don't expect perfection of myself anymore. It's just not sustainable. I have set the bar lower this time around and know I can do this: be the best mother I can be for my daughter.

'I've got you, baby,' I say. 'I'm going to make sure you'll be all right.'

When I look up, Alex is standing before me, his face glowering in the dark.

'What are you doing?'

'What does it look like I'm doing?'

'Don't be smart,' he says and a sliver of fear tears at my throat. 'Do you really think trying to breastfeed her is a good idea?'

There it is again, the subtle questioning that *seems* so innocent.

'She's taken to it straight away this time,' I say.

'Your supply has been going down. There's less and less in the bottles every day. How can you be certain she's getting enough?'

His questions could conceal a real concern, I suppose, but there's something perturbing about his judgemental tone, his seeming righteousness. My dad used to speak to my mum in the same way. No wonder Mum used to doubt herself too.

'It's okay,' I say, suddenly aware of the automatic docility in my voice, a strategy I'd learnt growing up. I hadn't realised, until just now, how much I instinctively placate Alex when I sense his anger threatening to emerge. 'If she's not, we can give her formula top-ups.'

'That's a lot of extra work.' For himself, he's obviously thinking.

'I'll make sure to offer her a top-up after the feeds.'

'She won't be getting your breastfeeds during the day. Do you think it's a good idea to be mixing it up?'

And suddenly I understand. Breastfeeding is something he cannot do, something of mine he cannot appropriate.

'Do you think it would be better for her if I stopped breastfeeding then?'

He rubs his chin with his palm. 'Less confusing for her.'

'You think it might be too confusing for her switching between the bottle and the breast?'

My questions have a practised air of naivety, of faith in him, of self-doubt.

'I think so. I think consistency is best.'

He is wrong. Clearly wrong. I'm an obstetrician. It's because I know this topic back to front that I can finally see him for what he is. Children's clothes, bathing, formula feeding are not my areas of expertise, but breastfeeding – at least the essentials – was taught at medical school. And then there's my maternal instinct. It's taken a long time, but I am finally beginning to trust it, to trust in myself. Even so, I'm not ready to muster the courage to speak up to him, to highlight his lack of knowledge.

'I hear you,' I say.

He looks at me pointedly.

'Let me finish this feed?' I ask, softly.

He shrugs and leaves the room.

'Night,' I call. I listen for his footsteps returning to our room, his body slumping into bed.

'I'm sorry, Charlotte,' I say. 'One day I'll be ready. No matter the repercussions, one day I'll speak up for what's best for you.' And, I say silently, for myself.

19

THREE DAYS EARLIER

The harsh ding of a text message wakes me from my morning nap. Charlotte is in my arms, fast asleep after her morning feed. Without waking her, I check my mobile. It's from Natalia.

Can we talk?

I exhale and the tension I've been holding in my body since discovering the bruise yesterday softens. My god, do I need Natalia's help.

Rising from the recliner, I settle Charlotte in the cot, turn off the volume on the baby monitor and call her number. If I know Natalia, she'll be at home, cooking a wholesome Sunday brunch in her sunny kitchen, the major chords of a female folk band pumping from her stereo in the background.

She answers right away, turns down the music.

'Hey. I'm really sorry about yesterday. I was thrown by Alex's phone call. I've done a lot of thinking, and I want you to know I'm here for you.'

'Thanks. That means a lot.'

'You okay?' She has clearly noticed my shaky voice.

'Not really. There's a bruise. On Charlotte's lower back. It's purply-brown, so a few days old.'

'God. What happened?'

I grip the phone, steeling myself. 'I don't think Alex believes me when I say I have no idea how she got it.'

'But you've been at work. You've hardly been home.'

'Right. When I get home, she's asleep. Alex is getting up to her most nights. Then there's barely time for a quick cuddle in the morning before I leave. He's been her primary carer and Magdala has only just arrived. Apart from me, Alex is the only other person who has been around her.'

'Maybe there's a simple explanation.'

'I don't know, Natalia.' I close my eyes as a wave of panic courses through me. 'I'm afraid.'

'Of course you are.' She's trying to convey concern, but I can hear how torn she is. I'm well aware that her role as a social worker means that if she has a reasonable suspicion of child abuse, she is mandated to report it to the authorities. 'Look, you know you didn't do it, right?'

'Right,' I say, but a numbness begins to spread throughout my body. I have some sense of how much I have blocked out, both on the day of Billy's death and ever since. I open my eyes and focus on the fish mobile swaying slightly above Charlotte's cot.

'You need to stand up for yourself. If you're certain you haven't done something, it's important you don't get talked into saying that you did.'

Stand up for myself. I can do it in a work context, when I feel strongly enough about an issue. But when I'm at home, with people I care about, my tongue has a tendency to freeze up and I find it so much harder to defend myself.

'I'll try,' I say. 'But I think both Alex and my mother-in-law believe the bruise is my doing.'

'Sounds to me like more of Magdala's gaslighting,' she says. 'Intentional deception to try and make someone question their own sanity. Does that feel right?'

'Yes,' I say, well aware of the nuances of the definition from dealing with my mother-in-law over the years. 'There's something else. The car the neighbour saw at our place last week.'

'The Peugeot?'

'The neighbour says she's seen an identical car at our house several times before. I mentioned it to Alex, but he dismissed it.'

Natalia speaks almost hesitantly. 'It does sound peculiar. I was surprised to get a call from him. I have to say – not many of my friends' partners call me up, not even in my line of work. Particularly if I've barely met them before.' I've never heard her like this. She's usually so confident, but today she is struggling to articulate her words.

'Wait, are you okay?' I ask after a pause.

She inhales deeply. 'You remember that patient complaint from a few years ago, how I freaked out?'

'Yes,' I say.

'I couldn't talk about it then, but things got way worse.'

'Geez, that's awful . . . I'm so sorry. I had no idea.'

'It's okay – there's no way you could have known. I wasn't allowed to say much at the time. But it'll be coming to a head next week. It's about to hit the news.'

'Oh, Natalia. We can discuss Alex another time. Do you want to talk about it?'

'Thanks, sure, yes, if you don't mind? It would actually be a relief to talk about it now that I finally can.'

I settle back into the recliner, gently stroking Charlotte's hair as I push my own fears into a sealable box in my mind. Natalia has always been there for me. Time to support her now.

She takes a deep breath. 'It didn't seem like a big deal at the time. Run-of-the-mill family violence during pregnancy. Like your guy the other day – not that commonality makes it okay, obviously.' She pauses.

'Go on,' I say.

She clears her throat. 'So, I referred the family to child services while the woman was still pregnant. The perpetrator gave me a hard time, wrote repeated complaints to my bosses, even started stalking me on social media. I was accused of all kinds of things: being a family wrecker, abusing my position . . . once he even called me a lesbian – as if that was an insult! But then it got personal. Emails threatening to track me down, make me pay for what I'd done to his family. I'm ashamed to say that I was so freaked out, I didn't follow up the case quite as pedantically as I usually do. Then, a few months after my last contact with him, he killed his family in a horrific murder–suicide. Gassed them all while they were sleeping. I felt so responsible. I mean, there were other services and clinicians involved – I knew intellectually that it wasn't all my fault. But I still felt awful about the whole thing. I thought I'd almost worked through it. Then I got the subpoena. The coroner's case is scheduled for next week. I have to give evidence about my involvement. So, I guess you could say I've been feeling a tad overwhelmed. I'm sorry.'

I blink. Even though I'd heard about the complaints she'd received, and remember the case being reported in the news,

I hadn't connected the two. 'Oh, Natalia. I'm so sorry for what you've been going through.'

'Thanks. I wasn't allowed to talk about it to anyone except my therapist. Confidentiality. I thought to tell you what I could, but I've also been mindful of what you're up against. New baby, returning to work . . . After everything you've been through I didn't want to put more stress on you. But if it's okay, I'd love to call you next week, after the hearing.'

'Of course,' I say. 'And before, and during too, if you'd like. Call me anytime. Please.'

'Okay, I will. Thank you, Laur.' She inhales sharply. 'He really got under my skin, you know? When I was caught up in the middle of it, it began to feel like I was the one with the problem. I kept finding myself believing his point of view, even when it conflicted with my own. And I know about this stuff, right? Like how cognitive dissonance works against us. It's in my training. So, I just had to keep reminding myself: if I don't remember doing something I'm accused of, the most likely explanation is that it isn't true.'

I don't respond to this comment as she continues to vent, but despite her formal training, I'm aware it can also be more complicated than that. I know firsthand about trauma, about denial – about how memory can block things out when they're too horrific to recall. It's a protective mechanism, the psychiatrist had told me, and it was why I didn't have a clear memory of the hours before Billy's death.

What I do remember is that the two of us had had a marvellous swim, cooling off in the pool, me spinning him around and around, him splashing me. He was exhausted. I was too. The last thing I recall was the soft smile on his face as I placed him in his cot for his nap. Then I lay down on the sofa. I don't remember anything from there; at least, not until several hours later, when I awoke to find the sliding door ajar.

You don't recall leaving your son unsupervised? the police officer had asked.

You don't recall leaving the gate of the swimming pool open?
You don't recall leaving the back door ajar?

'Laur.' Natalia's voice snaps me back to the present. 'Promise me you won't admit to anything you're not sure of. Okay?'

20

Session notes, psychiatric services intake

16 December, 11.56 a.m.

Amila Sanchez, RN, intake clinician

Phone call from client's husband Alex De Vale.

Private patient of Dr Georgiou (on leave until late Jan).

12 weeks postpartum.

Husband calling re: concerns regarding wife's erratic behaviour, not sleeping, recommencing breastfeeding in presence of declining supply – same symptoms immediately prior to death of first baby – drowned at 12 months of age under wife's care.

Wife Lauren texting/calling repetitively from work anxious +++ about wellbeing of baby.

Bruise found on daughter's back yesterday, Lauren denies inflicting it, however cause unknown.

Baby otherwise well, will be seen by GP early next week.

?Child Protection report.

Grandmother (A's mother – retired child services worker) present in the home full-time, able to supervise L with baby.

Both A and grandmother have concerns about wife's safety with baby.

A reports L is quick to become frustrated.

Episode when first baby, B, rolled off change table as an infant, retrospective concern from husband that it may have been intentional?

No expressed suicidality/homocidality from wife.

No family violence.

PLAN: discuss with psychiatrist on call to facilitate urgent assessment and ?mother–baby unit admission.

21

We're late to the barbecue, but not embarrassingly so. Rebecca greets us at the door of her modern home, a stately two-storey house approximating a mansion. 'Lauren, hi. So good to see you after all this time. And Alex! Welcome to mothers group! This is Charlotte? Hello, gorgeous.' She tickles Charlotte under her chin and is rewarded with a small smile.

She ushers us through a series of open-plan rooms – walls strung with tasteful Hanukkah decorations, a menorah on the dining table with candles as yet unlit – to the back of her house and outside onto the patio. Parents stand in small clusters beside an ornately decorated fresh-cut Christmas tree, the tips of its branches already wilting in the muggy heat. The scent of pine tingles my nostrils with nostalgia, a hint of happier times when the holiday season was joyous and fun.

I joined this mothers group when Billy was born, though for obvious reasons I stopped attending. I'm still in their online group chat, privy to photos and stories of their growing families. Even though their messages have often left me feeling hollow and lonely, something has stopped me detaching myself completely from the group. These women had been there when I found motherhood such a challenge. And they'd tried to help after Billy died, with casseroles, texts and visits, even though I symbolised every parent's worst nightmare. For a long time I put the group chat on silent and refrained from checking it. But since Charlotte's birth, I've felt the pull of reconnection. Perhaps this is a chance to begin again, around people who know me and understand all the challenges and joys of parenting. An opportunity to surround myself with people I can trust, who might help me rebuild my trust in myself.

Alex greets the other parents with handshakes. He had appeared undisturbed when I pretended to re-read the invitation in the car and 'realised' partners were also invited, almost as if he had somehow known.

Rebecca holds a glass of champagne towards me. I start to protest, but she insists. 'Just the one won't hurt. To help cool you down. How's it all going?'

As I take the glass from her, Charlotte begins to stir against my chest and I shift my weight from foot to foot, desperate for her to settle so I can focus and connect. My eyes sweep the manicured backyard as I try to recall how to make small talk. 'I love what you've done with the space,' I say, then groan inwardly at how pathetic I sound.

Rebecca grins. 'We're delighted with how it's turned out. There's a lot more we want to do. There's room for a pool, but we decided . . .' Her voice trails off. 'You're back at work already?'

Awkward comments, people saying the wrong thing. It's why

I've avoided social settings since Billy's death. From the other side of the porch, I catch Alex glaring at me.

'Yes,' I say. 'We thought it was a good idea this time around.'

'Of course,' she says and my feeling of never being quite good enough resurfaces, here amid Rebecca's spotless home, her perfectly shaped garden, her photogenic family. 'I was planning to go back to work myself but, oops—' she indicates towards her belly, a small bump already visible, '—another one on the way. Number three.' She gives a flawless, white-toothed smile.

'Congratulations.' There's a sense I am lagging behind in a race that I never wanted to be part of. I press Charlotte closer to me and she whimpers. Perhaps her bruise is bothering her. I adjust my hold.

'And you're a stay-at-home dad, I hear. Good for you, Alex.'

I hadn't noticed his approach. He now stands beside me, appearing remarkably composed despite the stifling heat. 'Should be more stay-at-home dads,' he says. 'I love it, but it's full on. Luckily, Charlotte is a great baby.' He reaches out his arms for her and I hand her over mechanically.

Natalia's words come to mind. How easily he dismisses all my concerns, how readily and willingly I forget. 'Yes, he's even had time to set up a new business and take on home renovations while he's been looking after her.'

'My, Alex, you are a superstar.'

He glances sharply at me. 'I arranged to get some blinds installed. Blackout blinds, so she can sleep better.'

Before I have a chance to reply, Rebecca interjects. 'Great idea. I've been begging Tim to get blackout blinds before this little one arrives. I'm praying for a good sleeper. Sounds like you have yourself one.'

'I had thought so.' The words slip out before I can stop them. 'But our neighbour has been hearing Charlotte crying for hours.'

I can almost sense Alex's hackles rising and I realise now why I have attended today. I'm reality testing. I've been away from other mothers for so long that I have very few outside perspectives on my experience. Without them, I realise with a start, I have been casting too much doubt on my own interpretation of things. In essence, I have been gaslighting myself.

'Good god, Lauren,' Alex says. 'I told you the neighbour was out of line.'

'She doesn't look like a baby who cries all day,' Rebecca says, making faces at Charlotte. 'She looks very happy with her daddy.'

'She is.' Alex's eyes are dark as he stares at me.

Other women start to congregate around us, admiring our baby.

'Isn't she gorgeous?'

'She has her daddy's smile.'

'She likes being with him, doesn't she?'

'Charlotte, what a beautiful name.'

Yes, a beautiful name, though one Alex had put undue pressure on me to accept. He'd been adamant, even as I'd suggested my own favourites: Sophia, Eleanor, Lily. He had dismissed them all. Yes, Charlotte was a lovely name, but not one I'd felt I had a say in choosing.

I have the overwhelming urge to grab Charlotte and run – far away from here, away from Alex and Magdala, away from my home that now triggers so many traumatic memories for me. But where would we run to? Where could we possibly hide?

22

I catch sight of Elspeth seated on a wooden bench under the only tree remaining in Rebecca's bare yard. She's a slight woman, diminutive in stature with gleaming shoulder-length honey-brown hair. I walk towards her, noting the young girl huddling by her knees. I recall she has recently separated from her husband, and that, long ago, she'd once dated Alex.

By chance, her name had come up early in our relationship. We'd been discussing my work colleagues and Alex had admitted that they'd briefly dated back in their university days. Even though he'd assured me that it hadn't been a serious connection, I'd felt slightly perturbed around her from then on. Each time I'd found myself working alongside Elspeth at the hospital it had been awkward, and it was worse the day she showed up to mothers group. Yet of all the women there, I'd found her the easiest to talk to – perhaps because, by then, I'd come to know her a little from work and had begun to like and trust her.

'Thanks for your help at the caesarean the other day,' I say, standing in the shade of the silver birch.

'Oh.' She looks a little bothered.

'Okay if I join you? I promise not to talk shop.'

'Um, of course.' She shuffles to one side and gives me a weak smile as I sit on the bench next to her, placing my bag between us.

'You remember May?' she says, gesturing to her daughter.

'Of course.' I smile at the shy, delicate-faced girl, who watches me with a neutral expression. 'How's things?'

'Not too bad. Work's busy as always.' Her eyes search mine for judgement. 'Especially being on my own. I imagine you heard?'

I nod. I know everyone has their secrets, things they prefer to leave unspoken, so I don't probe, but she continues.

'I remember talking to you about my marriage years ago. Patrick didn't want any more kids. I did. Ultimately that's what broke us. Sometimes I wish I could turn back time . . . I'd definitely have made different decisions if I'd known how hard this would be, working full-time as a single mum. Thank god for my mum. I wouldn't be able to work without her support.'

My chest hums. If only my mother were still around. *She's gone and she's not coming back*, Dad had announced in a gruff voice when I was all of ten years old. Though Mum had threatened to leave before, she'd never followed through. Each time, I had wondered if she were to leave, what it would mean for me. Dad's announcement made it clear: she had never intended to take me with her. *She went off with some guy from the west coast*, he continued. *Don't expect to hear from her again.*

But I did expect it. Every day I came home from school hoping to see her face or hear her voice. Occasionally I'd catch a glimpse of her: in a shopping centre, on a busy street. Then I'd realise my error and my heart would collapse in on itself just a little more.

'You wanted to talk to me about something?' Elspeth asks as May continues tugging at her sleeve. Distracted, she'd not realised my mind had been elsewhere. I focus on the present, reminding myself that I know Elspeth – she is someone I can open up to, someone I have confided in previously. She is a fellow doctor, a paediatrician – someone who is used to hearing and keeping confidences.

I glance back towards the patio where Alex remains surrounded by a sea of wives. 'Yes,' I say. 'I do have a minor concern.' I hesitate briefly, then decide to launch straight in. 'I found a bruise on Charlotte's back yesterday. A small one, I suppose. Alex swears nothing happened, but I can't help worrying.'

'What are you concerned about?'

'I know it wasn't me who caused the bruise. And I know babies don't bruise ordinarily. Alex is the main person around her. I just can't help wondering—'

'Alex wouldn't do that.' The sharpness of her tone strikes me.

'What makes you say that?'

She hesitates, then: 'Maybe Alex hasn't told you.'

From the patio my husband is observing the two of us. He squints over Charlotte's head as she bounces in his arms.

Elspeth rests her finger on May's cheek, already tinged pink from the sun. 'Alex reached out to me after your son died.'

'Really?' I had no idea. Alex had never mentioned that to me.

'He knew I was a paediatrician. He wanted my advice.'

'Advice?'

'Whether all would be okay next time, I suppose.'

I'm at a loss for words. Finally, I stammer, 'What did you say to him?'

Elspeth's face flushes. 'I'm not aware of all the details – and I don't need to know, either,' she says, reassuring me; she clearly saw me flinch. 'But I told him childhood drownings were a rare occurrence. Without a pool, the chance of something untoward happening to a second child, even in cases of maternal attachment issues, was minimal.'

Maternal attachment issues. 'You think Billy's death was my fault,' I say, noting the beads of sweat on Elspeth's temple.

'Attachment issues didn't cause your son to drown,' she says. 'Terrible accidents can happen in the most careful of homes.'

The most careful of homes. And she is right: I *was* careful. I'd known that what I was feeling for Billy wasn't normal. Of course I had read up on it, had even spoken to Elspeth about it back in the early days of mothers group. I recall her reassuring me it wasn't uncommon to find it hard to bond, but that babies couldn't tell the difference between a parent who was faking love and one who truly felt it. She assured me that, with time, natural bonding would spontaneously arise, and that until then I should 'fake it till you make it'.

And so, going through the motions of love is what I'd done: holding buttercups under Billy's chin and telling him it meant he liked butter, playing peekaboo, tickling him and blowing raspberries on his belly each time I changed his nappy. He had cooed and giggled in reply. At times, I'd even caught myself genuinely smiling back.

Elspeth's daughter tugs again at her mother's blouse.

'We'll be going soon, honey,' Elspeth says. When she turns to me, she averts her eyes. 'Alex was desperate when he reached out.' She chooses her words carefully. 'He was concerned for you. I reassured him that women with postnatal depression almost always recover. And then . . .' Her voice is strangled, her expression hard to read.

'And then?'

'And here we are. You with your new baby, me with my daughter. You with your husband. Me a single mother.'

I feel my neck pulsing. Why is she telling me this now? I suddenly remember the mystery woman at our house. And I recall that Elspeth and Alex had once shared a romance. I wonder why he would suddenly decide to confide in her. 'Has something happened between you and Alex recently?'

'No!' Her face burns red. 'I only wanted to be upfront.' She puts her hand on my arm. 'Look, Lauren, I've been thinking about reaching out to you. It's been pretty quiet for me these last few years. I mean, Rebecca and the others are great, but, frankly, I've missed spending time with someone who gets the challenges of being a doctor and a mother. I always appreciated you being so open with me. I would like us to hang out more.'

She looks tired and heartbroken. I want to help her, be there for her, like she was for me. My tense smile begins to loosen for the first time that day as we make plans to catch up for coffee in a few weeks. It will be interesting to see how Alex responds to the news of our blossoming friendship. Unless . . . I look up and see he's still staring at Elspeth and me.

Needing to escape his constant gaze, I offer to help Elspeth carry her things to her car. She points out a half-empty bowl of rocket salad on the table and a pair of salad servers. I toss the wilted leaves into the bin and give the bowl and cutlery a cursory wipe clean. I keep a careful eye on each step as I exit the front porch, so I don't trip down them. When I look up to locate Elspeth, I gasp as I see her opening the boot of her car. A blue Peugeot. I have to stop myself from blanching.

I had promised myself I would stop discounting my gut. Despite what she'd said, could Elspeth be the reason Alex had been so keen to start attending mothers group? She must be his mystery woman. My breath suddenly tightens inside me. Even in this group, I am on the outside. I am alone.

23

The car ride home is silent. After all the excitement, Charlotte is asleep in her car seat. I don't bring up Elspeth, but her comments keep surfacing in my mind. I've always known she and Alex dated years ago, and that they'd remained Facebook friends. When we'd discussed it in the past, he'd assured me he had no residual feelings for her. But I hadn't known he had reached out to her after Billy died. How often were they in touch? She drives a blue Peugeot. My instincts are screaming at me that Elspeth is the woman who showed up to our house the other day. But as we've only just reconnected, the prospect of our friendship deepening has me desperate for it not to be her.

I still haven't read Karla's notebook. Hopefully Karla has included other details about the woman's appearance that will give me some clues about her identity, so I can determine if she is a match with Elspeth. I must read it. It's critical I find out who this Peugeot woman is once and for all – if only for my own sanity.

We pull into the driveway and Alex steps out of the car, turning towards the back door where Charlotte is sleeping in her car seat. 'I'll transfer her inside,' I call through the window, as Alex begins to lift the handle.

He gives me a quizzical look, but leaves me to it. 'Don't take too long. Mum texted me. Dinner's already on.'

Once in the nursery, I settle Charlotte in her cot as she sucks contentedly at her thumb. She's always remarkably calm in her own company. 'Just like your mummy,' I whisper, even though there are no shared genes between us. I run my hand through the soft fuzz of her hair, contemplating her genetic heritage. The egg donor's name, date of birth, her answers to questions about her family's medical history, a baby photograph that looks remarkably like Charlotte: this is all we know of her maternal heritage.

Months after Billy's death, Alex had made a suggestion. Another child would give me a sense of purpose, he'd said, perhaps help me start to feel normal again. At first, I couldn't even contemplate it. But he brought it up most nights, despite my attempts to avoid the topic. Eventually, I caved. The path of least resistance yet again.

So, we tried. And we tried. Yet month after month, the pregnancy tests lit up with a single line. The fertility specialist was blunt when my blood tests came back. *Premature menopause*, she'd said, her face grim as if she were expecting me to start protesting. But there were no more tears left inside. Instead, a twisted smile curled at my lips for the first time in nearly two years. I couldn't believe the cruel irony; it seemed that even nature didn't trust me with another child and had simply switched my ovaries off.

Alex, however, had other plans. 'Donor eggs,' he said, without skipping a beat, before I could ask the specialist any further questions or had a chance to understand the implications of my diagnosis. He sounded sure and firm, like he'd been considering the option for some time. The specialist immediately directed us to the donor team, who warned us it was likely to be quite a wait. But that didn't seem to deter Alex. He was already researching every detail about egg donation on his phone as we walked out of the clinic. And I didn't have the heart, or the energy, to stop him.

Joint counselling sessions, reams of information to digest. And then, the seemingly endless wait. Two years later, I answered the phone call from the clinic with some trepidation, expecting further bad news. But finally, it was positive, the nurse announcing we had reached the top of the waiting list. We were offered two anonymous donors to choose from, and although I read both profiles at length, I remained uncertain. So, once again, I let Alex decide.

The procedures, the injections, were unpleasant, particularly in my never-ending fog of grief. But it was all worth it when I finally saw Charlotte's heartbeat on an ultrasound. Even though she carries none of my DNA, I have loved her wholeheartedly since that moment. I have no doubt her growing in *my* womb has impacted the expression of her own genes to some small degree; at least, that is what current science supports. My pregnancy euphoria could possibly have contributed to Charlotte's sunny temperament. And my care of my own nutrition and well-being may well have switched on her own health-related genes. So, despite my fleeting concerns about my lack of direct input into her DNA, I know she is every bit my daughter, my own. She is our miracle baby. I will stop at nothing to keep her safe.

I turn the volume on our regular baby monitor down to the lowest setting. I don't want Alex to become curious about what I'm up to and interrupt my reading of Karla's notebook. Damn, I realise, I need to look for the other monitor that was concealed beside the memory chest and switch it off too.

I scour the top of the bookshelf. It's not there. I delve into the box. Nothing. Change table, chest of drawers, nappy bag. I even look under Charlotte's cot. There is no sign of the monitor. Where, and why, would Magdala – or Alex, for that matter – have hidden it?

'Lauren. Dinner.' Alex's voice is faint but firm, echoing down the hallway. I smooth down my wrinkled shirt and call back.

'Coming.'

As I leave the nursery, I hear the *ding* of his phone from across the hall. He must left it in the black linen jacket he wore to the barbecue. He used to keep the jacket on the hallway coat rack, but these last few years he has taken to hanging it in the cupboard on his side of the bed.

I tiptoe across the hall into our room. Just as I thought, his jacket is hanging in his cupboard. I reach into his inner pocket, my heart racing, as he has always been insistent on me not checking his mobile. Now, with the screen of his phone lighting up with a message, I can see why.

Elspeth. *Good to see you today*, it reads, *and your other child*. There's a photo attached, a thumbnail of Elspeth hugging May. But when I attempt to open the message to enlarge it, it asks for his fingerprint or a passcode. I think quickly. His birthday. Charlotte's. Billy's. Mine? My fingers fumble as I try each of them in turn. None of them work.

'Lauren, where are you? Dinner's getting cold.'

Crap. 'I'm coming,' I call again.

What the hell does her text message mean? Have there been other text exchanges between them recently? And now, come to think of it, if their friendship is so harmless why did he so obviously keep his distance from her at the barbecue today? Now that I have finally opened my eyes, the more I learn about Alex, the more there is that simply doesn't make sense.

24

It's just past 11 p.m. From the bedroom, I can hear the clock ticking in the hall. Seconds pass, then minutes. I've been waiting the best part of an hour for Alex to fall into deep slumber.

Finally, I creep around to his side, reaching for his mobile in the dim light. I can't help questioning my own morals – perhaps I am stooping as low as Alex with this deception. I take a deep breath. Despite my ethical concerns, I know this is the best way to determine the truth of his relationship with Elspeth, and how frequently she may have been visiting our house.

His right hand is dangling over the edge of the bed. Pressing the screen against his fingerprint, he stirs slightly, then gives a deep sigh and resumes his regular breathing. And I'm in. I head for the ensuite.

Inside, I lock the door behind me and settle myself on the edge of the bath. I click into the messages between Elspeth and Alex.

Elspeth: *I feel a bit weird about you coming to the group.*
Alex: *Believe me, so do I.*
Elspeth: *Then why are you coming?*
Alex: *For more support.*

I wonder what support he needs that he can't get from me?

Alex: *Lauren is happy about me coming*, he continues.
Elspeth: *She won't be for long.*

Elspeth is certainly right about that.

Alex: *She isn't very cluey.*

My limbs tighten.

Elspeth: *And when she finds out?*
Alex: *She won't.*

My heart begins to race as I allow the facts to coalesce. Elspeth, Alex, the blue Peugeot, their secret conversations. I read on, determined to find irrefutable proof of their affair. I can't allow myself to jump to conclusions and if I'm to confront Alex, I'll need undeniable evidence. I won't allow myself to be deceived – either by him or by my own insecurities.

Elspeth: *She was asking a lot of questions at the barbecue.*
Alex: *Really?*
Elspeth: *Something about a bruise on Charlotte. I tried to reassure her.*
Alex: *But she was still anxious?*
Elspeth: *Hugely.*
Alex: *Oh, god. I hope it's not happening again.*
Elspeth: *You're not worried about her with Charlotte, are you?*
Alex: *I really don't know. Jesus, I hope not. Not again.*

My breath sticks in my chest as I realise he is hinting to people – Natalia and Elspeth – that he is worried about me with my baby. Turning the spotlight on me provides him the perfect cover to harm her, or worse.

If I just sit idly by, am I allowing the potential for something more than a bruise to happen to Charlotte? Alex's ex, Therese – and her daughter Zoe – come to mind. My breathing is sharp and shallow. I try to slow it down.

I search the contacts section, and there she is: Therese. I quickly store the number in my phone, then flick to his messages and search her name.

The last message is from seven years ago, before we met.

Hope things went okay with the wake, Alex had written. *I'm sure your eulogy did her proud. Let me know how it ends up. Apologies I couldn't be there.*

There is no reply.

Magdala had hinted at a tragedy. It seems Therese's child Zoe died too. Just like Billy. I text Therese's number from my own phone.

Hi Therese. Please forgive me interrupting and sorry I have to reach out. I'm Alex De Vale's wife. I found your number in his contacts. I wondered if it would be possible to ask you a few questions?

They don't seem to have been in ongoing contact, so it feels unlikely she'll alert him to my message. Still, I keep an eye on his mobile, just in case. Nothing comes through. Then, within a minute or so, a message pops up on my phone:

I don't want to talk on the phone or text. Happy to meet in person. You name a time and a place.

My fingers are clumsy as I type back. *Thank you so much. Would tomorrow evening suit – say, 6 p.m.? Fairmont Pub, the beer garden?* I'll have to make the excuse of a work meeting so Alex doesn't try to come too.

Perfect. See you tomorrow, she replies.

All at once I feel goosebumps rising on my forearms. I have no idea who this woman is, what she might be like. All we have in common is that we have both been in a relationship with Alex. And it seems we have each lost a child. God only knows what stories Therese has to tell, what she knows . . .

I hear shuffling echoing from the bedroom. I tilt my head, listening. Nothing more. I'm just about to leave the ensuite when Alex's phone dings.

You still up? An unknown number. It's almost midnight – who would be texting him now?

His phone has timed out and locked itself again. I sneak out of the ensuite, towards the mattress where his right hand hangs over the edge. I kneel beside him and lean towards his index finger with his phone when – snap! – his palm encircles my wrist.

Shit.

'What the hell do you think you're doing?' He wrenches his mobile from my hand.

'I should ask you the same question.'

His eyes glimmer in the semi-darkness.

I hadn't planned to say it, but it rises from me now like a hot mist: 'Elspeth told me everything.'

'What the hell! What are you talking about?' He swings his legs over the side of the bed abruptly, rubbing his forehead.

'You're talking to her behind my back!'

'For fuck's sake. I reached out to her for support. There's nothing going on between us.'

Something inside me twists like a sea snake. 'Nothing?'

'I hardly know her, for god's sake.'

'You dated her.'

He stares, then continues, 'You knew that. You don't need to make such a big deal of all this.'

They dated back in their twenties; I would hope it meant nothing now. So, why is he acting so defensively?

Good to see you today and your other child.

I had assumed Elspeth was referring to Charlotte. But an image of May springs to mind now, her delicate cheeks, her blonde hair, her reserved demeanour. I recall Elspeth tucking her daughter into the car earlier, May's beach-blue eyes catching mine. And I realise, all at once: May looks nothing like Patrick, Elspeth's ex. She looks very much like Alex.

'Oh my god.' I throw myself onto the bed, unable even to sob.

Alex rises and stands over me, his breaths loud enough to hear. 'What the hell's the matter now?' he says. 'I don't fucking understand you.'

'There's nothing to understand. Get out.'

'For god's sake, Lauren, you're driving me crazy. And can you please keep it down? Mum will hear you screaming.'

'You fathered another woman's child!' I cry, before I can stop myself. 'A friend of *mine*. A colleague of *mine*. A woman from *my* mothers group!'

'Jesus fucking Christ.' He kicks the leg of the bed. 'You've lost it. None of what you're saying makes any sense. You need some serious help. I'm calling your doctor first thing tomorrow.'

'Alex, you can't deny it. I've read your texts.'

'What the hell? How dare you, Lauren. You accuse me of leaving Charlotte to cry. Of bruising her. Now you're saying I've had a child with a woman I used to date *years ago*. You break into my phone. You may as well accuse me of murdering Billy.' He stands erect above me, his face a thundercloud.

'No, Alex. That's what you think of me.' My voice is trembling now, while his is cold and full of fury.

'I've done *nothing wrong*.' He backs away slowly, seating himself on the edge of the bed. 'I won't let you say I have. You, on the other hand.' He shakes his head. 'Maybe if you'd been a better mother, we wouldn't be in this mess.' He inspects his phone. 'Fucking hell. It's late. I'm sleeping on the couch tonight.' He grabs the baby monitor from his bedside table and storms from the room, pulling the door shut behind him.

I slide under the sheet on my side of the bed and lie still, rigid, the fan above the bed rotating eddies of warm air onto my throat. Our baby, a bruise on her; Alex, furious at my questions, even as he is keeping so much hidden from me. Is Charlotte at risk from him? It feels impossible to prove. But even if he did cause her bruise, I can't imagine he would hurt her with his mother present in the house.

If you'd been a better mother, we wouldn't be in this mess.

In the silence and darkness, Alex's words echo through my brain. He's right. I should have been a better mother to Billy. I'm not a good mother to Charlotte, not a good wife to him. Why did I immediately jump to the worst conclusion? Why did I accuse him like that? I have no real evidence that he and Elspeth are having an affair. That they have a child together. Talk about escalation. All I know is that Elspeth drives a Peugeot and has been talking to Alex about my mental health.

You need some serious help.

God, maybe he's right. Am I losing my mind again? I'm imagining things in my head, jumping to ridiculous conclusions, worst-case scenarios.

And now I know something even more painful: he is furious at me for causing our son's death.

I had been worried Charlotte was at risk. But is he correct in his implications – is Charlotte actually at risk from me?

25

TWO DAYS EARLIER

Monday morning and I'm a little hesitant to leave the house and head to work, worries about my postnatal depression sitting heavy in my mind. But the clench in my jaw softens ever so slightly as I remind myself of my tendency to catastrophise. I attempt to reassure myself that the worst almost never eventuates. Even so, my mouth is dry as I kiss Charlotte goodbye.

This evening I plan to meet up with Therese. 'I'll be late tonight,' I tell Alex before I depart. 'Work meeting.'

He grunts from the couch.

Thank god the day passes quickly at the hospital, a blur of mothers in labour and in the antenatal clinic. I manage not to text Alex to enquire after Charlotte's wellbeing; I have to trust that between Magdala and Alex no harm will come to her for now.

By the time I manage to leave work, I'm running late. The pub is chock-full, clusters of people at the bar, animated like fireflies around a light. I head into the beer garden, where the air is dense with humidity. The tables are all occupied by groups of rowdy punters, sipping on presumably lukewarm pints of beer.

I pick my way down to the back of the garden where a slim woman sits alone at a smaller table, shoulders hunched as she scrolls through her phone.

'Therese?'

She glances up and I note the mousy hair and amber eyes, the trusting, vulnerable face similar to my own. Therese is Alex's usual type.

'Lauren. Hi. I was wondering if you were still coming.' She places her phone on the table next to a glass of white wine. 'I'm guessing he's doing it to you too. For you to reach out.'

Despite all my doubts these last few days, it's still a jolt to hear her speak like this. 'I'm not exactly sure what you mean,' I say, pouring myself a water from the jug on the table and gulping a few mouthfuls. 'What did he do to you?'

'It's hard to put into words.' She bites her lower lip. 'My counsellor is still helping me understand.'

My body, tense from the overheated location, has softened as she has been talking. Someone who gets it.

She speaks haltingly. 'I still question myself all the time. He questioned me a lot – whether I was thinking straight.'

Fuck.

'I kept justifying it to myself – that he knew things, knew better than me. That I was the one with the problem. After all, I was the one seeing a counsellor. I was the one on medication. And he seemed genuinely concerned about my wellbeing. Anytime I tried to talk about my issues with his behaviour, he would accuse me of being daft. I guess over time I just started to believe him. I was the problem. I must have been, because he said it so often.'

'I'm so sorry,' I say. I know all too well what that feels like.

She looks up at me, her eyes welling with tears. 'Does he do the same with you?'

I clench my hands together and slowly nod.

What a relief, this external validation. It's not me. This comes from Alex. He has been placing all the burden and fault onto me because he cannot face whatever lies deep within himself. My shoulders loosen. My neck straightens. A small smile of relief crosses my lips as, for the first time in a long time, I feel some sense of clarity.

'Did Alex ever cheat on you?'

'Nope. That wasn't the issue. I don't think that's his style.'

I hold doubt, but put it to the side for now. 'Did he ever try to hurt you physically?'

'No,' she says almost immediately, then, 'You?'

'No,' I admit. 'But I found a bruise on my baby daughter a few days ago. I can't help but wonder if he did it on purpose, trying to pin it on me.' Even as I speak, I realise how ludicrous my words sound. 'Your child, Zoe – may I ask what happened?'

'Nothing.' She looks almost startled.

'There was something in your texts with Alex about a eulogy.'

'Oh.' Her eyes soften in comprehension. 'That was my mother. She died soon after Alex broke up with me.'

'I see.' My mind races. 'I had understood there was some tragedy involving your daughter – or am I wrong?'

'It's kind of personal.'

'I'm sorry, I don't mean to intrude. I only ask because I was concerned it might have been related to Alex somehow – to him causing you, or your daughter, harm.'

She gives a quick laugh. 'Nothing like that. I mean . . . it's public knowledge anyway, so,' she sighs, 'I guess there's no harm in sharing.' She takes a moment to compose herself. 'Zoe's father was targeted by Immigration for overstaying his visa. He died in detention, so there was a lot of media. His death was brutal in a completely different way. Having to tell Zoe her father was gone was . . .' She falls silent, her face pale.

'I am so sorry,' I say.

'It's okay. I met Alex about six months after we lost Zoe's dad. It was hard because at first Alex presented like a dream. I was deep in grief. He listened to me, told me all the things I desperately wanted to hear. That he would look after my daughter like his own, take care of both of us. It was only later that I realised he wasn't helping out at all – maybe he'd never planned to or maybe he just wasn't capable? It took a while, but eventually I clocked that he'd given me a lot of empty promises and no follow through.'

She looks up, searching my eyes for understanding. I nod. How well I know.

'It wasn't physical abuse, but it was devastating to me emotionally. And it was so subtle. It's still hard to pinpoint what went on.'

'It sounds tough,' I agree.

'One of the hardest parts was that at first he seemed okay with my desire to have more kids. But when we started talking about it more seriously, he freaked out. He categorically refused to have a child with me. By then we'd been in what I thought was a pretty serious relationship for some time. I was confused, given he hadn't said anything earlier.'

Therese's hands tremble as she reaches for her wine glass.

'And then, I fell pregnant. It was unexpected and unplanned, of course.' She looks up, daring me to challenge her. 'But I miscarried a month later. Soon after, he broke up with me. I'm still trying to comprehend how we went from A to B so quickly. In love, or so I thought, to pregnancy, to the loss of my baby, then our relationship . . . And as much as I've since realised how emotionally abusive he was, I'm still not over him.' She shrugs, tears welling in her eyes. 'Stupid, huh?'

My mind is clouded with confusion. Magdala had told me it was Therese who hadn't wanted another child. But now Therese is blaming Alex? I shake my head – I'm not here to get caught up in their relationship; my main concern is Charlotte. I need to ask again, just to be sure. 'You never had any reason to doubt your daughter's physical safety?'

'No,' she says, shaking her head. 'Nothing like that. But the one thing that stuck with me was what a counsellor told me early on: trust your gut. It's the best marker of the level of danger you're in.'

26

It's approaching 7 p.m. by the time I leave the pub. I've had my eye on my phone the whole time, half-expecting a text from Alex. Sure enough, as I'm about to start the car, a message pops up.

Dinner's ready.

There in 10, I text back.

We'll be waiting, he replies.

I contemplate calling Natalia, to tell her what Therese has said. But no – I spoke with her just yesterday and right now she has enough on her plate. I wish there was someone else I could bounce this off, get their thoughts. I don't have many friends I can reach out to anymore. And when I look back, I see that I have been having difficulty maintaining friendships ever since I met Alex. Superficially, he was supportive of my social connections. But in reality, he would make derisive comments about my friends, question their closeness to me, belittle them.

I can't believe I haven't seen it until now. Somehow, I've allowed Alex's influence to impact my relationships – all of them.

Once home, I quietly enter the coolness of the house. Gentle laughter filters down the hallway: Alex and his mum, enjoying their dinner. I don't announce my presence. First, I must read Karla's notebook. It's time. I know I am now capable of handling whatever I find out.

I cast an eye over Charlotte in her room. She appears sound asleep, the curve of her belly rising and falling under her sleeping bag. I head for our bedroom. There is a lock on our door. I contemplate using it – but no, if Alex came to find me and saw it locked that would raise his suspicions even further. I leave the door slightly ajar instead. He has heavy footsteps; I should hear him approaching down the hall.

I tug Karla's notebook from my work bag and flip open the cover. I click into the search bar, then type in *blue Peugeot*. A raft of entries fills the screen. I force myself to take a deep breath. This car has been visiting too often for it to be a coincidence or some random tradie.

My brain floods with the shock of truth. What does this mean for me – for us? For Charlotte? My heart is thumping so hard I almost wonder if Alex and Magdala will be able to hear it. But I refuse to let my thoughts run away from me and get distracted. For now, I just need to gather all the facts.

I know I don't have much time, so I push on. With trembling fingers, I type the date of Billy's death into the search bar. My chest heaves as memories flash, but I push them back.

The page loads and I scan it, confused. It is blank.

My heart crumbles. It is likely I will never be able to fill in the missing hours, the gap in my memory. The pain in my chest is overwhelming; it's almost as if I'm losing him all over again.

There's a slight rustle in the hallway. I cock my ear but it's only the creak of the walls shifting in the December heat. I continue searching, mindful of the short window I have before Alex realises I'm home.

I flip back to start scanning the Peugeot entries for any physical descriptions of the person driving, when I hear Alex's voice calling through the baby monitor.

'Lauren! Is that you? Dinner's ready right now.'

I snap the notebook cover shut. Damn. I've let myself get distracted again. I must count how many times that car – that woman – has visited our house. And see if there's anything further that could confirm it's Elspeth.

Alex and Magdala are seated at the dining table, candles flickering between them.

'Feeling better?' Magdala asks. 'Alex said you had one of your migraines last night. So good of him to sleep on the couch.'

Alex gives me a gentle smile and I'm immediately perplexed. He is being confusingly kind after his outrage last night. Why would he lie to his mother? After all, she must have heard our heated exchange.

'You know,' Alex says, quickly glancing at his mother, 'while Mum's in town, she's going to visit her lawyer to update her will. It made me wonder if we should think about redoing ours too.'

What on earth?

'Just a suggestion,' he says. 'You can think on it. I can book an appointment with our lawyer if you think it's a good plan.'

I take a seat and Magdala settles a plate in front of me. Boiled gnocchi from a packet, topped with a creamy sauce. My stomach curdles.

'Thank you, Magdala,' I say. 'I'm not very hungry tonight.'

'Maybe you'd like some of this instead, Lauren,' Alex says, pushing a plastic container towards me. 'It's from the barbecue. Leftovers. Rebecca insisted we take it.'

I lift the container to my nose, inhaling the aroma of sweet plum sauce, almost tasting it at the back of my tongue. I salivate. Peking duck: my favourite dish. But I don't remember seeing it at the barbecue yesterday, nor do I recall smelling it in the car on the way home.

'Thanks,' I say.

'No problem. I thought you'd like it,' Alex says.

'Magdala?' I hold out the container to her.

'No fancy food for me,' she says. 'I prefer home cooking.'

Or processed supermarket food, I think to myself.

'I'll have more gnocchi, thanks,' Alex says.

I scoop a large spoonful of duck onto my plate.

'You both enjoyed the barbecue, I hear?' Magdala has a habit of speaking while chewing.

'It was great,' Alex says, observing me. 'I'll become a permanent member of the group in the new year. The honorary father.'

'You'll be taking Lauren's place.' Magdala winks at Alex, who nods.

'Something like that.'

I slice into the duck, lift it to my mouth and begin to chew. A dense bitterness hits my tongue and my nose wrinkles.

'Everything okay?' Alex seems almost unsurprised at my reaction to the food.

I keep chewing. Alongside the familiar sweetness is a bitter, almost metallic tang. 'All good.' I swallow, but it's not just the tart notes, the texture is off too. The sauce is grainier than I'm used to and is missing the silkiness I love.

I try another mouthful, trying to adjust my palate. Some people cook differently to others and I know I should be grateful. I've been craving this dish for some time, might even have mentioned that to Alex several weeks ago? But I can't avoid it – the bitterness is overpoweringly strong, even in spite of the plummy sweetness. Suddenly, I feel ill. I place my fork on my plate. 'I'm not feeling so hungry anymore. Sorry.'

'Peking duck is your favourite,' Alex says. 'There must be something wrong with you.'

'I suppose so. Maybe I ate something at the barbecue that didn't agree with me.'

'Yes.' He inspects me with suspicion. 'Lauren, you're fading away. You must eat.'

Why is he being so insistent? I push the plate away. I'm aware Alex has been frustrated by my mental health, and Magdala doesn't particularly like me, but surely, *surely*, neither of them would ever consider poisoning me?

Magdala holds out a bowl of gnocchi. 'Something plainer then?'

'No, thanks,' I say, the bitter taste receding. Could I be imagining it? Is it all in my mind?

No. *Trust your gut.* All of the strange occurrences – the woman, the crying, the bruise – spring to mind. 'I'm heading to bed.'

'Already? It's so early. And you've hardly eaten a thing.'

'It's been a big day.' I remember his mother's comment

about the migraine. 'My head is still sore and I'm feeling a little nauseous.'

'You've got too much on your plate,' Magdala says. 'Metaphorically, I mean. Lucky I'm here to help out.'

'Lucky,' I say, and give what I hope is a grateful smile.

Seated on my side of the bed, I check myself for any symptoms of poisoning. No dizziness. No racing heart. My vision is clear, my hearing perfect. Whatever was in the two mouthfuls of duck I consumed does not appear to be causing me any acute harm. If indeed there was anything. Perhaps it's only my paranoia kicking in again. I shake my head, so weary all of a sudden.

I place the baby monitor on my bedside table, volume as loud as it will go so I will hear anyone entering Charlotte's room. She has an apnoea monitor, positioned under her mattress, to keep an eye on her breathing. I insisted on it, after Billy. I didn't want to take any chances. The monitor beeps when turned on or off and sets off a screeching alarm if Charlotte doesn't breathe frequently enough. Both Alex and I have forgotten to switch it off on numerous occasions after lifting her from the cot.

My mind is spinning with confusion. Yes, I think my husband is having an affair. Yes, out of nowhere he just brought up redoing our wills. It is not beyond the pale to consider that my husband and mother-in-law might also be trying to poison me.

I sneak to Alex's bedside table. Top drawer: nothing unexpected. His Kindle. Tissues. Lubricant. Earplugs and eye mask. A few melatonin tablets. Nothing untoward that might explain the bitter taste. And no sign of the missing second baby monitor. I edge my fingertips up under the rim of the drawers. Nothing.

In the cupboard, Alex's coat hangers are all facing the same way. His clothes are colour coded. I'm reminded how organised he is, how different his approach is from my own jumbled style. I rifle through the pockets of his jackets, his pants. Again, nothing. Drawers of t-shirts, socks, jocks. I crumple each pair of socks in my palm, wondering if there could be something inside, but they squash flat without a sound. On the top shelf of his cupboard, a few boxes of shoes. I check inside each one, around the tissue paper. A box of birthday cards, sentimental items. Nothing strikes me as odd. Ties, cufflinks, belts. Argh. As the intrusive thoughts rear again that this could all be in my imagination, my blood runs hot in my veins. No, I force myself to recall: Alex is likely having an affair. He has just mentioned our wills. I owe it to Charlotte, and to myself, to continue the search.

I slide the ensuite door shut behind me, then check each drawer of the vanity: old toothbrushes, toothpastes, a few old combs. Under the sink, rolls of toilet paper. And on the top shelf, nestled right at the back, the first aid box. I pull it out, my shoulders tight, and rummage through the contents.

Both Alex and I hardly get sick, so we rarely have need for this kit. I can't recall the last time I looked through it. Ondansetron, for my morning sickness, at the top. Paracetamol and ibuprofen, bandages, bandaids. Nothing that I would expect to give a significantly bitter flavour to food. I sigh and replace the box on the top shelf of the vanity. There are no clues here.

I slump to the tiles, my back against the wall, my head in my hands. There *could* be a more likely explanation. Perhaps I can find out who brought the Peking duck to the barbecue, and whether the strange taste might just be down to poor cooking.

On my mobile, I click into the online mothers group chat. It's been a long time since I contributed, so it's hard to get the tone right.

Hey! Great barbecue yesterday, thank you Rebecca. Who brought the Peking duck? Keen for the recipe. Thanks and see you all soon!

Upbeat, not accusatory. They would have no idea something was seriously wrong.

The replies are rapid.

My dish was the cupcakes, all gone :(:)

Cupcakes so good! Didn't see the duck, maybe Sylvia?

Nah, I brought the noodle salad. Hope everyone is having a chill start to the week x

Not me, didn't see it unfort, would have lapped it up! Thanks all for coming, it was a stellar party ☺

So, Rebecca also denies having seen the Peking duck. Was it even served at the barbecue?

Another ding on the group chat.

Hi lovely ladies! And darling Lauren of course. So glad to be part of this group now.

Oh, shit. It's Alex. My heart heaves in my chest. When the hell did they add him?

I scroll back through the most recent messages, a series of photos sent after the barbecue, prior to my message.

There is his number, between photos of the food and of the gathering. He is infiltrating every corner of my life. And this means he will have seen my question.

The messages fly even quicker in response to his text.

So glad to have you!

Fathers so welcome :)
You're a great addition to our group x
Can't wait to see you and Charlotte at our next catch-up
Even Elspeth chimes in: *It will be great to see more of you.*
I bet it will.
Shucks, thanks guys. Sometimes I feel like I'm not quite nailing this parenting gig. Will be great to have such a talented group of women to ask for advice x

In the past, on the rare occasions he'd revealed his insecurities to me, I had found it reassuring, and flushed with feelings for him. Now, I wonder if it was just a baited hook, a way to get me – or others – to open up.

'Darling.' It's him, knocking at the ensuite door. 'Can I come in?'

'Just a minute.' I stand and flush the toilet, then rumple my hair. I feel the need to convince him I have no suspicions about him. When I slide open the door and re-enter our bedroom, it's he who has mistrust in his eyes.

'I'm not feeling so good,' I say.

'You think it was the duck? So soon after tasting it.'

'I was trying to work out if anyone else was feeling unwell. You know, gastro.'

'I see.' He knows me all too well, can read my attempts at deception too easily. 'You seem to have got over me supposedly fathering Elspeth's child pretty damn quick.'

'I overreacted,' I say. 'I'm sorry I accused you of that.' My words finally do have the ring of truth.

He shrugs. 'Mum's gnocchi is in the fridge if you're hungry later. We're going to watch some TV now. Are you going to sleep it off?'

'Yes,' I say, then quickly, 'I can do the evening feed tonight.'

'Are you sure that's a good idea if you're feeling unwell?'

'She'll be getting my antibodies through the breastmilk, Alex. Even if she catches what I've got, she'll be okay.' I slide into bed and pull the doona up over my chest; no need to let him know I actually have zero intention of doing *anything* that could put Charlotte at any risk.

'If you insist.' He reaches for the baby monitor. 'I'll come and get you when she wakes.'

I place my hand on his arm. 'I've got it.'

'We'll see.' He leaves the room, clearly perturbed.

My mind swirls. He has been cooking for me for years now, right back through the pregnancy with Billy, after the birth, after Billy died, through Charlotte's pregnancy too, and every night since her birth. Has he been lacing my food this whole time?

I track back through the meals he cooks. The usual staples: spaghetti bolognese, tofu stir-fry, beef stroganoff. I've never been stopped in my tracks before by such a bitter taste. Except – he could have been concealing the taste in something else: my morning latte, for instance. Or in the port wine-flavoured jelly he occasionally makes for dessert.

Pulling out my phone, I google *bitter-tasting medication*. A list of possibilities lights up my screen. Antibiotics, antihistamines, antipsychotics. And then a thought surfaces. Before we met, Alex trained as a pharmacist. He had then sidestepped into IT for a pharmaceutical company. His previous career never comes up in conversation, and he talks about that time in his life so infrequently that it rarely comes to my mind. Until now.

I squeeze the doona in my fists. Alex would say this is more of the same, more paranoia. Perhaps he'd be right. I squeeze my eyes shut and bring Natalia to mind. Therese too. *Trust your gut*, they'd both said. My gut is literally screaming at me.

I google *poisoning food*. All of the articles describe wives poisoning their husbands. Nothing about husbands poisoning their wives. One website lists all the usual suspects: arsenic, belladonna, rat poison, antifreeze. I go to start a fresh search, then stop. Worse than being an ex-pharmacist, Alex is in IT. He probably knows how to locate my search terms and access my browsing history. He purchased a new router recently – he could have been observing my internet access all along, monitoring me even now. I quickly shut down the page, erase the search history then press my palm against my forehead, trying to think.

Whatever medication he has been using on me – if he has – must be concealed somewhere in the house.

I hunker down under the doona, feigning sleep.

Amid all the uncertainty, there is one thing of which I am sure: I *know* I have done nothing wrong.

27

ONE DAY EARLIER

I wake with a start. Despite the anxiety pulsing through my veins, it seems I fell into a deep sleep. Six a.m. Crap, I've been asleep for hours. Perhaps that bitter element in my duck was more sinister than I thought?

Alex is slumbering beside me, snoring softly. Still, I should have an hour or so before he stirs. There's a shuffle from the baby monitor, then silence. I rise and place the monitor in my pocket, then head into the hall. Poking my head into the nursery, I note Charlotte is settled, asleep.

I pad to the kitchen. Nothing in the fridge that's out of the ordinary, nor the cupboards, either. I run my eye over the orderly rows of crockery and tableware, all selected by Alex. He has trained me to arrange the plates just so. The glasses too. Easier to find things, he says.

The pantry is chock-full. It seems that Magdala has brought an assortment of foodstuffs with her. I can tell which are hers by the boxes and tins that are in disarray. Alex hasn't yet neatened her goods up. Perhaps this is a sign that he is expecting his mother to move on, take her pantry items home with her. Or maybe he just hasn't had a chance to make her things orderly yet.

My eyes flick over the shelves. Alex's stacking and organising are evident at the back of the pantry. Herb jars arranged alphabetically. Flours and sugars neatly placed side by side. Soups and tins at the very back, labels facing front. It's almost like a pharmacy. Almost.

The untidiness is the clue. If Alex has used something to lace the duck, he is likely to have carefully replaced it, possibly displacing one of Magdala's contributions in the process. My eyes scan the shelves with the same efficiency I use to scan ultrasounds, looking for the ugly duckling, the odd thing out.

Magdala's items: bottled pasta sauces, untidily stacked fettuccine packets, salted cashews – Alex's favourite. Also capers, anchovies, tinned pineapple and a few pizza bases. There's a box of oats on the herb shelf. Alex will soon remedy that. And then a gap. Behind the gap, the salt container. We usually use rock salt crystals in the grinder and rarely use iodised table salt – only for red wine spills on carpets, or cuts that need disinfecting. I pick the container off the shelf and examine it. It feels almost empty; strange, I can't remember using any for the longest time. I spin open the twist-top lid. Inside, white powder. I tap a small volume of it onto my palm. It's a ground-up substance, sure, but most definitely *not* salt.

I raise my palm to my nose. No odour. I wet one fingertip and press it into the powder, then lift it to my mouth and take a tiny lick. It is tasteless – so definitely not salt, nor bitter, like last night's dinner – but the texture is strikingly familiar; it is the graininess from the Peking duck. What the hell is it?

There's a faint cry on the baby monitor in my pocket.

I need to get the salt container back in place, in case Charlotte wakes Alex. I tip the powder from my palm back into the salt tin and screw the lid on tight, then replace the container on the shelf in exactly the position I found it. I listen hard for any movement in the house. Nothing, just a dense silence; Charlotte has settled. My job right now is to confirm what that powder is. The packaging should still be around somewhere.

Recycling. The bins went out last night. It might well be in there.

I sneak through the sliding door that makes less noise than going through the front, into the morning air heavy with moisture. It's already light enough to make my way along the perimeter of the house, past the iridescent lawn overlying the filled-in pool, under the window of Magdala's room, into the street. Our yellow-lidded bin sits beside our driveway on the nature strip.

I glance up to Karla's window as I tip the bin onto its side and pour the contents onto the grass. One by one, I replace the items back into the bin. Milk cartons, yoghurt container, soup tin. Cream from the scaloppine. Foil. Gnocchi packet. Nothing of interest. Then, as I gather up a soup tin to place back in the bin, a smaller pill bottle tumbles from it to the ground. I pick it up and inspect the label. *Cabergoline, 1 mg*. Not a medication I know much about; I'll have to look it up as soon as I get a chance.

I thrust the rest of the recycling into the bin as quietly as possible, making sure I'm not missing anything in my haste, then lift the bin to standing – not a moment too soon, as the recycling truck rumbles up the street. I slip the bottle into my dressing gown pocket and make for the back door.

Alex is in the kitchen, stacking the dishwasher.

'Where have you been?'

'Just putting something in the recycling before the truck comes.'

I can feel his eyes on me and I turn towards the coffee machine to conceal the shape of the small bottle outlined in my dressing gown.

'You're sweating,' he says.

'It's already pretty warm out there.' Then, 'You're up early.'

'Not as early as you, it seems. Although you did forget to feed Charlotte overnight, despite insisting that you would.'

'I fell asleep.'

'Luckily, I woke up. But you will be careful, won't you? Mothers have suffocated their babies by falling asleep while feeding.'

In the past, I would have taken this as legitimate concern. Now I can feel the warning for what it is: an attempt at control. And a threat.

'I'll keep that in mind.'

I place a cup under the coffee spout and press the button. The smell of freshly brewed coffee floods my nostrils, a reminder of the bitter powder from last night.

'What's for dinner?'

'No idea. Mum's going to cook again.' He passes me a mug. 'Would you make me one?'

'Have this.' I pass him the cup I've just made, then insert the mug beneath the spout, letting the coffee run as I froth milk for my latte. I'm careful to keep the cabergoline bottle in my pocket hidden from view.

'You feeling better?' he asks.

'Much. Thank you.'

'No one else fell sick, it seems.'

'No,' I say, feigning a modicum of surprise.

'And you're sure you're over your little flipout?'

'You mean about May? I'm sorry. I don't know what got into me.'

'Glad to hear you've come to your senses. I only wish you didn't keep losing them in the first place.' He lifts his eyes to the ceiling. How long have I been unaware of his contempt, his disrespect? He continues, not even glancing at me: 'I'll have a shower then.' He carries his coffee down the hall to the bedroom. I add frothed milk to my own and shake chocolate powder over the top. Soon I hear the ensuite shower running. It is only then that I tug the medicine bottle from my pocket and inspect it more closely. A sticky label affixed to the side has the prescriber's name on it: the patient is Magdala De Vale. I unscrew the lid. It's empty; no tablets inside. I screw the lid shut and stuff the bottle back into the pocket of my dressing gown just as Magdala walks into the room.

'Morning,' she says.

I hold out the mug as a distraction. 'Coffee?'

'Yes, thank you. But no milk for me.'

I don't know what part she is playing in all of this. But she and Alex are close. I mustn't give anything away to her.

'Let me make another for you,' I say, placing a clean cup beneath the spout. 'You'll be around all today?'

'I'm not going anywhere. I don't have anywhere to go.'

'Okay,' I say as I consider whether it is safe for me to even be leaving Charlotte with her. I have no concrete reason not to trust her. Except: it might be her medication that was given to me. I offer her the freshly brewed coffee. 'Charlotte has been a little unsettled. Can you let me know if you have any concerns?'

Her eyes are wide as she takes the cup from me. 'You know Alex will be here too, right?'

'He'll be occupied with his business, I imagine.'

'Perhaps.'

'There's enough expressed milk for Charlotte today.' I open the fridge. The two full bottles of milk I expressed yesterday and placed on the top shelf are gone. 'Where are they?'

'Where are what?'

'The bottles of expressed milk. They were right there.'

'Oh dear. Is this your memory again? Alex told me it's been particularly bad of late.'

Alex and Magdala seem to be in cahoots to sabotage my attempts at breastfeeding. And clearly, I must stop providing Charlotte with breastmilk – there's always the risk it could be contaminated by anything administered to me. My heart tightens, even as I know I am making the best decision to keep her safe.

I head for the bedroom, ensuring the medication bottle is concealed. Alex is out of the shower.

'Do you know where the milk I expressed yesterday has gone?' I call though the ensuite door.

'How would I know?'

I tuck the bottle into the top drawer of my dresser and cover it with some underwear.

Alex enters the bedroom, towel around his waist, and I am struck by his torso, the definition of his pectoral muscles, his biceps. Since Charlotte was born, he has frequently grumbled that he hasn't had much time to work out. His physique tells a different story. Has he brought his mother here so he can go to the gym too?

'My expressed breastmilk has gone missing. Twice.'

'You're accusing me of something else, are you?' he snaps.

I remain silent.

'I don't remember you expressing yesterday,' he continues, clearly annoyed. 'You were at work all day, then you forgot to get up overnight.'

I try to think back. It *was* a busy day. But I still found the time. 'I expressed twice at work.'

'You seem sure of yourself.'

I nod.

'Fine. Let's go and see.'

I trail Alex down the hall. He has already tugged open the fridge and there, on the top shelf, are the two bottles. Magdala had removed, and now replaced, them. But why?

She eyes me closely, identical to the way Alex often does.

'Please, Lauren,' Alex says. 'You have to see someone, get yourself sorted out. I don't want to have to let your work know what's going on.'

I feel a familiar, automatic shrinking inside from the veiled threats that in the past have kept me quiet.

'I'm sorry,' I say, fighting the instinct to cower, trying to keep the strength of my convictions in my mind. 'I guess I was mistaken.'

'You were,' Alex says, calmer now. 'You're so often mistaken. But I'm very understanding. We're very understanding, aren't we, Mother?'

'Yes, we are,' she says. 'We understand how easy it can be to get things wrong.'

28

Tuesday 18 March, 08:30

Dear Magdala,

Thank you for contacting Child Protection Services and for the information provided just now. Confirming I was able to locate the details of your previous notification on our system regarding your daughter-in-law Lauren De Vale's second pregnancy, which we will also take into account as we consider next steps.

Thank you again for contacting us and please don't hesitate to reach out again if any further concerns arise.

Kind regards,
Martha Cox
Intake Clinician
Child Protection Services

29

Alders Lawyers
Craven Lane, CBD

18 December

Dear John,

I'm writing to ask about booking an appointment with yourself for legal advice.

I'm considering separating from my wife of five years. We have one child together who was conceived with an egg donor. I'm unsure if the fact an egg donor was used may potentially impact on custody arrangements.

We didn't sign a prenup prior to marriage, so I am seeking advice on how assets might be divided in the event of separation/divorce. I'm also keen to know how custody would affect the division of assets, and how my wife's mental illness might impact both custody and asset division. Similarly, I would be interested to know the possibility of any future partner obtaining legal guardianship of our daughter given my wife's mental illness.

Are these issues for which you could provide legal advice?

Yours sincerely,
Alex De Vale

30

My hospital workload is hectic, yet something of a welcome distraction. The caesarean list passes in a blur. The women are all well, their babies too. I praise Devan, who tries to conceal his obvious pride.

I've snaffled a half-hour over lunchtime, before afternoon clinic begins. The weather forecast is suggesting a heatwave, so Natalia proposes we meet at our second-favourite place, the hospital's non-denominational chapel. It's always cool and usually quiet, the perfect place for a private chat.

Today, the light inside is dim, the stained-glass window dull and the chapel empty. Natalia is delayed a few minutes, so I use my first free minutes of the day to pull out my phone and google *cabergoline*. Pharmacology has never been my strong suit, and though its name is vaguely familiar, I can't recall having ever personally prescribed it. The page loads: *Cabergoline is used to reduce high levels of prolactin, a hormone in the blood, to treat certain menstrual problems, fertility problems in men and women, and pituitary prolactinomas (tumours of the pituitary gland).* I almost click away, but the last line catches my eye. *Can be used as a breastmilk suppressant.*

My face flushes. So, Alex has been dosing me – he must be trying to suppress my breastmilk supply. Or his mother is. But why? And how could they be so cruel? Then I remember his expression when he caught me feeding Charlotte. Breastfeeding has been a part of my relationship with Charlotte that he has been unable to fully control.

Frantically, I google the taste of cabergoline tablets: *tasteless*. So then, the tasteless white powder in the salt container is likely the cabergoline, made ready to lace my food and drink. It would explain the graininess in last night's duck, but not the bitterness. Perhaps that was simply down to bad cooking. If Alex *has* been feeding cabergoline to me in my meals, that would explain my waning breastmilk supply.

I drop my head to my knees. It's hard to breathe and almost impossible to believe, even as I am confronted with the reality of this situation. Power. Entitlement. Attempts to control me and my breastfeeding.

I desperately need time to think through my options and make a plan of how to extract Charlotte and myself from this terrible mess.

With a mixture of grief and relief, I recall it's the anniversary of Billy's death tomorrow. I've taken the day off work as usual. Alex and I usually spend the day engaged in our own tasks in separate rooms at home; early on, we came to an unspoken understanding that it was easier that way, to process our grief alone. If I can just get through the next few hours,

I'll have a whole day to think, plan and strategise my next move.

'Sorry I'm late.' Natalia shuffles down the aisle to the front of the chapel. 'Hey, are you okay?'

'Not really.' I'm numb, beyond tears. 'I found something in my recycling. A pill bottle. Cabergoline.'

'What's cabergoline?'

'A breastmilk suppressant.'

'I don't understand.'

'Alex has been administering it to me. Without my consent.'

'God, Laur. Are you sure?'

'Almost certain.'

'What reason would he have for doing that?' She looks incredulous.

I rack my brains. Who knows the multitude of excuses he would come up with to explain away his actions. He's worried about my sleep. He's worried about me breastfeeding. He's worried for the baby. He thinks I'm becoming unwell again.

I used to trust him. Not anymore.

But this is the kicker. Other people *would* trust him.

I am the one who has been deemed mentally unwell: postnatal depression, anxiety bordering on paranoia. Having a past history of diagnosed mental illness means I can be accused of almost anything. I can be locked away, medicated without my consent. I can have my medical licence revoked or suspended. A simple word from him, or his mother, and any of those things could occur.

I glance at Natalia. 'Has he been in touch with you?'

'Not since that first time. I told him not to call me again.'

Even as she regards me with an open face and wide eyes,

it's hard to completely trust her on this. Has there ever been anyone I could truly trust? My mother, perhaps. At least, for as long as she stuck around – though some might argue that her abandoning me was so great a betrayal that I should never have trusted her in the first place. Aunty Sal, I suppose, but we lost touch years ago. After Mum left, Aunty Sal popped round to our house a couple of times with her homemade chocolate cake. The first time, she barged her way into the house and demanded to know where Mum had gone. From my bedroom I heard shouting in the kitchen, but I turned up my music and pretended I couldn't hear. Aunty Sal was gone by the time I came out.

The second time, Aunty Sal arrived before Dad got home from work. When I answered the door she engulfed me in one of her usual crushing hugs, before presenting another chocolate cake. On that occasion, there was time to make a pot of tea. We sat drinking it on the back patio, surveying what had become of the garden that was now a weed-filled tangle.

'You haven't heard from your mum?' Aunty Sal said.

'No.'

Aunty Sal frowned. 'Did she ever give you any details about going away?'

I racked my memory. Perhaps she had, but my recollections of her had become so muddled with the things Dad said that I no longer knew what the truth of it was.

'She *might* have mentioned a friend on the west coast,' I offered.

She nodded slowly.

When Sal was leaving, I sensed something different in the hug she gave me. That was the last time I saw her.

'I'm concerned about you.' Natalia's voice shakes me back to the present. 'Are you saying your husband is forcing you to take medication without your consent?'

I realise how ridiculous it sounds. Accusations of poisoning – a sign of delusional thinking, a hallmark of psychosis. Perhaps that is exactly why he is resorting to this method. The more I protest, the more unwell I sound, such that any harm that befalls Charlotte can be pinned on me.

'You think I'm reading too much into this.'

'You know, I was thinking after last time we spoke,' Natalia says, 'about how easy it is for people to lose trust in themselves, in their intuition. How when you're bombarded with abuse, there's no time to think, and it's hard to know who to trust.' She studies the back of her hands.

'I'm so sorry you've been going through all that,' I say.

'No, I'm sorry.' She puts her hand on my shoulder and squeezes it. 'I'm not sure how to make sense of what you're telling me . . . but I know you're a wise woman, Laur. Don't second-guess yourself.'

I reach down into my bag. 'I took my neighbour's notebook,' I say. 'I want to show you something. Another set of eyes would definitely help.'

She frowns as I rummage through the bag. Laptop and diary, my purse and mobile, an assortment of pens, papers and folders galore; I really must clean out this bag. But despite all these items, the notebook is missing.

'It was here,' I say.

'You're sure?'

'Absolutely.' I'm certain I replaced the notebook in my bag after ever so briefly skimming it last night. Where the hell could it be? My pulse quickens. I pull out the contents of my bag, one by one, and line them up on the pew, inspecting each one carefully. Then I completely upend my bag. Empty.

I haven't had a chance to make a copy, can remember only the most minor details of its contents. I hadn't yet found any descriptions that could confirm whether the regular visitor was Elspeth. Nor do I have access to the figures that could tell me exactly how many times the blue Peugeot came to our house. Where the hell has the notebook gone?

'I know you haven't invented it,' she says, her brow furrowed. 'It's just – it's not like you to steal things, Laur.'

'I didn't *steal* it,' I say. 'In my mind, I was *borrowing* it. I was always planning to return it.' God, I'll need to find it before Karla comes demanding it back.

Natalia gathers her bag and cardigan. 'Look, I've got to rush back to work. Keep me in the loop, okay? You've got a lot going on and I'm here for you.'

'Thanks,' I say. 'I know I'll always be able to count on you.'

31

Hi Natalia,

I hope it's okay to email you. I understand you're a good friend of Lauren De Vale. I just wanted to reach out as I know Lauren through our mothers group, as well as through work, of course, and I saw her over the weekend at a Christmas function. No doubt you've heard about the bruise on her baby Charlotte – obviously a concern given what transpired with her son Billy.

When I spoke with Lauren, she seemed somewhat guarded and preoccupied during our chat, as well as suspicious of her husband's intentions, and it had me wondering about the possibility of emerging postnatal psychosis. She didn't mention or display any other features of concern and, unfortunately, due to it being a social event and my child being present, I wasn't able to ask her any pertinent questions (perhaps not my role anyway).

I wondered if you'd be willing to have a quick chat about this, just to discuss whether it warrants a child services notification, as well as any implications for our shared workplace, maybe even an AHPRA notification. I'll speak with my medical defence as well, but I'd be grateful for any insights you may be willing to share or any thoughts you have regarding next steps. I'll wait to hear from you.

Kind regards,
Dr Elspeth Lim

32

Clinic is almost done for the afternoon. I take a moment to check my phone.

Nothing from Alex, but no messages from him isn't necessarily a bad thing.

There is, however, a text from Devan: *Would you have time to speak to Bella Parnos's parents in special care nursery before you head off?* Devan had sounded nervous last time he ran through his decision-making process on her caesarean case. *They're still asking lots of questions about why their surgery was delayed.*

Heading to you now, I write back.

As I take the elevator to the fifth floor, I remember that it's Natalia's day in the nursery. With a pang of guilt, I realise that in my hypervigilant state, I neglected to enquire how she was going with her coroner's case at our lunchtime catch-up. I'll have to apologise for my insensitivity when I see her.

I swipe my way into the nursery and head for the nurses

station. Christmas decorations are dangling from the ceiling and tinsel rims the edge of each computer monitor. There is no sign of Natalia.

Devan is waiting for me. He shuffles from foot to foot.

'You okay?'

'I wish I had the answers.' He shrugs. 'The parents are really sticking the knife in.'

'You *know* this wasn't your fault, don't you?'

'I'm sure there's something I could have done differently.'

I am all too familiar with this type of self-recrimination. 'Of course, you're reflecting on your process. That's because you care,' I say. 'Remember you can only do your best with the knowledge and information you have at the time. It's much easier to judge decisions as errors with hindsight.'

He nods, his face solemn.

'Lauren?' It's Elspeth, immaculately dressed as always in a pressed suit and heels. Geez, I always forget how small this hospital is; I should have considered the possibility of running into her here.

'Hi,' she continues, a blank expression on her face. 'Four times in a week. We usually don't see each other nearly so often.'

'Hi, to you too,' I say, then point to the whiteboard. 'Baby Parnos – Bella? Devan's keen for me to speak with the parents.'

'Okay,' she says. 'We don't believe Bella will have any lasting physical or cognitive impairment, and even though she's struggling a little with feeding, we're expecting her to make a full recovery.'

Devan's shoulders soften a little as he hears this.

'Elspeth, can I ask you something?' I move her away from Devan's hearing. Her scent of lemon balm is pleasant – and oddly familiar. I had returned home last week to the same smell: unexpected but lovely, I'd thought at the time. I rack my mind to match dates – I'm almost certain it was the same day Karla had seen the woman visit our house.

'Go ahead.'

I take a deep breath. 'If you prescribed cabergoline to a mother who wanted to stop breastfeeding, would you be concerned about any effects on the baby?'

Her eyes narrow. 'What do you mean?'

'I mean . . .' I begin to stutter. 'Can cabergoline in breastmilk harm a baby?'

'Let's go somewhere more private?' She indicates the workroom behind the nurses station, usually reserved for doctors writing up clinical notes.

'Sure,' I say, even as I am uncertain why she would suggest this.

Devan gives me a puzzled wave as I follow Elspeth into the bland room. Given her stern expression, it might be a good idea for me to lead with the fact that I know about her communicating with Alex. I then lean back against the white laminex desk.

'While we're here, I wanted to ask, why have you been texting my husband?'

'What do you mean?' Her eyes crinkle.

'Sunday night, after the barbecue. I saw the messages.'

It's her turn to look nervous. She rubs her nose. 'I didn't mean anything by it, Lauren. Alex is obviously concerned about you. To be honest, so am I.'

'And what is it that you and Alex are so concerned about?'

'About you.' She looks down at the back of her hands, avoiding my eyes. 'There were things I wanted to tell you.

But I wasn't sure it was my place. And it never seemed quite the right time.' Her voice is quiet. 'I should have said something. It was a long time ago. But Alex and I . . . we were quite serious. We were engaged and then – I ended up getting pregnant. Alex tried to talk me out of a termination but I was still studying and not ready to become a parent. Afterwards, he was upset I'd gone behind his back, so we broke up. It was quite an intense time for both of us, obviously.'

Even as Elspeth looks devastated, a shudder of betrayal strikes through my chest. I recall that at some point early in my pregnancy with Billy, Alex had mentioned how devastating his partner having a termination had been in an earlier relationship; I'd had no idea he'd been referring to Elspeth.

'Wow, Elspeth. That's a lot,' I say. 'Obviously, I knew about you and Alex having dated, but not that.' I shake my head slowly, trying to take it all in. 'Back in mothers group, I'd hoped we might become friends,' I admit. 'I didn't understand why it was so hard. I guess now I do.'

'I'm sorry,' she says, the corners of her mouth drooping. 'I'd wanted us to catch up more, back then, too. But I always felt a little awkward because of . . . I didn't know what Alex had told you, how much you knew.'

'He hadn't told me any of that,' I say. 'Though,' I flush, unsure if I should proceed, 'the other night I convinced myself Alex was May's father.'

Two red dots bloom on her cheeks. 'What? That's ridiculous.'

I feel the truth behind her words, and shrug. 'It was silly of me.'

She sniffs. 'He's a good guy. He's worried about you because he loves you.'

'What makes you say that?'

'I know you've been concerned he might have bruised your baby. But he's not the type, Lauren, believe me.' She pauses. 'That medication you're asking about – cabergoline – it wouldn't be given to mothers who are still breastfeeding. It would only be administered to a mother who's had a stillborn baby. Or whose baby dies while she is still breastfeeding.'

I push down the grief threatening to engulf me. After Billy's passing, my breasts had swelled to the size of melons, hard and firm. I had only just started trying to breastfeed again right before he died. I could have done with some cabergoline then, I suppose.

'What if it was administered without a woman's knowledge or consent?'

She purses her lips, then opens her mouth. 'Look, if this is about Billy, it makes sense any anxieties would all resurface after having another baby but—'

'It's not that,' I interrupt her, then realise I need to change the topic before I say too much. 'I'd better get to those parents.'

'Absolutely.' With a concerned expression, she opens the door. 'You take care of yourself, Lauren.'

I glance through the glass windows of Room 4. The mother, standing over the cot, has recovered well from her caesarean and has already been discharged from hospital. The father has his arm around her waist, as he too leans over, gazing at their baby.

I push any thoughts I have about Elspeth's motives to the corner of my mind, just for the moment. It's time to sort out the parents' complaints. I take a deep breath and knock lightly at the nursery door, then enter. The parents look up at me, confused.

'I'm Dr De Vale, the obstetrician from the caesarean,' I clarify. 'Dr Joshi has been keeping me up to date with Bella's progress. How is it all going for you?'

'We thought she'd be fine by now. We didn't expect any of this.' The father's eyebrows are set in a deep frown.

'When will she be able to come home?' the mother asks.

'The paediatricians will be able to let you know the best timing of discharge,' I say. 'I wondered if you'd like to discuss any issues around the birth?'

'We keep asking why it took so long to have the caesarean,' the father says gruffly. 'No one has been able to give us a satisfactory answer.'

'Good question,' I say, avoiding – as we're trained to – criticising the patient despite the fact his wife had refused a caesarean for more than twelve hours, only capitulating to Devan's pleas for intervention at the last possible moment when their child's heart trace turned critical. 'We were finishing up another emergency caesarean when yours was called. It's not ideal, but we performed your surgery as quickly as practicable.'

'Shouldn't you have two operating theatres available to perform caesareans for exactly this situation?' the father asks.

'We can call in other doctors in this scenario,' I agree, 'however, in this case it would have taken even longer to get another whole operating team set up. It was faster to proceed with the operations back-to-back.' My heart flutters a little as I recall my own prolonged departure from home that morning, which may have ever so slightly delayed things, even though Devan has insisted my tardy attendance had no impact on proceeding with either of the operations. Despite my attempts at reassurance, Bella's parents seem even more irate than when I entered the room. The father is clicking his tongue, while the mother is tapping her nails on the plastic top of her daughter's humidicrib.

'We're not satisfied,' he says. 'We'll be taking this further.'

'Of course. I can give you information on how to make a complaint,' I say, my last resort in these situations.

'No matter. The social worker has already provided that.' And he looks to the door.

There in the doorway is Natalia.

'Lauren,' she says, her voice dull and her face flat, 'can you please come with me?'

33

Natalia leads me into the interview room – or the 'bad news' room, as the staff have nicknamed it. No Christmas decorations on display in here. She indicates towards the couch against the far wall. I perch myself on the edge of a cushion and wait for her to sit beside me, but she remains standing by the door, her expression blank.

'I've been mulling on what you told me at lunch, what you're going through,' she says.

I wait, biting the inside of my cheek.

'It's been a rough few years for you. Believe me, I know. Billy. Fertility treatment. Now a new baby. I can't imagine the stress you're under.'

'I'm fine,' I say. 'I'm coping okay.'

'That's what I wanted to talk to you about. I'm not convinced you are. You've got massive bags under your eyes. You've lost weight. I haven't seen you eat during any of our catch-ups.

Plus, you're stressed out of your head about Charlotte. When you were talking about that bruise on her, I've got to admit, I was worried. Not about her. About you.'

I go to protest, but she puts up her hand and continues. 'I should have stepped in last time with Billy, when you mentioned what you were doing with the breastfeeding, and when you told me about Karla. I failed you that time. I won't make the same mistake again.'

It hits me then. I can't believe I didn't see it before.

'He's spoken to you again, hasn't he?' I'm almost certain I've never mentioned Karla's name to Natalia. It can only have come from Alex.

'I'm aware of your concerns, Laur. Believe me, I hear you. I'm keeping an open mind about him, of course I am. And I'll keep a close eye on you too.'

On you too. I've always thought I could trust Natalia. Turns out, I was wrong.

Her voice softens. 'You're not yourself at the moment. Usually, you'd have soothed parents like that within a few minutes. But they seemed more upset than ever.'

She doesn't mention that she had provided the parents with the avenue to make a complaint before I'd even had the chance to address their concerns. This has nothing – or almost nothing – to do with my capacity to practise obstetrics. It's hard to believe how rapidly Natalia has turned.

'And that woman you referred to me the other day – Jody. She thought you were a little pushy. Not aggressive – she didn't say that. But she did comment that she felt slightly nervous around you.'

This is news to me. I try to take it all in. It is conceivable that Jody found me pushy I suppose, but anything I said or did was out of concern for her safety.

'I don't understand,' I say finally.

'I know.' From her despairing voice, I can hear how conflicted she is. 'I know you'd hate for all this to affect your work. And I guessed you'd deny there was a problem. But Laur, the medical director called me just now. He said several staff had approached him with concerns about you.'

Elspeth? Hardly surprising, but still . . . and who else has been speaking with him?

'There are lots of signs things aren't quite right.' Natalia looks sheepish. 'I told him I'd speak with you about having some time off. I thought that might be easier for you, rather than having to go through official channels. I'm so sorry, Laur.'

Fuck, fuck, fuck. Less than a week back at work and I'm already being forced out on sick leave? This is not going to go down well on the unit. People will talk. There will be even more concern from my colleagues than there was before, gossip about my capability to perform my job.

Now, with Natalia standing firm, I don't know what to say. If I defend myself, they'll accuse me of not seeing reason; if I play along, I'm essentially admitting their accusations are right. *Their* accusations? This may all be stemming from Alex – and Elspeth. Maybe, just maybe, some leave will give me time to deduce what is going on. And get Charlotte and myself to a safer place.

'I wouldn't want to be obstructive,' I say. 'Of course, I want the best for my patients.'

'I know.' Natalia gives a slight smile. 'I was certain you'd do the right thing. I'm only concerned for you. We're all concerned. And this way, you'll get all the help you need.'

34

I hit a speedbump and despite the seatbelt I'm launched upwards towards the car roof. In shock, I slam on the brakes.

I've been driving absent-mindedly, not paying attention to my surroundings, since leaving work. Without realising it, I've been heading towards the outer suburbs where I grew up. I check my mobile. The battery has died. Great. Just great. Now I'll have to use my already impaired memory to remember my way home.

In front of me is a refurbished playground with pastel pink climbing frames and purple swing sets, next door to a milk bar that looks strangely familiar. It appears that I've ended up in the vicinity of my childhood home, a few blocks away from my aunt's old house. I pull the car to the kerb and switch off the engine, and, with a jolt, I'm reminded that Mum and I would walk this exact route home from the playground – when it was fitted out with far less fancy play equipment – before Dad would get home from work. Around the corner from the milk bar, down the street, through the back alley towards our front gate.

Aunty Sal's house was directly opposite the alley so sometimes we'd pop in for an unannounced cup of tea. Sal would always make me one in a miniature teacup and saucer, decorated with the same rose pattern as the adults' set. I felt like a proper grown up. And she would always serve just the right biscuits – Raspberry Shortcakes, with their circular spray of rich raspberry jam, Butternut Snaps, with their reassuring crack on biting into them, or Orange Slices, where the orange icing could be licked straight off the biscuit. And of course, on more scheduled visits, there was Aunty Sal's homemade chocolate cake . . . While she and Mum gossiped, I would make up stories with the china animal figurines she kept on her hall table. I would catch words here or there – *booze*, *drunk*, *aggro* – but they would lower their voices if they thought I could hear.

Now, here I am, with the playground before me. After all this time, Aunty Sal might not even live in the same house. It was – what, almost thirty years ago that Mum left. Which would make Sal about seventy-five. Old enough to have downsized, moved into a retirement village, or even to have passed away.

Out of curiosity, I restart the car, turn the corner and cruise down the street at low speed, air conditioning blasting. It's a more genteel neighbourhood now, with manicured lawns, freshly painted fences and the occasional lush hedge. The alley I remember is on the right. I pull up at the house opposite. The old oak in the front yard is shading the house from the northerly sun. My breath catches in my throat. A battered VW is in the driveway, the same sunshine yellow as Aunty Sal's old one, albeit faded.

With some hesitation, I climb out of the car into the blistering heat. The garden is unchanged from my youth, pruned roses in garden beds surrounded by a low-cut lawn. There's a plastic wreath on the door, coated with faded holly and replica pinecones. I reach out for the doorbell, but the door swings open before I can press it.

'Is that my Lulu?' It's her. She is shorter and her face is more wrinkled than I remember, but otherwise, she is still the Aunty Sal I recall from my childhood. A plaid cotton shirt barely covers her middle, revealing practical denim shorts bursting at the top button. She reaches for me before I can reply, encircling me in a hug that, just as it had in childhood, causes me to catch my breath. Freshly cut grass – she smells exactly the same. 'It's hard to believe it's really you,' she gasps, looking me up and down and nodding.

I can't help but smile. 'I could say the same about you.'

'Come in, come in,' she says. 'We need to get you out of the heat.'

She directs me inside and down the familiar hallway to her kitchen, switches on the kettle and brandishes an open tin of biscuits. Some things haven't changed.

'I must have all your news.' She rubs her hands on her shorts and then looks at me expectantly as I take a seat at her green formica kitchen table.

I want to ask why she'd never been in touch all these years, but my throat feels too tight to speak. Instead, I reach into my pocket, hoping to provide a photographic update. Damn, that's right. My mobile is dead. Short of images, I begin a verbal recap of the last thirty-odd years. I include Charlotte, but skip the parts about Billy and my psychiatric hospitalisations.

Went through a bit of a hard time these last few years seems like a reasonable summary, in the circumstances.

She tuts and fusses at all the right times and it's as if I'm simultaneously both the ten-year-old me and my mother, having adult chats with my kindly relative over a cup of tea. All those years, I realise. All those lost years.

She must be having similar thoughts, as a darkness sweeps across her face. 'I'm ever so sorry I didn't reach out.' She rubs her temple. 'Your father told me harm would come to you if I ever tried to speak with you again.'

So, it was because of him. My heart doesn't even skip a beat.

'I wanted to,' she continues. 'It's one of the reasons I stayed in this house, so you could always find me, and on the off chance your mum . . .' Her voice trails off.

'Well, we're here, finally,' I say, a heaviness settling in my chest. 'I'm glad I can be with you again.'

'Me too, my dear.' She dives into a cupboard beneath the bench. 'I saved these. I always planned to give them to you, in case you had children of your own one day.' She hands me a small cardboard box. I prise it open and inside, four miniature teacups and saucers with rose print on the rim. The set from my childhood.

'Thank you,' I say, my voice cracking.

She places a teapot before us and slides a brown knitted tea cosy over it. 'You never heard from your mum, I take it?' Her tone is hesitant.

I shake my head as a distant memory tugs at me, and questions that have long been stifled within me gush out. 'Why did she leave? *Was* there some guy in another state?'

'That's what your father always maintained.' She pours milk in my cup, then reaches for the sugar bowl, the same solid white china one from my youth. 'Still have one sugar?'

I shake my head.

'I've never believed your mother had anyone else, my dear,' she says, then knocks the milk jug over with her elbow, the white liquid spreading across the tabletop. 'Dearie me, dearie me.' She heads for the sink, picks up a rag and mops at the mess. 'No use crying, I suppose.'

I never did, at least not in front of anyone else. Crying was a sign of weakness in my father's eyes. I didn't even cry when he died, out of misplaced respect. It occurs to me: 'You weren't at Dad's funeral.'

'I was in hospital.' She taps her chest with the palm of her hand. 'Breast cancer.'

'I'm sorry.'

'Thank you, my dear. It's cured, I'm told.'

'That's good,' I say in genuine relief.

Aunty Sal sighs. 'I'm sorry. I thought to reach out, after he passed. I know I should have . . .' I watch her waddle to the sink again, her careful gait reminding me so much of my mother.

'Mum – is she . . . ? Do you think she's happy?'

Aunty Sal wrings out the cloth into the stainless steel sink. Her back is to me. 'I don't think so, my dear.' Her words hang like wet washing in the air.

'I mean, she *is* alive, isn't she?'

She pauses, then speaks in a whisper. 'No.'

'No?' My body turns to stone. 'Why? How do you know?'

Her hands are shaking as she pours tea into both cups through a strainer. 'There was an inquest.'

An inquest? Like Billy's. My body sinks into the chair. 'What do you mean? What inquest?'

'Your dad applied for a death certificate, seven years after she left. The inquest happened a few years later. Because she hadn't accessed her bank accounts or engaged with any government agencies, and none of us had heard from her, the coroner ruled she was most likely deceased.'

'Dad knew she was dead?' When I'd visited him in the hospice on his deathbed fifteen years ago, I had so wished for some sort of reckoning, a moment of repentance for his behaviour over the years. Although that never came, I can't comprehend how he could have failed to mention Mum's death to me, even at the end. 'Why didn't he tell me? Why didn't *anyone* tell me?'

She encircles her teacup with her hands. 'When I didn't see you at the inquest, I thought maybe you were trying to create some distance, or that you didn't want anything to do with the past and losing your mum. I didn't know what had happened to you. I wanted to believe you were overseas, living your life, chasing your dreams away from your dad. I'm sorry. I should have tried to track you down.'

'I had no idea.' I'm almost not shocked by my mum's death, but remain taken aback that no one thought to let me know. However, Sal is right – I would have been overseas around that period, working in the UK in some half-hearted attempt at freedom. I had changed my surname to Mum's maiden name when I left home to try to distance myself from my father. I can see now that both of those decisions might have resulted in anyone – authorities included – finding it harder to contact me. Then again, besides Dad and Aunty Sal – who must have each had their own reasons for not reaching out – who else was there?

'What happened? How did she die?'

Her voice is soft, almost inaudible. 'There was no communication from her. No records, no doctor or dental visits. She vanished. I believe you were the last person to see her alive on the day she left.'

I see Mum's elbows on the wooden kitchen table, her head in her hands. The long sleeves, the scarf around her neck, on that hot summer's day. She hadn't met my eyes as I'd wrapped my sandwich in gladwrap and stuffed it in my lunchbox.

'Goodbye, darling.' Her final words to me.

Ten-year-old me was annoyed she hadn't moved from her chair since I'd entered the kitchen that morning, hadn't helped me with breakfast or preparing my school lunch. I didn't kiss her goodbye. My last image of her has a different frame now.

'Do you think she's at peace?'

She shuts her eyes. 'Maureen, your mum's best friend, you remember—'

I nod.

'Maureen and I think she might be up in the bush where your parents used to go camping before you were born. Me and your mum's friends went up there several times over the years, scouting all around, but we never found anything. I don't know . . .' Her voice trails off.

'Why would she be in the bush?' An image of her walking beside a creek lined by eucalypts used to be a common daydream of mine.

And then it hits me.

Dad. It was him.

'How the hell could you have let me grow up with him?'

Fury over his treatment of me and Mum, which I've kept shoved down inside all these years, threatens to boil to the surface.

Aunty Sal covers her face with her hands. 'I'm so sorry.'

'You knew, and you didn't protect me?'

'What could we do?' Her voice is desperate. 'Back then, the authorities wouldn't have listened to me. They wouldn't have listened to any of us. Your dad . . . I was concerned for your safety if it all came out. I know now it was wrong. But going along with his ultimatum – I thought that was the safest thing for you. Appease your dad. Let you get through your university studies.'

'Were you ever going to tell me?' My face simmers with heat.

'I don't know. Afterwards, it all felt like it was too little, too late.'

It's the most honest answer she could give. I place my palm against the cool of the formica. 'You need to tell the police.'

'I did. After he died. It felt safe, then.' She stares into her cup of pale tea.

It strikes me how fearful Aunty Sal must have been of Dad, how frightened Mum must have been too. How these women didn't not act from a lack of care, but rather from a place of distress, and a misguided concern for my wellbeing. How Mum might have stayed because of me. How I had lived with terror for so many years that terror had begun to feel like home.

It wasn't just me, though. Adults had been afraid of him too.

I don't want to believe it, even as it all makes sense. My father muttering under his breath as he drank himself into a stupor. His removal of her photographs. The way I instinctively knew it wasn't safe to mention Mum's name. The way he never spoke of her again.

'Fuck.' How the hell did I never consider this an option? I have been aware of my ability to put things in mental containers and close them off. And yet, this feels bigger than that. It is beyond the comprehension of most people to imagine one of their parents killing the other. It had been a truth too hard to consider.

'They haven't found her.' It's a statement more than a question; I already know the answer.

Sal shakes her head. 'I'm sorry. The police said the area was too vast to cover.'

Numbness spreads out over my ribs, flowing down into my limbs. 'They never contacted me,' I say. The void of sensation intensifies like a protective shield. I can see now, there was almost never anyone there for me. Mum had wanted to support me – I know she loved me – but she hadn't been able to keep me safe. Not even Aunty Sal had been there for me. I had been completely alone.

I shake my head, trying to break the foggy sensation shrouding me. I need to be present, proactive. I cannot allow Charlotte to grow up as I did.

As the frozen feeling in my brain starts to defrost, I can feel my limbs again. But my breath catches as I remember that I'm sure Alex has been lacing my food. I am in danger just as my mother was. Do I seriously want Charlotte in a house where her mother's life is under threat?

I dig the heels of my hands into my eye sockets. This is almost unbearable. I have to get out of this situation.

'I'm in a bad spot,' I say, noting my relief to speak those words aloud.

'Sweetheart, I'm so, *so* sorry,' Sal says, and all at once my numbness completely drops away and I realise how different it could have been, had someone been there for me back then. Thank god I can be there for Charlotte now.

'I think I have to leave, with my daughter, as soon as I can.'

'Oh, my darling.' She places her arm around my shoulders. My muscles soften beneath her touch. 'Where will you go?'

I stare out through the kitchen window at a eucalypt in the backyard, its branches pitching to and fro in the hot summer air. 'I have no idea.'

'That's settled, then. There are spare bedrooms here.' Her eyes are determined and her tone resolute. 'You can stay for as long as you need.'

35

EIGHTEEN YEARS EARLIER

Alex,

Please stop calling me and waiting outside my house. I don't want to see you. We're done.

36

FIVE YEARS EARLIER

It's been a long time. I never stopped thinking about you. I get why you cut off contact back then. I should have been more supportive, I know that. I wasn't there for you. I'm sorry.

I've thought a lot about our time back then. How easy it was, how good it felt – remember that night by the pool under the full moon, as the New Year's Eve fireworks started? I know we were young, but I've never had anything like that, before or since.

I get it's hard now – things are different. But I'd love to reconnect. Reminisce about the past. Who knows, maybe even relive the magic. Let me know if you're willing to give us a chance.

Alex

36

FIVE YEARS EARLIER

37

My heart pounds as I slip through the front door. I tiptoe to Charlotte's room and ease open the door. Soft music; Alex must have set up a new sound system. Her room is pitch black. I switch on her night-light and creep into her room, already preparing myself for what I might find. I peer into her cot.

It is empty.

My stomach twists in agony.

I sprint out of her room and down the hallway. Bursting into the living area, I see Magdala and Alex standing at the sink, their backs turned to me, looking out the kitchen window at the side of the house where the pool used to be.

Alex turns and for a moment I see him holding Billy – lifeless, pale, his eyes rolled back in his head. Then I refocus and see Charlotte, pink-cheeked, cooing. Alex and his mother are staring at me as if the devil itself had burst in. I catch sight of my reflection in the window, hair wild from the wind, clothes wrinkled, makeup smeared from crying on the drive home. Charlotte's face turns, her smile receding to a pout and she begins to whimper. It's me. She is afraid of me.

I stare at him, this husband of mine who has things so carefully planned, who has excluded me, and I can see that he does not even need poison; he only needs to separate a mother from her child long enough to create that most devastating of wounds – a child who is not attached to, does not feel safe with, the person who birthed her. I need to get Charlotte, and myself, to Aunty Sal's as soon as I possibly can.

'You're home late. Are you okay?' Alex says, and his voice is so calm, so apparently full of concern, that for the briefest of moments I almost collapse into his arms and tell him the troubling events of my day. Then I remember.

'How was she today?' I keep my voice steady, even as my shoulders tighten. Submissive, Lauren, I remind myself. Submissive, and smart.

'Mum looked after her. I had to pop out to do a few errands. Then a little work on my business. But she spent most of the day sleeping.'

'That's nice.' And terrifying. A baby shouldn't be sleeping quite so much. If Alex has been feeding me cabergoline, I hardly want to think about what he's giving Charlotte. It's making me wonder now why she sleeps so soundly, and for much longer periods than Billy ever did.

'You should eat something,' Alex says.

He's right; I skipped lunch to make sure I'd be on time to meet Natalia. Apart from some biscuits during antenatal clinic, and few more at Aunty Sal's plus some cups of milky tea, I've had nothing else all day. I'm starving, and annoyed at myself for not having at least grabbed something at a drive-through on the way home.

I hold out my arms for Charlotte, but Alex shakes his head.

'I don't want you to drop her. You haven't been getting enough sleep. And you haven't been eating. You need to eat first.'

I lower my hands, incredulous. 'That's what you told Natalia, right? That I wasn't sleeping or eating. You spoke with her.'

He shakes his head, presses his lips together.

'You could have talked to me.'

'You won't listen to me, Lauren.'

And the problem is me, again. Always me. Fuck. Fatigue sweeps over me, not physical but emotional, from the reverberating shocks of the day.

'Please, have some dinner. You need to eat to breastfeed,' Alex argues.

'I thought you didn't want me to breastfeed anymore?'

'I'm not trying to stop you breastfeeding,' he says.

I pause. I didn't say anything about him trying to *stop* me. He *has* been speaking with Natalia again. Presumably it's due to his intervention that I've been put off work.

'You don't look well,' Magdala says, gesturing to the outdoor area. 'The cool change has just arrived. Go take a seat. I'll bring some food and drinks out. I'm sure you've had a hectic day.'

'Just tap water, please.'

'A glass of wine too?' She fills the water jug from the tap.

'No, thanks.' I hold up my mobile.

'On call again?' Alex rolls his eyes.

The year we met, I had just been made a consultant, finally reaching my long-term goal of obtaining an obstetric position in the hospital system. The hours were long and taxing, but Alex had initially appeared understanding about my on-call roster and the demands of my job. When he suggested we live together after a few months of dating, it seemed only natural. He could support me with meals and shopping, he said. We could get a cleaner. Maybe even try for a baby together. I laughed at that – *not for a while*, I'd told him – but something in me thawed a little. I had to admit, I did want to have a baby eventually. And with this man more than with prior boyfriends, I felt secure enough to consider raising a family together down the track.

It was only when we'd moved in together that I started to wonder about his promises. I was working long hours, overtime and on call. But it seemed like Alex wasn't home as much as I'd expected. He was constantly out of the house, at the gym or catching up with friends after work. I hadn't met most of the people he talked about. I hinted that I'd be keen to get to know them, but the dates never seemed to align. And then I was pregnant.

Funny, an obstetrician not properly considering birth control. Of course I should have thought about it, but I'd never been particularly careful in previous relationships and there hadn't been any accidents. So, I had put the bloating, the nausea, the tender breasts down to premenstrual tension, and kept waiting and waiting for my period to come. When realisation finally hit, I locked the clinic door and pressed the ultrasound machine to my belly. I took the measurements, my racing heart almost in time with the baby's. Fourteen weeks. Bloody hell. How could I not have realised? A pregnancy hadn't been part of my plan so soon into the relationship. But fourteen weeks was too late for a regular termination. And anyway, seeing that tiny heart beating on the screen, I could no longer contemplate one.

Yet despite this, the maternal feelings didn't come. My ever-growing belly was simply a reminder of all I was about to lose, all I was risking. My career had only just begun. How could I have been so careless?

As the pregnancy progressed, Alex started to resent my gruelling work roster. I did my best to explain that it came with the job, that it was imperative I fulfilled the obligations of my role, particularly as I had only recently been made a consultant and would soon be going on maternity leave. But I can see, now, how my long hours and on-call requirements might have left him frustrated that I wasn't so available for him.

Magdala ushers me outside, to the patio overlooking the area where the pool had been. 'Sit,' she says, placing the water jug on the table before me. It feels like an order.

I obediently take a seat on the wooden bench and pour myself a glass of water. I've just seen her fill the jug, plus it's filtered; there can't be much wrong with it. I gulp down the whole cup.

As Alex slides Charlotte into her highchair beside me, I realise the attentiveness he and his mother are showing me might be because they've been informed of my work situation. Natalia, again.

'I imagine you've heard,' I say to Alex as Magdala places a plate loaded with cold roast chicken and pasta salad before me. The chicken should be safe to eat, at least.

'Heard what?' Alex looks genuinely confused.

'I've been placed on leave. They think I've come back to work too early. They want me to have more of a break.'

Saying it now, as Alex fastens the buckles on Charlotte's highchair, feels like a relief. I will be around him and his mother, able to keep my eyes on Charlotte, while I figure out the best way to extricate us both from the house. Nothing is going to happen to her on my watch.

I catch Alex and Magdala glancing at each other. I wonder if he is only just realising how his efforts to impact my work may have inadvertently disrupted his plans to attend the gym, work on his new business undisturbed, see Elspeth, and continue disrupting my attachment to Charlotte. He clearly didn't think that one through.

'Sorry to hear that,' Alex says. 'It's paid, I hope?' He watches me closely as I remove the skin from a chicken drumstick and begin to nibble at the white flesh. There's no bitter aftertaste, no grainy texture. It feels okay to eat and I can't deny it's a relief to have home-cooked food, even if my anxiety about it being laced remains sky high.

'I only have two weeks of sick leave left,' I say. 'Because of all the time I took off after . . .' My voice fades as the impact of Billy's death, and then the attempts at pregnancy, hit home. Essentially, ever since Alex entered my life, my career and financial independence have taken a huge hit.

'You'll make it work,' Magdala says.

'I thought, your new venture . . . when it takes off . . .'

'I'm still nutting out the details,' he says. 'It'll be some time before it kicks off.'

'Could you go for a position at your old job in the meantime?'

'Maybe,' he says.

Charlotte gives a short cry and I swivel to face her. She looks like she could do with a cuddle.

Magdala raises her eyebrows. 'So, you'll be around a bit more then, Lauren?'

'Yes,' I say, resting the drumstick on the tray table of Charlotte's highchair as I reach for the buckle.

With a violent thrust of his arm, Alex snatches the chicken away. 'Fucking hell, Lauren, what are you thinking? She could choke on that.'

He's right of course. 'I'm sorry,' I say quickly. 'I didn't think.'

'Mistakes like that could kill her. You need to be more careful.'

His voice doesn't even flinch on the word *kill*.

I gulp down a mouthful of water, feeling the coolness in the back of my throat. Careful, Lauren, I tell myself. Be non-confrontational, remember. Otherwise, you might put Charlotte, and yourself, at risk.

Magdala places several packets and bottles of pills from her handbag onto the table. 'My damn pill box has decided to go into hiding,' she says. 'Have you seen it, Lauren?'

I shake my head.

'Could have sworn I brought it with me. But, maybe I left it at home.' She pops one tablet from each packet, tips her head back and drops them into her mouth before taking a swill of wine.

'Mum,' Alex says, 'should you really be washing those down with alcohol?'

'What the doctor doesn't know won't hurt him,' she offers, reclining the chair.

'But it might hurt you.'

She gives him a stern look. 'Your old mama can take care of herself.'

Even as I hesitate, I need to ask. 'What are you taking, Magdala?'

'Let's see.' She picks up the medications from the table one at a time, pronouncing their names with some difficulty. 'Ram-i-pril for my blood pressure. At-or-vas-tatin for my cholesterol. And—' she fumbles through her handbag but comes up empty handed. 'Some new medication for my Parkinson's.'

'The specialist told Mum that her Parkinson's can be managed with medication for now. Is that right?' Alex stares at me, waiting for my medical input.

'I'm sure her doctor knows what they're talking about,' I say. And for a moment, it feels like we're having a regular family conversation in our backyard.

Nothing is wrong.

Perhaps my husband isn't poisoning my food with his mother's Parkinson's medication. Or perhaps Magdala coming to stay has just made things that much easier for him . . .

38

Australian Health Practitioner Regulation Agency

This form helps us manage complaints or concerns about registered health practitioners. Very serious, or repetitive concerns that demonstrate there is an ongoing risk to patients or the public can be investigated.

Getting started

All concerns are recorded on our database.

*Do you want to continue?

Yes

No

We will ask you details about what happened and then about you, including your contact details.

Sharing your contact details means we know who you are. We won't tell anyone else you're the one who told us what happened unless you give us permission to do so. (We'll ask you this later.) You might choose to use a name that is not yours (a pseudonym). That's okay too. What we do ask is that you give us a reliable way to contact you so we can talk to you.

You may still decide that you want to remain anonymous. This means:

- we will not know your identity
- if we need more information from you, we will not be able to contact you
- there will be limited things we can do in response, and
- we will not be able to keep you informed about the progress and outcome of the concern.

You can call us to talk about this. We're available Monday to Friday 9 a.m. to 5 p.m. local time.

*Do you wish to remain anonymous?

   Yes

   No

39

THE DAY OF

When I wake, the shutters are open, daylight streaming in. It's my first day at home since I was forced to take time off. I check my phone. 19 December. Billy's anniversary.

Despite the sunny weather, my heart closes over. It's always a quiet, sad day we spend at home. Alex and I don't speak Billy's name, don't visit his grave or look through old photos. In some ways, it's a shared denial – as if by avoiding the topic, we can pretend it never really happened. But sometimes I wonder if it is Billy's death, or his brief life, that gets lost in our collective silence.

Today's anniversary is different. We have Charlotte now. I roll over. Alex's side of the bed is empty. I head to the cupboard to gather my clothes for the day. Opening my underwear drawer, I register that the cabergoline bottle is gone, just like the diary. Are these messages from Alex? *Don't mess with me.* I glance back at our bed, the doona crumpled. Where is he now?

The faint sound of giggling echoes down the hallway from the living room. Dammit, I slept so deeply, I missed the overnight feed again. Even though I won't be able to breastfeed Charlotte any longer, I still cherish our precious time in the half-light.

Could my heavy slumber be the result of some other medication Alex is administering to me without my knowledge? But, no – I didn't eat or drink anything last night apart from a few mouthfuls of chicken and tap water. And . . . I also drank from my water bottle through the night. Dammit. I hadn't thought of that. He could have added anything into my drink bottle. Maybe he's been administering me with sedatives for some time now without me realising it. My hands go clammy and, suddenly, I'm relieved I am no longer giving Charlotte my breastmilk. And then I freeze involuntarily as it strikes me.

Breastmilk.

Billy.

Mirtazapine. The antidepressant – prescribed to me during my first inpatient admission to help manage sleep and anxiety – was found in my bloodstream, and in Billy's, on the day of his death. Yet, I'd been sure I hadn't been taking it at that point.

Oh, crap.

I shake myself, trying to collect my thoughts. If my hazy memory from that period serves me correctly, I had only just recommenced breastfeeding Billy a week or so before his death. I had been confused when Alex reported he had found a packet of mirtazapine on the kitchen bench the day Billy died. He insisted I must have taken a dose, that Billy must have ingested it through my breastmilk. It didn't make sense to me as I was certain I had stopped taking it months before but, consumed with grief, I had felt unable to explain the blood results – either my own, or Billy's – in any other way.

Wait – my records. I had obsessively kept track of the feeds – and documented any medications I'd taken while breastfeeding. I should still have that journal. I hurry across to the nursery and tug Billy's memory chest from the bookcase. I rifle through it. No way I would have thrown out those notes. There, at the very bottom, is the small journal in which I wrote down every detail. Times, dates, even graphs. Admittedly a little over-the-top, but back then it had felt like some sort of warped measure of my worth as a mother. How sad, I can see that now. Partly because of my inability to bond with Billy, I had felt breastfeeding was my only tangible measure of maternal 'success'.

It's all there in the journal, every agonising, exhausting breastfeed. The feeds had tailed off when Billy was around six months old, due to my waning supply and my concerns that he wasn't getting much milk, plus the fact he had begun eating solids. It is possible, I realise now, that Alex could have been administering cabergoline to me then too, in an attempt to reduce my milk supply. But with a pang of sadness, I realise that there is no possible way, now, to find that out.

I inspect the later entries, which confirm my vague recollection: I had indeed re-established breastfeeding a few weeks prior to that fateful day. And I'm right – I'd been obsessive about recording any medication I took here too. Tracing back through my records, I see the capital 'M' inscribed against seven dates in a row, right after my discharge from the mother–baby unit back in the June of the year Billy died.

I took it for only that first week after I got home from hospital. All it did was make me drowsy – which made it harder to look after Billy. So, I'd stopped taking it without telling anyone.

There are no other days I took mirtazapine recorded here.

I flick to the final entry. 19 December, four years ago. The day of Billy's death.

12.15 p.m. normal feed.

No capital M on this day, either. No wonder I was confused when the police reported they had found mirtazapine in my blood and in Billy's too. I'd tried to tell the officers interviewing me that I had stopped taking mirtazapine months before, but they were insistent; they had the blood test results. In the fog of grief, I had gone along with Alex's and the police's explanations, agreed that I must have taken one that morning and concurred that Billy had ingested some through the breastmilk. At the time, it seemed preferable to the far worse alternative conclusion the police could have drawn: that I had intentionally poisoned Billy. Besides, I told myself, whether I had taken mirtazapine or not, I was the one who had been responsible for Billy's care at the time of his death. Either way, I was the one who had failed him.

Now, with the journal's records corroborating my memory, I scan my recollection of mirtazapine's taste. I faintly recall its overwhelming bitterness, which I had learned to neutralise with mouthfuls of coffee. My hands tighten their grip on the journal as I realise that the taste of mirtazapine is identical to the intense bitterness of that Peking sauce. My eyes well up, even as fear grips my insides.

'Darling? Would you like some breakfast?' Alex's voice travels down the hall.

'No, thanks. You go ahead. I'll have a shower.'

'Don't be too long. I'm sure Charlotte would love to see you.'

'Okay.' I'm unnerved. It seems likely Alex is attempting to drug me with mirtazapine again. Given he knows I had restarted breastfeeding, he must be aware Charlotte had been receiving some of the mirtazapine too. I inhale deeply. So, why is he suddenly encouraging me to spend time with her? What does he have in store?

I sneak across the hallway into our ensuite, my breastfeeding journal tucked into my pyjamas, and lock the door behind me. The other day, I hadn't thought to look *behind* the first aid kit. I remember concealing the box of mirtazapine there, not wanting to be constantly faced with the shame of what I had deemed as 'evidence of my failure' at motherhood. I know it was still there after Billy died; the police had taken the single blister packet Alex had found on the kitchen bench, but not the other sheets of tablets within the box. I had gone looking for the mirtazapine box in the weeks after Billy's death, trying to deduce whether the medication had indeed been mine. I recall the shock of finding it right here, one sheet of tablets missing, realising with horror that it *had* been my blister pack of mirtazapine tablets on the kitchen bench the day of his death. I must have been so unwell, I concluded at the time, that I had taken a tablet and not even realised.

I bend down and, reaching into the vanity, I grab hold of the first aid kit again. I pull it out and squint at the back of the top shelf. It's empty. The box of mirtazapine that definitely *was* here after Billy's death is now gone. I realise this is more evidence: Alex must have removed the box in the intervening years. He administered me with mirtazapine in the Peking duck. He somehow sedated me last night; perhaps other nights, also.

And, far worse, he must have drugged me with mirtazapine on the day of Billy's death.

I slide down the wall until I reach the floor. The cold of the tiles seeps through my pyjama bottoms. How long might Alex have been lacing my food before Billy's death? Had he merely been trying to medicate my anxiety surreptitiously and non-consensually – or had he been purposely overdosing me with a more malicious intent? Regardless, Billy would likely have been at least somewhat drowsy on the day of his death, which might potentially explain his drowning. We had trained him to be as careful around water as was possible for a 12-month-old, with regular 'splash and play' sessions. Even though he had been found face-down in the deep end, it had been hard to believe he would have attempted to go in the pool alone. But no matter what happened – whether Alex drugged me or not – it was me who, in my drowsy state, must have left the pool gate propped open, and the back door ajar. Billy's death was still essentially all my fault.

'Lauren? What's going on with you? You hardly ate any dinner. Now, no breakfast. Was it something you ate at the hospital yesterday?'

Thank god I remembered to lock the ensuite door. 'I don't think so,' I croak back. He is monitoring my food intake, presumably because he's lacing my meals.

I haul myself to my feet and turn on the shower taps. Think, Lauren, think. I replace the first aid kit in the vanity. I tuck the journal into my pyjamas for now. I have to find a good hiding place for it.

Then I realise: cameras. Alex must have cameras throughout the house. He is all over IT security and is totally into the latest technology. He once boasted to me that cameras could be hidden in something the size of a pinhead. Which means . . . I wheel around, taking in my surroundings. Toothbrushes, soap dispenser, towel rack. I examine each item in turn, looking for a possible lens. Then I remember a YouTube video I saw years ago about how to locate microcameras in holiday accommodation. Turn off the lights, and sometimes a pinpoint red light will be visible. Alternatively, shining a phone torch in the dark will reveal a reflection.

I flick off the light and with no windows in the ensuite, the room is plunged into darkness. I scan the walls, the vanity, the shower itself for a red light, then switch on my phone light and scan again. Nothing.

A banging on the door.

'Lauren. What's going on?'

With creeping awareness, I look above my head. On the ceiling, where the fan sits, is a small red light.

I grasp at the basin, my head reeling. I am effectively trapped. If I turn on the light to start dismantling the fan, he will catch on. Can I somehow cover or disable it? Again, he will know.

I'm *not* imagining this. He *must* have been watching me all this time, aware I have been reading my journal and checking for the mirtazapine box. He may know I am putting clues together, forming connections in my head. No wonder he knew when I'd breastfed Charlotte – there must be a camera in Charlotte's room, too. He was aware I had searched his phone – a camera in our bedroom too. And most likely, the kitchen. Which means he probably knows I have discovered the cabergoline in the salt container. But surely, he can't be watching me at all hours – he has to sleep, take care of Charlotte – perhaps that's why he brought his mum here . . .

'Migraine,' I say. 'I've had to turn the lights off. I thought to get some medication, but I think I just need a lie down.'

'What . . . on the ensuite floor?'

I can tell from his tone he's agitated. Uncertain, perhaps, just how much I know. And beneath his concern, I hear a trace of anger, because he can't control me in here. And maybe, I realise, noting this for the first time – maybe he is beginning to comprehend that he can't control me out there, either.

'It's cool on the tiles,' I say. 'I just need some space.'

'Okay,' he responds, his voice cold. 'But why is the shower still on?'

He wants the shower off. Not just the shower – the fan too. No doubt when it's on, his view of the room is significantly impaired, from condensation and the spinning blades. The ensuite, then, will be my place to sit. To hide. To think.

'I'm sitting down in the shower,' I call.

'Do I need to get you some help?'

'No. I'm fine. I'll be out soon.'

'Okay.' But he doesn't sound convinced. His tone is curt when he speaks again: 'Just as long as you're not going to accuse me of anything else. Like fathering another woman's child.'

I'd almost forgotten. Elspeth. The Peugeot. So, how, exactly, does she fit in with all of this? I scan through every possible motive until there is one that clicks like a jigsaw piece: Alex wants to be with Elspeth. If he can cast me as an unfit, incapable mother then he can be with his lover and gain custody of Charlotte. That explains Elspeth's car being outside our house last week, as well as all the other times she must have visited our house.

But it's not just Elspeth – Magdala is involved in this too somehow. She has been hiding my breastmilk, supplying the cabergoline to suppress my milk supply and god knows what else. Which means . . . Elspeth, Magdala *and* Alex might all be involved in trying to separate Charlotte and me. I know Magdala would do anything to keep her son happy – but causing her daughter-in-law to appear like such an unfit parent that she loses custody of her child? Hmm – perhaps it's not such an outlandish theory after all.

Fucking hell.

I clutch at the breastfeeding journal tucked into my pyjama pants. I must not lose this. With my history, and the ease with which Alex calls my memories into question, people are unlikely to believe me when I try to explain my situation. My number one priority is Charlotte's safety. And that necessitates prioritising myself – a lesson I learned from my mother only too well.

40

I emerge from the bathroom wet with just a towel wrapped around me, my pyjamas bundled up to conceal the breastfeeding journal.

'Darling.' Alex is reclining on our bed with Charlotte. They're both fully dressed. 'We've been waiting for you.'

I place the pyjamas on top of my chest of drawers as Alex jumps to his feet. 'Let me help you,' he says, reaching out.

I snatch my pyjamas away, push them into the top drawer and grab my underwear. 'I need to get dressed.'

'Go right ahead.'

'I'd like some privacy.'

'From your husband?'

'I don't want to get changed in front of Charlotte.' It's untrue – I'm fine with nudity – but it's the best I can come up with.

He looks at me strangely, then picks Charlotte up and heads

for the door. 'Take your time,' he says. 'Let's go, Charlie. Lauren needs to get dressed. We'll leave her to it.'

Since when did we decide to call our daughter Charlie? And why did he refer to me as Lauren rather than Mummy?

As soon as he's gone, I scan the room for cameras. There's nothing obvious, but I feel safer in the dark. I close the shutters, switch off the light. It's almost pitch black thanks to Alex's recent addition of blackout blinds in our room too. I can only imagine him cursing himself now for having purchased those.

In the darkness, I hurriedly dress myself, then remove the journal from the drawer and shove it under my jumper and t-shirt against the skin of my belly to conceal it. I need to get it somewhere safe, somewhere he won't be able to find it.

I switch on the light as I leave the room and head into the hall. The front door creaks a little as I ease it open, but then swings wide. As I don't have my keys with me, I pull it closed behind me just so it doesn't quite latch – I'll need to let myself back in before Alex realises I'm gone.

The wind is blustery, the sun already scorching overhead as I rush next door and ring Karla's bell.

Her door swings open almost immediately.

'Please,' I say, almost falling over her threshold. 'Can you help me?'

'Of course.' She surveys my damp hair and crumpled clothes. 'Are you all right?'

'No.' I thrust the journal at her. 'Can you keep this safe for me? Please don't let anyone have it. No one. Especially not my husband.'

She pulls the door closed behind me and begins to flick through the pages. 'What is this?'

'My journal from around the time of Billy's death.'

She nods, a confused expression on her face. 'Okay.' Then her eyes tighten. 'And about my notebook – I know you took it. I need it back. You're lucky I have another one for backup.'

'I'm so sorry,' I say. 'I was planning to return it as soon as I could, but he stole it from me.'

'He?'

'Alex. But please don't say anything if he comes here. I'll get it back from him, I promise. I'm just—'

There's a harsh knocking at the door. Alex's silhouette is visible through the frosted glass.

'Please hide my journal. *Please.*' I stare at her in despair.

She frowns, clearly angry. 'You stole from me and now you want my help.'

'I know. I'm so sorry. I'll keep looking for it.'

She places the journal on her hall table, beside a small bowl of keys. 'It's against my better judgement, but just this once.'

'Thank you,' I say, then lay my hand on her forearm. 'And – I need to know – can you describe the woman who visited our house in the blue Peugeot?'

Karla looks even more confused. 'I guess she was about our age,' she says, then pauses. 'Lauren, what the hell is going on?'

Alex bangs again on the door. 'I know you're in there, babe. Open up.'

'I'll be all right,' I gasp, 'but you'd better let him in.'

Karla nods almost reluctantly and opens the front door.

Alex's face is all smiles. 'Darling – your migraine – should you be up and about?'

Karla looks back at me and I give a half-smile, half-grimace. 'False alarm,' I say, trying to think of a reasonable excuse for being at the neighbour's house. Nothing comes to mind. 'I thought one was coming on, but it hasn't, thank god. I feel much better.'

'Oh, good,' he says. 'So, what are you doing here?'

'She was just returning something she borrowed,' Karla interjects. 'Which is what we should all do, isn't it?' She looks back at me.

'Of course,' Alex says, his eyes flicking to the hall table. His brow furrows as he catches sight of the journal before him. Its cover, a photograph of sailboats, will be familiar to him. 'We'd better get going, Lauren,' he says. 'We need to leave for our daytrip.'

'Huh?' I say.

'We're going out for Billy's anniversary. A tribute. I told you, remember? The car is all packed.' He flashes Karla one of his charming smiles.

My mind spins in dizzying circles, trying to take in his words. 'It's the first I've heard of it.'

'Her memory struggles sometimes.' He speaks directly to Karla. 'It's not her fault. It's since the . . . well, you know.' Karla nods and I can see that, like everyone else, she's taken in by him.

My eyes lock on my journal. Even if I survive the day, how can I trust that it will be safe with Karla? Alex could come back at any time and insist she give it to him.

'I can't possibly go out for the day. What about Charlotte?'

'Come on, darling. Have a little faith. You know I always have her best interests in mind. Yours too. But let's not discuss this in front of our neighbour. I'm sure she has a lot to do.'

'Don't worry. I'll be here if you need any help,' Karla says. I'm not sure if she is trying to reassure me or is just being polite.

Not for the first time, I wish I had got to know her better, spent more time with her over these last few years.

'Thank you so much,' Alex says. 'You've always been such a great neighbour.'

Boy, is he turning on the charm. I can only imagine he is suspicious about my connection with her. And, given he likely took her electronic notebook from my workbag, it may well have been him who deleted the entry from the day of Billy's death – in which case he would be aware that Karla knows more about what happened on that day than he would like. Which means – my god, she could be at risk too.

'I've mentioned to Lauren I'd be happy to help with baby-sitting if you ever need,' she adds.

'Thank you, Karla, but we're very fortunate my mother is here to help out. Darling—' Alex reaches into the hallway and grabs my hand, 'we really should be going. We don't want to be late.'

Karla has her gaze firmly set on me. 'Please take care of yourself,' I say to her.

'You too,' she says with concern in her eyes as Alex pulls me away.

Back in our house, my backpack is resting against the hall table, stuffed full and zipped closed.

'You packed for me?'

'Yes,' he calls as he heads for the living room.

I unzip the bag. Inside is a neatly folded towel and my bathers. Surely, this isn't a daytrip that involves water. He must know that would be triggering for me, today of all days. Unless that is his intention – to upset me even more.

When Alex returns carrying Charlotte, my breathing is quick in my chest.

'Is she coming too?' My heart lightens.

He shakes his head. 'Just us. She'll stay here. Mum will mind her.'

'Can't Charlotte come?'

'I thought it might be best just us.' He speaks slowly. 'You know, almost like a date. I thought you'd prefer it that way.'

I could argue, insist on staying home. But I know Alex. Once his mind is fixed on something, he's impossible to shift. In years past, I would have been happy to spend a day-date with him. But now, with everything going on, the idea chills me to my core. It's very unlike Alex to arrange a day out for us, let alone a tribute to honour Billy's anniversary. It has been so long since we did anything like this together.

He kisses Charlotte on the crown of her head. 'Who's excited about a little time with Grandma?'

She smiles and gurgles.

A surge of heat pulses through me. This is part of Alex's plan, then – divide and conquer, separate mother from baby. I shouldn't be allowing this to happen. Yet the words of protest stick in my throat as a sense of hopelessness fills me. I'm outnumbered, with nowhere to turn. For now, I can only submit, attempt to maintain safety for myself, and for Charlotte, as much as I can. 'Where are we going?'

He grins. 'It's a surprise. A good one. You'll see.'

Alex turns up the music playing on the car radio as I sip the coffee I brought from home and mentally run through the information from the limited family violence training I have attended over the years. I'd never paid it much heed, always figuring I could call one of the hospital social workers for assistance if circumstances required. Counselling people about family violence has rarely been part of my remit. Now, I curse myself, wishing I'd paid more attention.

Keep a bag packed with important documents in it. I'll do that, as soon as I get home. Fortunately, my journal is safe at Karla's for now.

Let a friend, family member or neighbour know what's going on. Have a safe word or emoji you can use if you need them to contact authorities. Ordinarily, I would speak with Natalia, confide in her. But after yesterday, I can't trust her. Karla appears somewhat supportive. Perhaps I can be more transparent with her, ask if she'd be willing to contact the police should the need arise.

Leaving an offender is the most dangerous time. I can sense that in my bones. The more I become aware of the danger Charlotte and I are in, the more I feel push back from Alex. Hence the need to appease him until we can safely escape.

Be wary of leaving traces of contacting family violence services on your electronic devices. I hadn't even thought to reach out to this type of service, had assumed they would pay me no heed. After all, both times this same anxiety arose, I was admitted to a psychiatric ward and fed antidepressants. It was understood *I* was the problem, that it was all in my head. But maybe, just maybe, I could contact them anonymously. If I can find a way to circumvent any monitoring of my devices, that is. Alex's specialty is IT after all.

Alex is humming along to Eminem beside me. At the end of the song, he pauses. 'You have your phone, right?'

That's it. Another phone. A different SIM card. One he doesn't know about.

'Yes,' I say, already formulating my plan. 'Can we stop at a supermarket, though? I forgot to bring pads.'

His eyes narrow. 'You haven't had a period for years.'

'Incontinence pads,' I say without a blink. 'Since the birth, I've been leaking on and off.' Smart, Lauren.

I glance at his face: expressionless. It's hard to judge what he is reading into my actions. The bottle of cabergoline. Karla's notebook. The mirtazapine. My breastfeeding journal. I guess the cameras are a way for him to gather evidence that – what? – I'm mentally unwell? But more than that, they give him good reason to suspect I am closer to figuring out his possible contribution in framing me for Billy's death. Which puts me directly in his firing line.

He pulls up at the next shopping centre without comment.

'Back soon,' I say with an innocent smile.

In the chill of the supermarket air conditioning, a tinny version of 'We Wish You a Merry Christmas' blares overhead. I scuttle through the aisles, grabbing the first packet of incontinence pads I can locate, then head for the front counter. Fortunately, the supermarket windows are covered over with white spray paint and seasonal messages of good cheer; I won't be visible from the car park. The mobile phones are in a plastic cabinet behind the counter. I clear my throat.

'How can I help you?' the server asks in a languid drawl.

'I'm in a rush,' I say. 'My husband is waiting in the car. I desperately need a new phone and SIM card.'

'Not a problem.' Dangling from her earlobes, Santa earrings with red LED lights flash on and off. 'Let me unlock the cabinet for you.'

Energy thrums through my chest. The slowness with which she untangles the chain of keys from her belt and reaches for the lock of the cabinet is almost unbearable.

Behind me, a queue of shoppers is building at the 'eight items or less' check-out. I glance to the front door. No sign of Alex.

The server's movements are concrete-slow as she removes three mobiles from the cabinet and places them on the counter in front of me.

'I'll take the cheapest,' I say. She indicates an inconspicuous black mobile before me. 'And a SIM please.' I glance at the front door again. 'It's urgent.'

She finally gets it and scans the phone packaging and a SIM card from the rack. 'Here we go, sweetie.' As she passes me a form to complete the purchase, her eyebrows crinkle with concern. 'Are you all right?' she asks.

'I truly hope so,' I say.

41

Alex's face bears a smug expression as we pull into the driveway of the complex.

'Hot springs,' he says. 'I thought it might be just what you need.'

As the heat of the sun pours through the windscreen, I squish my hands into fists beneath my sticky thighs. How could he possibly pretend that he thought a spa, a pool, would be of benefit for us on the anniversary of Billy's death?

The car park is almost empty – midweek, of course. As he unloads our bags from the boot, I survey the surrounding landscape. The complex is more than a little luxurious, with a sweeping view across an elegant lake, surrounded by serene pools of all shapes and sizes perched in private nooks among low scrub. In any other lifetime, this would be a place of heavenly luxury. For me, now, in this baking summer heat, it resembles a deathtrap.

My skin is slick with perspiration as we enter the large, cream-coloured modern building. At reception, beneath a metallic foil *Merry Christmas* sign, a staff member slides towels and white robes across to us.

'You're booked for lunch before you bathe,' she says.

At least, here, I'll be able to eat without worrying what Alex is going to feed to me.

'I've booked us a massage for later as well,' Alex says.

My shoulders tighten. He knows I don't like massages.

His phone pings in his pocket. He checks the message and gives a short laugh. 'Rebecca says enjoy your special day.'

'You mentioned this to the mothers group?' I ask casually.

He shrugs. 'I thought you'd want them to know.'

While I haven't checked the thread in a day or so, I imagine the mothers will all be drooling, wishing their husbands were as thoughtful as Alex. But I know his MO: keep your friends close and enemies closer. I dig my fingernails into my palms, a reminder to keep my wits about me.

Lunch is a casual affair, with picturesque views across the lake. Alex and I appear to have missed the dress code. Unlike the rest of the patrons in their white fluffy bath gowns and disposable white slippers, I'm wearing a silk shirt and Alex has dressed up too. At least there are no reminders of Christmas in this part of the complex.

'What would you like for your entree?' Alex says.

'I don't mind. I wonder how Charlotte is.'

'She'll be fine.' He places his fingertips on the back of my hand. 'You needn't worry so much.'

I press my lips together, recalling my kiss on Charlotte's forehead as I had bid her goodbye. *See you soon, baby girl.* She had turned her face into Magdala's shoulder as I left. My eyes prickle as I realise that if something were to happen to me now, I can't be certain she would even remember me.

Alex checks his phone at the table. 'See, no messages. I'm sure all is fine.'

Our first date in so long. And our first time out together since Charlotte was born. It feels desperately wrong that this is happening on the day Billy died, of all days. I wish with all my being I was happy, contented, relaxed. Instead, I'm trying to contain an avalanche of terror inside.

'I'm sure everything is fine too,' I say, blinking back tears.

As Alex scans the wine list, I consider: what is his scheme for this trip? What's it really about? And – my blood runs cold – what possible reason did he have for wanting to pin Billy's death on me? Did he feel so guilty about whatever role he felt he'd played that he couldn't handle it and had to lay all the blame on me? Or was it more callous that that – he wanted me so racked with guilt that I'd be pliable and submissive, do whatever he desired? None of this makes any sense.

An image of my darling daughter jumps into my head. She is the spitting image of Alex. After only a few days back at work, I can see how easy it has been to start feeling disconnected from her. I had told myself that genetic heritage was of no importance, that I could love a child no matter their origins. And I do. But maybe Alex believes it is easier to sever that attachment when there is no genetic link. Step-parents might miss the child when separating from the other parent, but they often struggle to maintain a connection. Is that how

Alex hopes it will be with Charlotte and me? Or – and this thought horrifies me – is he like my father with my mother, wanting me dead, so he can have Charlotte all to himself?

The writing on the menu wavers in front of me.

'You order for me,' I say in a shaky voice and he does so without hesitation.

My heart tightens and I know what I want, what Charlotte means to me. I am her mother. I will always be her parent, no matter what the DNA says.

Alex glances up at me. 'Starting to feel more relaxed?'

I give a half-hearted nod and sip at the champagne that has been placed before me.

When the food arrives, the servings are minuscule: a few oysters and scallops circled by coloured blobs of sauce, a few scattered edible flowers on the rim. I dive right in.

'Slow down,' he says. 'It's like you haven't eaten in weeks.'

The room spins a little on its axis. The champagne has gone to my head. At least I am certain there's no way it could have been spiked.

I look at Alex, seated opposite me, as he slices into his scallops, then slides them into his mouth and swallows effortlessly. In many ways, he is a stranger. We eat in silence. There isn't much to talk about that doesn't feel loaded with grief and pain.

There was a moment, I recall, a week or so before Billy's death, when everything changed between my son and me. I was napping on the couch when I woke with a start. It had been quite some time since I had put Billy down. I called his name, ran to his bedroom, then into each room in the house. As I returned to the living room, I saw it: the sliding door was open. I raced outside. The pool gate, usually secured shut with a heavy garden pot, was swinging in the summer breeze.

In that moment, lightning ran through me. My first thought: *Alex is never going to forgive me.*

Billy was standing at the side of the pool, seeming tempted by the water, despite us having taught him to never go in without us.

'Billy!' I sprinted to him, lifted him to my chest and hugged him so tight I must have squeezed the air right out of him.

Something cracked inside me in that moment. As I carried him inside, I realised how easily I could have lost him. My fear of Alex's wrath transmuted into self-recrimination. How could I have been so stupid as to leave the pool gate unsecured and the back sliding door open? I had no memory of leaving the door ajar. Sure, its latch was weak, had been for years. But it was unlikely to slide open itself. Had someone been inside the house? I simply couldn't figure it out. As for the latch on the pool gate, it hadn't been working since Magdala had vacated the house. Rather than letting the gate slam back and forth in strong winds, we had taken to wedging it closed with a heavy garden pot, mindful that Billy was too young to get to the poolside unaided.

Except suddenly he was crawling and then walking. I had kept meaning to get the pool gate repaired. After my swim earlier that day, I could have sworn I pushed the plant pot back in place to secure the gate closed – and yet the only possible explanation is that I didn't. It really was all my fault.

That night, I lay in bed, restless.

'You okay, hon?' Alex had asked.

'Yep,' I replied, not keen to disclose the day's events, fearful of the repercussions. Finally, bracing myself for his anger, it spilled out. 'Something happened today,' I said, then bit my lip in the darkness.

'Oh, yes?' His tone was cool and casual, almost unconcerned.

'Billy almost died.'

I could hear Alex's rapid intake of breath.

'I found him in the pool enclosure. He was staring at the water as if he might jump in. I caught him just in time.'

'What a relief,' he said, though he didn't turn towards me.

'I could have *sworn* I closed the sliding door. And put the pot back in place.' There was such a desperate, pleading tone in my voice.

'I guess we all forget things sometimes,' he said finally, then fell into silence.

Now, looking back, I can see how strange it was that Alex didn't ask any further questions, made no enquiries as to what or how it had happened. It's almost as if he didn't need to ask, because he knew.

As Alex fell into sleep, the sight of Billy by the side of the pool, staring into the depths of the water, consumed my thoughts. Perhaps more shocking to me than the memory itself was the lack of emotion I had felt in that moment. What did it show about how impenetrable the walls were that I had built around my heart? And it hit me then – that if *I* couldn't keep my heart open to my son, who would? I was his mother. He needed me. There was no one apart from Alex who ever would, or ever could, love him more than me. It was my job – my responsibility – to give him that.

The following week with Billy was beautiful. It seemed that my heart had been cracked open by the threat of losing him. And he responded to the change. His smiles were mesmerising, his sky-blue eyes so beautiful and bright. He could finally feel my love – I am sure of it – as much as I could feel his. We finally had the connection we both deserved. I had thought everything was finally going to be all right.

Alex smiles. 'Charlotte will be waking up from her nap about now.' He slides his phone face down onto the tablecloth. I wonder what he is trying to hide. 'So, I've been doing some thinking.' He gives a subtle smile and takes a sip of his red wine. 'You know how I mentioned our wills the other day? Well, Mum is getting on a bit and clearly unwell. I've been thinking we should appoint a legal guardian for Charlotte – someone who could take care of her in the unlikely event of something happening to both of us. It would just mean adding an extra clause to our wills.'

'Our wills?' My brain is reeling. Today of all days is not the right time to bring up our wills again. It is the anniversary of our son's death. He is clearly scheming to get rid of me. The situation is as ominous as my worst fears.

'Oh, darling.' His grin is plastered on, and I realise that for all these years I've had no idea what goes on inside my husband's head. 'I know it's been a lot. That's why I thought I'd make this easier for you. I've spoken to our lawyer about it and had him draw up the papers. They're right here if you'd like to sign them.'

He sets a sheaf of pages held together by a bulldog clip before me on the tablecloth. 'Here, have a read. Don't sign them until you're satisfied. And not until we've entered the name of the guardian we've agreed on.'

Trying to stop my hands from shaking, I reach for the papers. 'I'm not sure I understand. Are you suggesting we do this right now?'

'The sooner the better, I guess,' he replies.

I clear my throat. 'Who are you suggesting we appoint as guardian?'

'It would have to be whoever you're comfortable with. I thought perhaps Natalia would be your preference? Otherwise, Elspeth? They're both good with children and have your medical experience. I briefly considered Karla but she's just a tad too interfering, so . . . probably not?' He gives a quiet guffaw. 'Anyone I missed?'

I try to think of an appropriate answer. 'Maybe we can discuss this again another time?'

'Of course.' He takes another sip of his shiraz and his smile widens.

And I realise, then, what I am to him. I am not a wife. I am an incubator. Does he really believe that a luxury day spa, fine dining and expensive champagne are all that is needed to seduce me into signing over guardianship of my beautiful baby? To Elspeth, no less. What does he take me for – an absolute fool? Of course, after that, there'd be no benefit to keeping me alive. I shudder to think what his next plans are.

The mains are placed in front of us. The duck dish he's chosen for me, with its bloody centre and plum sauce, reminds me of a placenta. Recalling the last time he served me duck, I gag.

'Are you okay?'

I want to escape to the bathroom, but I cannot trust what he will do with my food, my water. Still, I really need some time alone to get my bearings.

'You eat,' I say. 'I'll be back in a tick.' He doesn't reply as I stuff the papers into my handbag, clutching it to my chest as I head for the door.

Instead of turning right to the bathrooms, though, I veer left, out through the main doors. I gulp at the cloying, humid air. A small fountain bubbles beside me. The location feels menacing. I shake my head and check my phone.

A brief message from Devan: *Hope leave is going well. Not much to report. Patient JG was back in clinic today requesting you, was disappointed to find you were on leave.*

My brain is a scramble, trying to recall what Natalia recounted yesterday about the patient named Jody. Yes, I recall – her surname began with a G. Jody had reported that I was 'pushy', Natalia had said. But now I'm hearing a different story.

Patient is feeling a lot stronger now and wanted me to pass on that she was safe and truly grateful for your help. Said I'd let you know.

Grateful? Well, that doesn't sound like she felt nervous around me or that I was 'pushy'. So, why on earth did Natalia tell me that? Is she in on this with Alex too? Why else would she try to convince me to doubt myself?

I must find out what Alex has been up to. I place a call to our lawyer.

'Hello, how can I help?' A young woman's voice.

I speak quickly and quietly. 'It's Dr De Vale. I need to speak with Martin urgently.'

'Of course. I'll see if he's free.'

As the hold music plays its tinny tune, my shoulders drop ever so slightly. Maybe there is still hope I will get out of this nightmarish situation alive, along with my daughter.

'Martin Stilinovic speaking. How can I help you?' His voice echoes down the line.

'Hello, Martin. It's Lauren De Vale. My husband has just presented me with a new will. Do you know about this?'

'Why, yes,' he says in a pleasant voice. 'Alex asked me to draw it up yesterday.'

'Did he give a reason?'

'He said you haven't been well. His mother, also.' He pauses. 'You sound well.'

'I am,' I say quickly. I was right; this is about Alex attempting to collate more evidence that I am mentally unwell, as well as securing his custody of Charlotte if anything were to happen to me. 'Can I ask what changes were made?'

'He only wanted the addition of a clause nominating a legal guardian for your daughter.'

'Did he say who he wanted?'

'He did. But he asked to leave it blank for now. He was waiting to discuss it with you before confirming the name.'

'Can you tell me who it was?'

'I can't recall offhand.' I hear him shuffling paper in the background, then keystrokes. 'I'm sorry – I'm just about to go into a meeting. If I can't locate it now, I'll email the name through later today.'

'Thank you so much. You have no idea what this means to me,' I say.

'Tell me,' Alex says from behind me, his voice hard, 'exactly *what* it means to you.'

42

EIGHTEEN YEARS EARLIER

PHARMACY STUDENT EXPELLED FOR ABORTION PILL THEFT

A final year pharmacy student has been expelled from his university and is facing criminal conviction following allegations he stole a medication commonly used to terminate pregnancy.

A 20-year-old man from Taylors Bridge is being questioned by police over the alleged theft of misoprostol during a recent student placement.

Police are making enquiries into the recipient of the medications. Further details are yet to be released.

42

EIGHTEEN YEARS EARLIER

43

Alex takes me by the elbow and moves me with silent fury along the clifftop path. The pinch of his fingers on my skin stings. I try to pull away, but he clenches harder.

'Where are you taking me?'

'To the changerooms,' he says. 'We're going to fucking make the most of this day, whether you like it or not.'

It sounds less like an ultimatum and more like a threat. Thank god he didn't overhear the whole phone call, only my final comment, which I was able to explain away as a hospital-related issue. He appeared to believe me.

To the right of the path there's a sheer drop to waves churning against the rock face. It would be so easy for him to push me over the edge. An innocent slip. A stumble. So many ways things could go wrong.

Another couple approaches, laughing, hand in hand. They pause to allow us to pass, nodding at us. I can see they're trying to read the dynamics between Alex and me. I dip my head to avoid their gaze.

Their voices fade as they continue down the path. That is how a normal couple interacts, while I'm wondering whether at any moment my husband will attempt to throw me to my death.

Outside the changerooms, Alex points me to the female section. 'I'll be waiting out here,' he says. 'Don't take too long.' His words are laced with menace.

I glance overhead as I enter. There's CCTV above the entrance to the changerooms. None above the door to the female area. I wonder if there will be cameras throughout the complex, but surely he would have thought of that, factored it into his plans.

The changerooms, with long views across the valley out to the horizon, should feel serene, but I can hardly focus on my next step, let alone the picturesque view. A few other patrons are changing into their swimwear. I imagine how I might appear to them, face flushed from champagne, hands shaking from adrenaline, pupils constricted like bullseyes in the centre of my wide, terror-filled eyes. I want to scream, beg for help, anything to get me away from danger. But I need to be smarter than this. If I can calm my breath, I will be more able to strategise, make a survival plan.

How did it come to this?

In, out, Lauren . . . in and out. That's it. I speak calmly to myself, the same way I speak to Charlotte when she cries, just as I imagine my mother might have done with me.

The lockers in front of me shift into focus as a plan forms in my head. I need to pretend everything is fine and avoid putting myself in a position where Alex could harm me. I'll keep my new phone – the one Alex thankfully didn't clock when he snuck up on me just now – hidden until I have a chance to call the family violence service. And I need to let someone else know what is happening, so if the worst does befall me, my death won't be put down to an accident.

I flick through the contacts on my old phone, trying to decide who to call, who might understand.

Until Natalia's recent betrayal, I had always been able to rely on her in difficult times. I reflexively dial her number, hear her familiar recording: *Let me know who you are so I can get right back to you.* Normally I find her voice reassuring, but today all I can hear is her cool tone from yesterday's remonstration. I hang up the phone without leaving a message.

Women from my mothers group? But there's no one I can really trust to keep this confidential in the event that nothing comes of my fears today. Most definitely *not* Elspeth.

Devan, perhaps – but as a hospital colleague, I have no idea what he has been told about my mental health; he may not take me seriously.

Karla – I don't know her well enough to reach out with this.

Of course – Aunty Sal!

I go to text her, then realise I forgot to get her phone number. Dammit. How the hell could I have neglected such a simple, but vital detail? At least I know her address – something Alex doesn't.

From my new phone, I text my old mobile number. I am, perhaps, the only person I can truly trust: *I'm in the changing room at Manuka Hot Springs. I believe my husband is going to try and kill me. I wish for my daughter's legal guardian to be –* I pause.

Aunty Sal is too old to take on the care of a baby. So, Alex is right – Natalia probably would have been my first pick until recently. The fact that she is unable to advocate for me doesn't bode well for Charlotte, and clearly, after yesterday, she's siding with Alex.

How *dare* Alex suggest Elspeth as a suitable caregiver for our daughter. It's apparent he wants to do away with me and allow Elspeth to become Charlotte's surrogate mother. Well, fuck him. And fuck Elspeth.

My body stiffens with fury. Karla might not be my first choice, but she's the only person who makes any semblance of sense at this point. I type her name then press send, and the text pops up in my old phone. I read it back and realise how ridiculous the message sounds. No one would believe me, even if I had someone I could reach out to.

Steeling my shoulders, I sling my new phone along with my old one into my backpack, catching sight of the legal papers as I do so. I pull them out and flick to the final page.

I nominate _____ as my child's legal guardian in the event of my death.

Grabbing my eyeliner, I'm about to scrawl Karla's name, then panic. Fuck, what is her surname? Think, Lauren, think. My mind is blank. *My next-door neighbour Karla* is all I can manage. I scribble in the empty space, then roughly sign my name before replacing the sheaf of paper in my backpack.

Alex won't be able to retrieve these from the women's changerooms. And if something happens to me, hopefully the authorities will be suspicious enough to check my belongings and my mobile records. I've created as much safety for Charlotte as I possibly can.

My mission is to play the innocent card. Try to smile. I change into my bathers, place my clothes in the locker and click the door closed.

For now I just have to pretend that everything is going to be all right.

44

Alex is waiting for me by the door when I exit the changeroom, his face deathly calm.

'Follow me,' he says.

My chest constricts. I have no choice but to obey.

He leads me away from the main area of the springs, where several patrons are soaking in pools of various shapes and sizes, then winds his way up a series of hot concrete steps, through a slew of eucalypt saplings, towards the top of the hill. I can just make out glimpses of the sparkling ocean through the host of leaves. The large pool at the end of the path is oval-shaped, rimmed with natural-looking rocks. A couple is embracing at the far end of the pool; the area is otherwise deserted. Alex sits on the nearest edge and dangles his feet into the water.

'Come in,' he says. 'It's very pleasant.'

'After you,' I say.

'Chicken.' He slides in, up to his knees. 'It's brilliant.'

I hesitate. The other couple will provide a measure of safety; I can probably afford to at least enter the water. I ease myself into the pool until my feet meet the concrete base. The water is barely lukewarm, enough to elicit a shiver. Goosebumps spring up on my skin. Alex's expression is smug.

I've never been a particularly strong swimmer. Alex is well aware of that. His motive for today wasn't designed to give me some relaxation time, nor to mark Billy's passing together. It is, as I suspected, designed to upset and coerce me. His plans have been strategised from the start.

He wades to the opposite side of the pool and beckons to me.

'This way, darling.'

'I'm okay, thanks.' I wrap my hands around my chest, shivering despite the sun's rays.

He heads back towards me, concern etched on his face. 'Oh, you poor thing. Let's get you somewhere warmer.'

Is his acting for other patrons, or for cameras? I glance around the pool's perimeter but there is no sign of CCTV. A large red button to one side bears a label that reads, *For assistance in the event of an emergency.* So, it seems we are very much unobserved.

When he reaches me, he encircles my waist with his arm and presses me towards the edge of the pool. He has never been physically abusive, never threatened me with violence of any kind. And now, I realise, he didn't have to. The words he uses, his tone, are similar enough to my father's that I instinctively obey him, almost without thinking. Our whole relationship I have expected him, allowed him, to be in charge. I have unconsciously believed he knew my desires and wants better than I knew them myself.

At the edge of the pool, he almost hauls me out.

'Come on, darling,' he says, his face rigid. 'I know just what you need.'

He leads me down the concrete stairs, through a nestle of trees, into a small clearing. This pool is smaller, isolated and empty, and, from the steam rising at its surface, I deduce it must be significantly hotter. The bottom is invisible, a swirl of froth coating the surface.

'A spa,' he says, and I note the button for the jets off to the side. There's another warning sign detailing in red-lettered capitals not to remain in such hot water for too long. 'Looks perfect,' he says.

He leads me to the edge. The water is fire-hot, scalding my skin. But his hand is on my shoulder, almost pressing me into the pool. 'Warm enough for you?' he taunts.

From the edge of the pool, he presses the 'on' button and the jets scream into life, bubbling hard against my buttocks and lower back.

My shoulder muscles soften automatically in the hot water. My eyelids flicker closed.

Shit. I force my eyes open. This is exactly what he wants. It's the heat, the champagne, as well as god knows what else he has, without me realising, managed to administer to me.

Alex eases into the water beside me.

'That's better, right?' he says.

I bite the inside of my lip, tasting blood.

He leans his head back against the edge of the spa. 'I hope you know you can trust me.'

Surely, he's joking. As I look into his eyes, creased in faux sadness, I force myself not to scoff. I could give him a hundred reasons why trust is the last thing on my mind.

Beneath the water, he reaches for my hand and squeezes it tight. 'I know things haven't been the same between us since Billy.' In his voice, I can hear some of the softness that first attracted me to him. 'I shouldn't have held it against you, I know that. I can see how much you care about Charlotte, how much you're trying. I'm sorry things have been so rough between us, really I am.'

Lulled by the soothing heat of the water, it's hard not to allow myself to relax alongside him. Yet, although his words are kind and his tone mellow, there's something else, a layer beneath that feels like a threat. I must remember what has happened, what he is capable of.

'I'm getting warm,' I say. 'I need to cool down.'

'Just a little longer,' he insists.

Despite the panic that has been coursing through me for days now, the hot water is so intoxicating. My muscles are jelly, making it almost impossible to move. I'm guessing he somehow laced my food with drugs that are not only sedating me but are also sapping my energy. Garnering all my strength, I rise to standing. 'Time to cool off,' I say.

'For god's sake, Lauren,' he snaps. 'Don't be such a spoilsport.'

A gust of wind slides over the beads of water coating my skin. As my core temperature drops, my body starts to recalibrate. 'There was a plunge pool at the bottom of the hill, wasn't there?' I clamber from the water. I can only imagine the darkness on his face as he emerges, grabs his robe and towel, then trails behind me down the stairs to the more populated areas of the complex.

The plunge pool is small, only a metre or so in diameter, but it must be deep; I can't see the bottom. I step straight in, falling through the icy water, my respiratory muscles seizing up in a protective instinct. My head drops below the surface, the coldness hitting the top of my scalp, and I see then an image of his plan, him holding the crown of my head under the scalding water, waiting for me to stop kicking. He wants me gone.

Underwater, I hold my breath, count slowly, seeing how long I can last. As the coldness seeps through the layers of my skin, my brain has a hard reset. The dullness that has permeated my mind for so long is clearing. I can think again.

My job is to survive, and to convince him I am no longer suspicious of him. Then I will be able to leave the relationship, and the family home, while securing Charlotte's safety. If I can procure enough evidence that he is a threat to her, I will be able to obtain custody. I will need to prove it wasn't solely me who was culpable for Billy's death. That I am a good enough mother. That I can keep Charlotte safe.

When I bob up from under the surface, he is crouching at the water's edge, waiting with furious eyes.

There are voices behind him. A female laughing, then a deep male voice that sounds exactly like Devan. I raise my head higher, searching for my registrar like a life raft, but when the man passes on the other side of a nearby pool, I see he's a stranger. Alex turns to follow my gaze and his moment is lost. I climb the ladder and emerge dripping onto the poolside.

'I feel much better,' I say.

He regards me, his smile tight. 'Good,' he says. 'That was my plan all along.'

*

We walk side by side towards the changerooms. I keep a safe distance from him on the clifftop path, well away from the edge. The wind is strong now, tugging the bottom of my towel from my thighs. My skin still cold from the plunge pool, I begin to shiver, and my soaked robe will only make me cooler if I wear it. Alex steps closer as if to throw an arm around my shoulder like he might have done years ago. I dodge and pull away. I don't think he would dare try anything here, but I don't feel safe. I hitch my towel tighter around me. By the time we reach the changerooms, I'm freezing.

'See you soon,' he says and I watch him head into the men's changeroom. The women's is empty. I take a moment to inhale deeply. At the rear, there's a sauna beside the showers. A minute or two in there is exactly what I need to bring my temperature back up again.

When I swing open the door, heat bellows out. Ahhh. I've always loved a good sauna. I pull the door shut and climb to the very top bench, lying myself out flat. The wood beneath me is warm to the touch, softening my muscles. Saunas are my happy place. The familiar smell of cedar is a pleasant memory of all the times I've sunk into this same enveloping heat and obtained a sliver of relief from the stress of work or home. The freeze inside me is already starting to thaw and I can contemplate what needs to happen next: retrieve my breast-feeding journal from Karla's house, find my own lawyer, then get Charlotte and myself out of that house and the hell out of that relationship.

I breathe the woody scent deep into my lungs. There will be a way to heal from all this, I know it. Today is only the very start.

Sweat is beginning to bead on my forehead as I hear a clunk at the door. I rise to sitting. Another clunk. Is someone trying to get in?

I climb down the benches to the floor and push at the door. It is stuck fast. What the hell?

I scan the doorframe for locks, but there's nothing, no slot for a key on this side. I push against the door, but it's fixed in place. My blood is pumping, not only from the sauna. Alex. I have no idea how he has managed to do this, but it can only be his work.

I lean my back on the wood, levering my weight against it, then begin to slam my body into the whole door. It is firmly stuck. I hammer it, kick it, scream for help as loudly as I can, then push my ear to the wood. Nothing. I sink down to the concrete floor, my hands pressing against the door.

The wan sauna light in the ceiling casts a faint glimmer across the tiny space. There's not even the smallest gap in the doorframe, not an inch of light penetrating from outside. There are no temperature controls in here either, no way to turn off the flow of heat. How could I have been so stupid? I press my forehead to the door.

The thick, humid air is causing my mind to fog as I run through options. Sweat dribbles down my temples, into my eyes. Think, Lauren, think. I've seen Alex use a credit card to open a locked hotel bathroom door once, years ago, but I don't have a credit card on me here. A bobby pin might come in handy, but I don't have one of those, either. What I do have – the flat tabs on the back of my bikini bra, clicked together. Is there a way of manoeuvring them to unlatch the catch mechanism that must be jammed shut?

With slippery fingers, I unhook and remove my bikini top, unconcerned about my nakedness. This is a race for survival, with no place for embarrassment. I attempt to flick one of the hard pieces of plastic into the gap between the door trim and frame, but the plastic is too thick, the gap too thin. I try higher up the door where there is more room, then run it down towards the lock in the jamb. It's still not thin enough. I will have to pry the wooden trim surrounding the door away from the frame to access the catch mechanism.

My breath is heaving as I use the plastic clip of my bathers like a chisel. The levering seems to be working, the wooden trim coming away, leaving a thin gap. As I give a final levering motion, the clip snaps in two in my fingers. *Fuuuck*.

I grab the other bikini clip. I must not break this last one. With shaking fingers, I stick it into the now-exposed gap between the door plate and the ball catch, jiggling it gently to try to release the catch.

It's getting harder to breathe, harder to stay upright. What I wouldn't give for a freezing plunge pool right now. I imagine myself there, a cool oasis in this desert of heat and it helps to slow my breathing, my thumping heart. I need to stay as calm as I can to get out of here.

Catch mechanism, bikini clasp. My fingers slip and I fumble, dropping the bikini top.

I rest for a moment on the concrete floor, trying to suck up any vestige of coolness into my skin before I rise and try again.

I can do hard things. I can do this.

I stick the clasp back through the thin hole, jiggling harder now. The ball catch pops with a sharp click and I can feel the mechanism give way as I push against the heavy door with the last of my strength. Nothing moves. The door is still stuck fast. Someone is on the other side, holding it closed. Alex has got me. I am never going to get free.

45

FOUR AND A HALF YEARS EARLIER

DISCHARGE SUMMARY

Lauren De Vale

2 August

Primary diagnosis

Postnatal anxiety

Progress

Although initial concern about postnatal psychosis was raised due to prominent anxiety related to breastfeeding issues and possible delusions about a next-door neighbour's behaviour prior to admission, there was no evidence of psychotic features during Lauren's inpatient stay. Lauren demonstrated significant improvement in mood and affect over the course of her admission, and noted improvement in both sleep and anxiety following the commencement of mirtazapine. Although Lauren declined participation in inpatient group activities, she reported that her enjoyment of interactions with Billy had significantly improved since being away from the stresses of the home environment.

Medications

Mirtazapine

Recommendations

Continue medication and regular psychotherapy with Dr Georgiou as planned.

Advised early psychiatric review with any further pregnancies.

46

When I come to, there is a crowd of people around me. One woman, identifying herself as a nurse, sits me up as she tries to pour cold water into my mouth. Another man drapes heavy, wet towels over my legs and torso.

'Get her outside, into the air,' I hear someone say and before I can utter a word, several people are hauling me to my feet and half-walking, half-carrying me outside, into the shade of the changeroom complex where they lower me to the ground.

'It's like that movie,' the same voice says in the background, 'where three people get trapped in a sauna. How the hell did she get herself out?'

'I moved the lockers.' Alex's voice, urgent, stern. 'I heard shouting. A block of lockers had fallen across the sauna door.'

My eyesight is still so fuzzy, I can't make out his expression. There will be time to dissect the sequence of events later.

Thank god that other people are around. I am protected. I am safe for now. At least, safe enough.

'I have a cold towel for you. That will help.' Alex places a hefty weight on my neck and back and although the coolness of the wet cloth seeps into me, the towel is pinning me down from behind, making it even harder to breathe.

'The ambulance is here,' someone says and before I know it, two ambulance officers are beside me, asking me questions, attaching leads and beeping monitors. I can hardly think, let alone speak. I mumble incoherently as a sharp prick needles the back of one hand and cold liquid suddenly seeps through my arm, ever so soothing.

'What's that?' I mumble.

'She's a doctor,' Alex offers, as if that makes any difference at this point.

'It's just saline,' one ambulance officer explains, 'to help cool you down.'

I close my eyes as they lift me onto the ambulance stretcher and cover my almost-naked body with a white sheet. My mind is starting to think more clearly. Alex is a pharmacist by training. I have plastic tubing heading straight into my vein, which will carry anything he injects directly to my heart.

'I'll come along,' Alex says as I'm wheeled towards the ambulance. I flick open my eyes. He is staring down at me with apparent care.

'She's more alert,' one ambulance officer says to the other as he loads me into the van, facing the back door. The walls are lined with shelves containing resuscitation equipment and drugs. I hear Alex climbing into the front seat of the ambulance.

At least there he doesn't have direct access to the medications – or my IV drip.

'Lucky escape,' the ambulance officer says as he seats himself beside me. 'Another few minutes might have been too much.'

'Lucky,' I repeat softly. The man appears friendly, trustworthy. He probably has a partner, possibly kids at home. In his job, he would have seen many incidents of family violence, would likely have completed training on how to handle this. But with Alex so close, how can I possibly convey the situation to him? And what's to say he would believe me anyhow? No – I need to stick to my original plan. Recover from this setback as swiftly as I can. Get Charlotte. And get the hell out of my house.

My backpack: the phones and signed forms confirming my choice of legal guardian for Charlotte. Shit.

'I left my bag back there.' My voice is husky, my vocal cords still rehydrating.

'Don't worry, darling,' Alex says. 'I have it here. They retrieved it for me before we left.'

How the hell did they know which locker was mine? And why, oh why, would they have given it to him?

'Can you pass it to me, please?'

'Later,' he says.

Control, as always.

I glance at the ambulance officer who must sense something in me. 'Pass it over, mate.'

I hear fumbling from the front seat.

'The whole bag, mate.'

There are good men out there, men who respect women, who don't try to control them, men who will stand up for what is right. Why the heck did I choose to marry someone so similar to my father?

The ambo beside me reaches into the front seat and passes over my bag. It's half-unzipped, so it's a relief when I grope inside and feel the sheaf of papers as well as both mobile phones at the bottom. A close call.

'What exactly happened?' The ambo's face is neutral, staring down at his iPad as he makes notes.

'A row of lockers must have fallen and blocked the sauna door,' Alex says from the front seat.

'I'd like to hear it from her,' the man says.

I scan my memory, trying to recall what happened between when the locking mechanism popped and when I passed out. There was a brief sensation of the door giving way outwards, as if someone had suddenly released their weight . . . but it *could* just as well have been Alex moving a set of fallen lockers. There's no way to prove his story is a lie.

'I don't know,' I say. 'It's all a blur.'

The ambo slowly nods his head. As he types a few words onto his screen, I reach into my backpack and retrieve my mobile from my bag. A text from an unknown number lights up: *Lauren! Karla from next door here. Magdala's unwell, so she's brought Charlotte here until you and Alex get back. Magdala said she'll be fine, she just wanted me to let you know.*

A photo of Charlotte smiling her cherubic smile. Thank god she's all right; and I am too. But now Magdala is unwell, which Alex had conveniently let slip to the lawyer – no doubt in a further bid to highlight everyone's impaired capacity but his own. A thought strikes me, but no – surely not his own mother . . . is he deliberately making her unwell too in order to secure

Charlotte's guardianship? And, what is he scheming next for me? My heart freezes.

'Your mum's not well,' I call through to Alex in the front seat. 'Karla's babysitting Charlotte until we get back.'

He spins around to face me. 'What the hell? Is Mum okay?'

'I don't know about your mum,' I say, 'but Charlotte looks fine.' I ponder whether I should ask Alex to go home and pick Charlotte up, but think again as I blink back tears. It seems she'll be safer for now with Karla than with him.

It's not long before we're pulling up at the hospital. As one of the paramedics wheels me through to a cubicle, Alex gets waylaid at reception providing registration details for me.

The ambulance officer draws the curtain around the space. 'Everything okay?' he asks, concern in his eyes.

'What do you mean?'

'Something feels a little off,' he says. 'You get a sense for it in this job.'

'If there were, what would happen?'

He stoops, fiddling with my drip. 'The hospital social worker could see you. Provide support. Make sure you and your baby are all right.'

Oh, crap. I've had enough conversations with Natalia to know how it could end up if the hospital social worker was to get involved. Child services, unannounced visits, children removed from the home if there's any concern about their safety. Besides, Alex is a master at charming people; I'm certain he'd have child services believing *I* was the problem. I might even be forced to leave the family home without Charlotte.

The ambo steps away from the gurney. 'Everything will be all right,' he says. 'You're going to be okay.'

Something in his demeanour, his tone, his reassuring words, settles me. He can see I'm frightened and knows not to push it.

A fresh-faced nurse with her hair tied back in a ponytail pushes the curtain aside and steps into the cubicle. As she listens to the ambo's handover, she takes my temperature with an ear probe.

'Almost normal now,' she says with a sigh of relief.

'I'd best be off. You take care,' the ambo says as he moves towards the curtain.

'Wait,' I say. 'Would you both mind witnessing a document for me?'

The nurse nods and the ambo steps forward. 'Where is it?' he says.

I indicate my backpack and he removes the wad of papers and inspects the front page.

'A will? Far out. Are you sure you're okay?'

I nod, tears now threatening to brim over. 'Could I borrow a pen?'

He and the nurse watch on as, with my head now clear, I manage to recall and inscribe Karla's full name neatly in pen alongside the eyeliner version on the final page. I sign my name with a shaky scrawl, and the two of them dutifully inscribe their details, followed by their signatures.

The ambo gives an encouraging smile as he steps back. 'I'm sorry for what you're going through. I hope you manage to have a tolerable holiday season. You are clearly a fighter, so stay strong and hang in there, okay?' he says, as he and the nurse depart.

I have no idea how he knew the exact words I needed to hear, but the sentiment bolsters me. My strength is returning as my core temperature is normalising. I am starting to feel like myself again. It has been a long time since I experienced the sense of someone having my back – longer still that I have been able to believe in, and back, myself.

Time to make my escape. I push my back against the thin hospital mattress, steeling myself for what is to come. I glance at the gap beneath the hospital curtains. No sign of Alex's shoes. There are no voices immediately outside my cubicle, only the occasional padding of footsteps, the beep of machines and the hum of distant conversation. For this one and only time, I thank god for understaffed emergency departments. The coast is clear.

I glance down at the back of my hand, where the IV has pitched my skin like a tent at its point of entry. In hospital, I am in more danger from Alex than anywhere. He could inject me with god knows what at any point and no one would be any the wiser.

By fiddling with the roller clamp on the IV, I'm able to bring the flow of fluid to a halt. Then I rip the cannula from my hand, pressing down hard with the heel of my other hand to stem any bleeding. I swing my legs over the edge of the trolley and ease myself to standing.

One thing at a time. I grab my bag from under the trolley, rifle through it and pull out my clothes. Blouse, underwear, bra, jeans. I slip them all on, grateful I won't have to make my exit in a hospital gown. I slide into my sandals and haul the backpack over my shoulder. My body is still lethargic from the heat. My legs give way a little and I clutch at the trolley beside me.

I take a tentative step, then another. I've got this.

Working my way along the wall, I reach the curtain and pull it slowly to one side. Over in the nurses station, staff are frantic as usual. I slip out from behind the curtain and head for the exit.

No one stops me. There is no sign of Alex.

I pass reception, adorned with masses of red and green Christmas paraphernalia, out towards the double doors that automatically open for me, then out into the smothering air, thick with December heat.

'Lauren!'

Alex. *Fuck.*

'Babe, what are you doing?'

How on earth am I going to explain this? 'They said I can go.'

'Really? Already? Did you see the doctor?'

'I'm stable enough to go home, they said. And it's chockers in there. Much sicker patients. They thought I'd be better off in my own bed.'

'Let me get the car then. You wait here.' He strides off in the direction of the car park.

A few spits of rain land on my forearms. I glance up at the sky. Flickers of late afternoon sun are filtering through the dark clouds – it appears another summer storm is about to break. I could flee, I know, but Alex would just hunt me down. He probably has trackers on my mobile, can follow my movements. At this point, I can't afford to be discarding that phone, with all the contacts and passwords it contains. But I need to let someone know what is going on. Once again, I will have to text myself.

Reaching into my backpack with shaky hands, I retrieve my new phone, then begin a message to my original number: *I got locked in a sauna today, and I nearly died. I'm just getting out of ED. I'm really scared.* I see Alex's car circling the car park. I text faster. *If anything happens to me, please, protect my baby from my husband.*

Alex pulls up next to me and winds down the window just as I manage to press send.

'Who are you texting?'

My brain swirls, desperate for an acceptable response. 'My aunt,' I say.

'Your aunt?'

'She just called me.' I avoid his eyes as I open the car door and slide into the front seat. Alex has always said he can tell when I'm lying; in his words I'm an 'open book'. Certainly not something I could accuse him of.

'I haven't heard you speak about your aunt for years,' Alex pipes up again as fat droplets of rain splatter against the windscreen. He flicks on the wipers. 'Why did she just call you out of the blue?'

He's right, I've hardly mentioned Aunty Sal in all our years together. It was an error to bring up her name just now. 'She reached out recently,' I explain, then all at once, I realise my mistake.

'You didn't mention it,' he says. 'What else aren't you telling me?'

'Nothing,' I respond, perhaps a little too quickly. 'It's Billy's anniversary. That's the reason she called.'

He grunts and pushes against the headrest of the driver's seat. 'You haven't asked after Mum.'

'Is she okay?' Heat rushes through me.

'She's quite drowsy. She might have mucked up her medication, she said. I told her I wanted to take her to ED, but she refused. She just wanted to sleep it off.'

Hmm – her drowsiness fits with Alex's MO. As hard as it is to fathom, my guess is he's been administering her with mirtazapine too. Still, Magdala is not my primary concern. 'Charlotte – is she okay?'

'She'll be fine. Karla seems to have it all under control.'

I nod in relief.

Alex finally turns into our driveway, where rain is slickening the bitumen.

'I'm sorry today didn't quite go as I'd planned,' he says with a grimace, then slides out of the car. 'I'll go check on Mum first, then I'll get Charlotte. You should rest. Let me know if there's anything you need.' He hurries up to the front door.

There is nothing I need from you, Alex.

47

Sunset is pink blossom-shaped clouds on the horizon, casting peach reflections in the puddles on our driveway. A little steadier on my feet now, I stumble out of the car. I hobble to the large eucalyptus tree in our front garden and rest my back against its damp trunk. Here, I'm hidden from view of the front of our house. Using my new mobile, I dial the number of the family violence service. They answer straight away.

My words come out in a jumble. 'I'm on my way to pick up my daughter. We're in danger. I don't know what my husband is capable of. I need some advice.'

'I hear you. Let's take it slowly,' the woman on the other end of the line says. 'I'm here to help.'

I detail the situation, my concerns.

She asks a few clarifying questions.

No, he doesn't have a gun. No, he doesn't use drugs or excessive alcohol. No, he hasn't threatened to kill me, our daughter or himself. No, he hasn't physically harmed Charlotte to my knowledge – apart from the bruise several days ago, which he blamed me for. No, he doesn't know I'm planning to leave.

I'm beginning to wonder if the woman taking my call believes the risk I am facing when she starts to speak. 'It's important you know that the time when a woman leaves her partner is when her safety is most at risk.'

It hits me then, the enormity of what I am about to do. Dangerous to leave. Dangerous to stay.

'Whatever your decision, you will be able to file for an AVO for yourself. But be aware, even if you have your daughter placed on the AVO, he may still be approved for contact with her down the track.'

'But how the hell can that happen if I truly believe he will hurt her?' I press the back of my head against the solid tree trunk.

'Child services will need to be involved,' she says.

Child services. Exactly what I had been dreading. Alex will disclose all the information about me, my hopes and fears, my mental health. Billy's death on my watch. I will come out looking like the dangerous one.

'I won't be able to keep her safe.' My voice cracks.

'You're doing your best,' the woman assures me. 'You may also wish to consider getting a second phone with a pre-paid SIM. There may have been apps installed on your mobile that can monitor GPS location, as well as tracking messages and webpage searches, even if the browsing history is deleted.'

This is what I had been concerned about. I mentally run through my recent outings, in particular whether I had taken my phone to Aunty Sal's place. With relief, I recall the battery had died. Alex will have no idea of her address.

A light comes on in Karla's front room.

'I'd better go.'

'I completely understand,' the woman says. 'Call us back when you can.'

I scurry up to Karla's front door. Cicadas whirr from the surrounding bushes, an eerie hum. Her outside light is on too, bathing the verandah in an orange glow. I knock at the door as quietly as I can.

No noise from inside.

I try again. And again.

No answer and no sign of movement through the frosted glass, even after I bang the door as hard as I dare, calling Karla's name.

I creep across the verandah to the front windows and peer into her loungeroom. Modern bookshelves lined with books. Leather couches. On the fireplace, several photographs.

No sign of Karla, or Charlotte. My heart pounds.

I peer closer at the photographs. Alongside that one with the tall handsome man in a hunting hat with his arm around a younger Karla is another baby photo, which had been hard to make out in the glare of sunlight on my first visit. Something about it catches my eye. It looks vaguely familiar, even from across the room. I squint through the glass, trying to make it out.

It's a baby in a bassinet. White plastic wicker, on four legs, eighties-style. I've definitely seen it before. Wait . . . The egg donor candidates were asked to include a baby photo in their profiles. I had admired the baby's eager eyes and goofy smile.

Oh, fuck. *This* is the photograph. Charlotte's egg donor. Please, oh please, tell me Karla is not Charlotte's biological mum.

48

EIGHTEEN YEARS EARLIER

MAN WHO PROVIDED PARTNER WITH STOLEN ABORTION PILLS WALKS FREE

A man who provided his partner with stolen abortion pills has escaped criminal conviction in Landover District Court today. Alex De Vale, 20, a pharmacy student at the time of the offence, stole the misoprostol from the pharmacy where he was completing a student placement.

His partner, Karla Walker, 19, knowingly consumed the medication. In the days following the ingestion of the stolen pills, Walker developed sepsis and was required to undergo a life-saving hysterectomy.

De Vale pleaded guilty to the theft of prescription medication as well as being unqualified to provide an abortion and received a six-month suspended sentence. Following the theft, he was expelled from his university studies and will face a hearing with the Australian Health Practitioner Regulation Agency (AHPRA) at a later date.

The Australian Pregnancy Advisory Service restated the importance of women having access to safe, legal abortions in order to prevent abortions endangering the health and wellbeing of women when performed by unqualified practitioners.

49

Someone holding a torch approaches, the light waving in jagged lines up Karla's driveway. I stumble, my back hitting the windowsill behind me.

'What the hell are you doing?'

It's Alex. The fury of deception, of betrayal, overtakes me. He had some hand in this, must have known Karla was Charlotte's biological mother.

'How *could* you?'

'What are you talking about? Why are you taking so long – where's Charlotte?'

I jab my finger at Karla's window. 'Her baby photograph. It's the same one in the pack for the donor we chose. The donor you *insisted* we choose. Remember?'

He glances between the window and me, then steps up onto the verandah and peers inside. When he leans back, I can see he is struggling to come up with an explanation.

We stand there, my husband and I, on our next-door neighbour's porch, twilight falling around us. So much I didn't know about what has been going on.

Alex lets out a long sigh. 'Karla had to have a hysterectomy years ago,' he says eventually. 'It wasn't her fault she couldn't have a baby.'

'Right.' My mind is running through all possible scenarios. 'You should have told me. Her fertility concerns weren't our problem.'

So, orchestrating our next-door neighbour to facilitate our baby-making *was* Alex's doing. I recall the certainty on his face that moment in the fertility specialist's office when he said the words *egg donor*. In retrospect, he must have already had Karla in mind. But why would he have felt responsible for taking care of a woman he barely knows? And why did he keep all this hidden from me?

Unless . . . 'Have you got feelings for Karla?'

His eyes flame red in the verandah lights. 'You're crazy.'

The front door swings open and Karla appears, her eyes narrowing as she catches sight of us both. She leans against the doorframe, almost melting into it, her lips widening into a smile.

'How nice to see you both,' she says. 'Charlotte's asleep. Let's not wake her just yet.'

No, no, this is not right. I need to get Charlotte out of here immediately.

'I should be able to resettle her as soon as we get home,' I say, my words falling out in a rush.

'Certainly,' she says. 'But first – your paperwork?' Karla holds out her hand.

Jesus – it was Karla pushing for this? My heart thumps in my chest as I realise the paperwork signing over Charlotte's legal guardianship to Karla in the event of my death is sitting in the bag on my shoulder.

'I already told you, Lauren is refusing to sign hers.' Alex's contempt is directed squarely at me.

'That's okay,' Karla says, her voice slick with charm. 'Yours should be adequate.'

'It's at home,' he says. 'Shall I grab it?'

'Yes, please,' she says. 'Bring me a coffee over too, babe?'

Babe?

'Of course,' he says. 'Back in a minute.'

As he turns and makes his way down the verandah stairs, my mind is racing. This woman has been sleeping with my husband. If it's these two who've been having the affair, that explains Alex's choice of egg donor. *Karla, not Elspeth.* Pressure is building in my skull as our porch lights flick on next door.

'How long have you two been fucking?' I snap. It's crude, but effective.

Karla's eyes widen.

'I've almost felt sorry for you, Lauren, watching you all this time. Fiction is nowhere near as strange as truth, I find. I worked so hard on that notebook, by the way. I do hope you found it pleasant reading.'

It hits me then: it was all a deception. The elaborate notes and timelines, the red herring of a woman in a blue Peugeot, designed to draw suspicion away from herself. I fell for it all. Now it makes sense why Karla allowed me to steal her notebook, and why she didn't rush round to get it. Blood thrums in my temples. How could I have been so naive?

'Look, can I please just grab Charlotte? I'll leave you alone. And I promise I won't get in the way of the two of you being together.'

Karla smiles sweetly. 'Maybe it's best if you leave Charlotte *here*,' she says.

Oh, fuck. This was her plan all along.

Charlotte.

She might not be my biological child, but despite what Karla seems to think, she is most definitely my daughter. Biology is not destiny. I have nurtured her, held her as she cried, soothed her to sleep, over and over again. She needs me. And I need her just as much.

My body aches as I contemplate a lifetime away from her. Mothers whose children were wrenched from them at birth, or later on. Mothers who lost children. Me. I've already had one child taken from me. It's not happening again. 'I'm taking Charlotte.' My voice falters as it echoes down the hall.

'Don't you understand,' she says, 'that as soon as I have Alex's signed paperwork, you won't have a choice?'

My body shudders. Alex nearly killed me just now. And I've stupidly, stupidly just signed paperwork that hands over care of Charlotte to Karla in the event of my death. The thought that he and Karla could become completely responsible for Charlotte's care is terrifying. I must destroy the paperwork – Alex's and my own – at all costs. But first, I must rescue my baby.

'I understand. Can I see her before I go? I want to say goodbye.'

There's a flicker in her gaze, the decision to placate me for tonight at least.

'Fine,' she says. 'Come inside. I'll bring Charlotte down. You can see she's all right. You can say goodbye.'

THE OTHER CHILD

With trepidation, I follow her into the house. She locks the front door behind us with a sharp click.

'Wait here,' she says, then heads down the hall and up the sharp flight of stairs at its end.

Karla has dumped her bag beside the front door. My eyes roam past it, desperately searching for anything that could help, but the stench rising from the bag snags my attention. I bend down, inspecting it. It has an odour of chlorine and sulphur, different from the smell of a regular pool, distinctive to that from hot springs.

My skin prickles. She was at the springs. *She* trapped me in the sauna. Karla was trying to kill me. So she could take Charlotte.

Karla and Alex are in cahoots. They are both trying to kill me. And now she has my baby.

I peer down the hallway. There's no sign of Karla, no sound of her footsteps or of Charlotte's cry. I must take this opportunity, before she returns with my baby, to destroy my signed will. I reach into my backpack and tug out the raft of papers.

At that moment, Karla's voice calls from the top of the stairs. 'I'll be a bit longer than I thought. Lauren, why don't you come back later on to say goodbye?'

Like fuck I will. There is no way I'm leaving this house without my baby, no matter what.

Charlotte's wail filters down the stairs. What the hell is going on up there? Could Karla be trying to harm her too?

I toss the papers back in my backpack and shove it under Karla's bag by the front door to conceal it for now. Then I sprint down the hall and take the stairs two at a time. Reaching the top in record pace, I rush to the door Charlotte's cry came from. I swivel the handle. Locked. Oh, fuck.

From downstairs, I hear the click of a key in the lock. Alex – he must have a key to Karla's house. Quickly, I bend down and peer through the keyhole of the door before me. I catch a glimpse of Karla, seated in a recliner, cradling Charlotte against the bare skin of her chest. My body seizes up. Karla has been breastfeeding my baby. The horror of seeing my baby being held to another woman's breast is overwhelming. But more more to the point, Karla doesn't have kids so how could this be happening? It comes to me in a rush: galactagogues – medications that can induce and stimulate lactation, even in someone who has never given birth. I bend down again, trying to stop myself from crying out in fury. Behind Karla, a large computer monitor with CCTV images of various rooms of our house. Oh. My. God. It was Karla watching me. After Billy. With Charlotte. This whole time, she has been plotting to take her away from me.

Alex is striding up the stairs. He reaches the top of the staircase in no time at all, a lidded coffee cup in one hand, a sheaf of paperwork in the other. His tall frame looms over me as he shakes the papers in my face.

'If you'd just signed the forms like I suggested,' he says, 'all this could have been avoided.'

'You mean, you could have killed me at the pools,' I say, 'rather than having to wait for me to sign the papers first?'

'*Killed* you?' Alex recoils, frowning. 'What the hell are you on about? For fuck's sake, I saved your life today.'

My brain tries to make sense of his apparent sincerity. Surely he has been plotting to kill me – the will, the mirtazapine, his veiled threats . . . 'The papers . . . you wanted me to hand over guardianship of Charlotte to Karla.'

He gives me a contemptuous look. 'It's about custody, Lauren. About who is best placed to look after Charlotte. Karla is her biological mother. She *should* have the legal right to take care of Charlotte if we weren't able to. No one is talking about *killing* anyone.' He raises his eyes to the ceiling as he shakes his head.

Alex is right; the paperwork would only take effect if something happened to both him and me. After all, without both of us appointing Karla as Charlotte's legal guardian, Magdala would be the first point of call. Wait . . .

'Did you drug your mother?'

He stares. 'Don't be ridiculous. As if I would ever try to hurt Mum.'

My brain scans for the solution. If Magdala and I were both disposed of, and Karla was in possession of Alex's signed paperwork . . . The pieces of the puzzle rapidly shift into clear alignment in my mind.

'Do you want your mum to live?'

The question disarms him enough that he pauses and glares at me. 'What the hell are you on about?'

'You'd better call an ambulance straight away. Karla has drugged her. She doesn't want your mum to have custody of Charlotte.'

'You're crazy,' he says. There's a flicker in the corner of one of his eyes, a sign of his anger. 'As if Karla would ever hurt *anyone*.'

Does he *really* have no idea what Karla is capable of? It appears she has manipulated him as skilfully as he has me. I have to speak the words; I can see no other way out of this. 'Karla – she has played you, Alex. She tried to kill me, and I'm sure she'll try again. Now she's trying to kill your mother. Once you give her those forms, what's to stop her from killing you next?'

'Shut up, shut up, shut up!' I see a fist before me as a shot of white light floods my vision and everything goes black.

There's a faint shimmering of light through my heavy eyelids.

'This wasn't in my plan. But I'm sure I can make it work.' From where I lie sprawled out on the landing, I hear Karla's muffled voice through the doorway of the nursery.

I can't summon the willpower to open my eyes. My limbs are immobile. I lie still, trying to make sense of the words filtering into my muggy brain.

'What are we going to do now?' Alex, agitated.

'First, give me your documents,' Karla says, her voice stern. 'And can you drink the coffee, please? I don't want it getting cold.'

I hear him take a few heavy gulps of liquid. 'What do the papers matter? I don't get your fixation on them.'

'You haven't shown up for me,' she says. 'I've had to take everything into my own hands. You told me you were writing letters, making phone calls. But nothing has changed. Your wife isn't certified. She's not in a fucking institution. She's living with my daughter. I need to make sure I have custody of my child. And I sure as hell don't trust you to do that.'

Alex grunts. 'How can you not trust me? I've done *every-thing* you asked.' I can identify the escalating rage in Alex's voice. 'I convinced my wife to use your eggs so we could make a baby together. I let you pick our baby's name. I gave Lauren the fucking Peking duck just like you insisted, even though you wouldn't tell me why. I've been lacing the milk for her coffee with Mum's cabergoline. I even got Mum to try and convince her to stop breastfeeding. I cut you a key to the house. I quit work to stay at home so we could spend more time together. You've been able to see Charlotte almost any time you liked. And because the plan to drive my pitiful wife crazy isn't moving exactly at your desired speed, I spent today trying to get her to sign the papers you insisted on. All of this, for *you*. Everything I do is to try and make you happy. What *else* do you want from me?'

Our baby? *Pitiful wife?* My head throbs as I lie as still as I can, trying to take it all in.

'Jesus, you're a moron.' Her voice is laced with venom. 'I just want your signed papers. I don't want anything else from you. Charlotte and I will be fine. I don't need you anymore.'

'What the *fuck*?' Alex gives a guttural growl. 'Are you *actually* threatening to *leave* me?'

'Don't be smart.' She sounds incensed. 'I know about you and Elspeth.'

Alex snorts. 'What the hell are you talking about? Jesus, Karla. Elspeth and I are friends.'

'Cut the crap. I *heard* you. I *heard* your conversations with Elspeth.'

'You *what*?'

'I had listening devices. Cameras.'

'What the fuck? You've been *spying* on me?'

'I've been watching my baby.'

'Is that what those screens behind you are for? Jesus.' He snorts with revulsion. '*Your* baby. I'm starting to get the feeling all you care about is Charlotte.' He grunts. 'And to think, I thought you wanted *me*.'

'Don't fuck around,' Karla says. 'I can see where things are going. Your long, intimate phone chats with Elspeth. All your pathetic requests for her advice about your worries with Lauren. And then her visit the other day . . . I know what you're up to. It's exactly how you started things with me.'

Her heels click over the floorboards, towards the cot. I stiffen, trying to hold my breath as I attempt to take it all in. The details are immaterial, I realise; the only thing that matters right now is Charlotte's wellbeing.

'You don't get it,' Alex says. 'I have been working on our plan.'

I hear a huff, then the sound of Karla placing Charlotte atop the cot mattress. Thank god my baby is safe, at least.

'That's too bad, Alex. Because I'm sick of waiting. I've been waiting long enough. I didn't manage to get rid of your bitch of a wife today. But don't worry. You've actually been more help than you thought. I have my own plan now. I just need those, thank you.' There's the rustling of papers, then silence.

'Hey.' Then, very slowly: 'What the hell are you saying? What do you mean about getting rid of Lauren? Are you trying to tell me you were at the spa complex?'

She lets out an exasperated groan. 'How else could I guarantee I'd get custody of Charlotte?'

'You tried to *kill* Lauren? Holy shit, Karla. Did you put the lockers over the sauna door?' I hear the tap of her heels on the floorboards again. 'Fuck, Karla. I thought the plan was just to frighten her into signing the papers. I had that all in hand.' There's a hint of grogginess in his voice.

My breath softens a little in my chest as I realise Alex's intention for me was marginally less malevolent than I had suspected. He hadn't planned or intended to kill me; amid all his abusive, manipulative behaviour, I suppose that's a sliver to be grateful for. As for Karla . . . my pulse beats fast and heavy in my throat.

'What choice did I have?' Her voice is thick with hatred. 'You clearly weren't able to get your wife out of the picture. I had to damn well do the job myself.'

'What – *kill* her?' His words are less clear, less sharp than they were just a few minutes earlier.

'You're not the only one who can dish out medication, you know.'

I open my eyes a fraction, trying to take in my surroundings. Through the doorway, inside the room, I catch sight of Karla holding a box of medication aloft. It's my mirtazapine. I only just stop myself from taking an audible breath.

'But . . .' Alex, for once, is speechless. Then a sharp intake of air. 'You haven't drugged my mother, have you?' His words are now slurring heavily. 'And . . . what have you done to *me*?' Every time he opens his mouth, it's harder to make out what he's trying to say.

For the first time since I blacked out, I open my eyes wide. From my position on the landing, I see Karla through the open nursery door. She is standing in front of Alex, her smile twisted with contempt and scorn.

He moves towards her, but stumbles to one side and catches himself on the wall.

'Oh, Alex,' she says. 'To think I used to believe you when you said you were going to leave your wife. You couldn't even convince her to sign the paperwork,' she sneers. 'You weak, useless man.'

Alex teeters against the wall, then slides down into a slump on the floor beside the cot with a faint groan.

I press my eyes shut and lie as still as I can, listening hard. I hear a few thumps, then Karla breathing heavily. When I open my eyes again, she has Alex by his legs, dragging him slowly over the floorboards towards a door at the side of the room from where I can hear the sound of water running.

'Five fucking years . . . what a fucking waste,' she says with laboured breath as she heads out of my line of sight, Alex in tow.

Gingerly, I ease myself off the floor of the landing and, holding onto the banister, haul myself to standing. My head feels like it's exploding. It's hard to think enough to concoct a plan, but I can hold onto the only thing that matters – I need to get Charlotte the hell out of here.

I take tentative steps into the appointed nursery. My baby is in the cot on the other side of the room. I slowly continue to pick my way across the boards towards her when all at once there's a soft gasp, then a heavy splash from the room next door – presumably an ensuite. The sound of running water ceases. An image of a sedated Alex being heaved into a bath flickers in my mind.

My guts twist. Part of me wants to rush in and confront Karla, stop whatever evil she is enacting. No matter how horrific Alex has been to me, he is still Charlotte's father, still my husband. He doesn't deserve to die. But in this moment I can – I *must* – trust my intuition: in my current weakened state, I simply don't have the strength to fight Karla off, and to save Alex.

I move as fast as I can towards Charlotte until I am finally by her side. She gives me a wide smile as I reach into the cot and raise her to my chest. I can get her away from here, get the two of us to safety; it's the only thing that matters now. I can't stop shaking as I begin to step back across the nursery as silently as I can.

I'm almost at the door when a floorboard creaks beneath my foot.

Oh, shit.

Karla emerges from the ensuite with a tight smile on her face.

Alex subjected me to many horrific things: contaminating my food with cabergoline so I wouldn't be able to breastfeed, criticising and gaslighting me into believing I was an unfit parent for the duration of our relationship, seemingly constant affairs. But Karla – she has been the mastermind behind all this. Alex has merely been her tool – one she is disposing of now he's no longer of use.

I slowly back out of the room, as fast as I dare. Karla strides across the room, advancing on me as I reach the landing at the top of the stairs.

In my most placid voice, I speak up. 'If you just let Charlotte and me walk out of here, I'll say everything was my fault. I promise I'll tell the police I killed Alex.'

She scoffs. 'You idiot. That's my plan anyway. I have your diary. It's all the proof I need of how dangerous you are.'

My head pounds. 'My diary?' God, I too played right into her sinister plans.

'How else did you think I was going to get away with this? I'll have to add in one more sentence about your fuckwit of a husband hitting you. Otherwise, it's all ready to go: murder–suicide. A nice bedtime story for Charlotte as she gets older, the story of what her supposed mother did to the rest of her family.'

I clutch Charlotte tight against my chest. 'We can discuss this. Let's talk about options.' I press my back against the banister.

'I'm not negotiating. Give her to me. *Right now*. You wouldn't want anything to happen to her too, would you?'

'Please,' I say, even as I am starting to see that handing over Charlotte may be the only way to keep her safe. As my mind wrestles with the inevitable, I hug my precious baby in close, nuzzling my lips into her fuzzy scalp, smelling her nectarine skin. 'I love you, my baby,' I whisper.

Karla's voice snaps. 'Now. Give. Her. To. Me.'

Raising one arm in a gesture of submission, I glance back towards the room Karla turned into a nursery for *my* baby, where she breastfed Charlotte, likely even bruised her, where she spied on me, enacted her plan to make me look like an unfit mother, all in a malignant attempt to steal Charlotte away. Yes, I could sacrifice my life to ensure Charlotte lives. But Karla will never be the mother Charlotte needs, the mother Charlotte deserves. Charlotte needs a mother who loves her. Karla cannot be allowed to take my daughter away from me – her mum. Charlotte needs *me*.

As I stand there on the landing in semi-shock, a plan begins to solidify in my mind – the only way I can see to escape all this, the only way to truly keep Charlotte safe.

'I haven't completed the paperwork. It's been witnessed, but the guardian is still blank. When Alex and I are dead, it'll be easier for you if both our wills appoint you as Charlotte's legal guardian.'

Karla looks me up and down, her brain ticking over. 'Where's your paperwork?'

'In my bag by the front door. But you'll have to be quick. Alex called emergency services for his mum. You'd better make sure I sign over Charlotte's care before they come here looking for him.'

She turns with a dismissive shake of her head, 'You never were a good mother.' And as she spins away from me to rush to the bottom of the stairs, a strength rises from within me – my own power fuelled by the strength of all the women like me: my mother and all the mothers who endured more than they should have; the unappreciated women taught to undervalue their strength, courage and power; the abused; the dead. And in that moment, I finally come to trust myself – my intuition – and that I *do* know *exactly* what is fair, just and right.

I channel all my power into my palm and thrust it into the left side of Karla's back, pressing my other hand into Charlotte's small body to hold her fast. There is a moment, a split second, when Karla is unbalanced, when I see her arms flail in front of her and I don't know if it will happen ... Then her body tilts, she leans into the slope of the stairs and plummets downwards, the side of her head smacking into the edge of a stair halfway down with a sharp crack. Her limp body tumbles to the tiled floor at the bottom.

She is still, finally. There is no breath apparent in her chest, no movement of her nostrils, or of her lips.

I encircle Charlotte in my arms, raise her to my lips, bring her in close and kiss her forehead, letting all the love from my heart infuse her tiny body.

'We're safe now,' I whisper to her, and finally, in the softening of my muscles, the slackening of my face, I can truly hear – and believe – my own words.

50

FOUR YEARS EARLIER

Karla's diary

The glint of light off the water was stronger than I had expected – I wished I'd thought to bring sunglasses. There was a fair bit of thrashing, and I started getting concerned there might be too much water splattering on the poolside tiles. Then I realised the sun was hot enough to dry off any splash marks fast enough. There was a fair bit of gulping, a few gasps. If I couldn't have Alex's baby, then neither could she. As the ripples on the pool surface died down, sparkling sunlight reflecting off the glazed flowerpot beside the pool gate made me squint, a fortunate reminder to drag it into place once I was done.

51

ONE YEAR LATER

It's cool for early spring. Light grey clouds tip the sky down to the horizon while daffodils, flattened after last night's rain, line the path. The cemetery is quiet. I scuff the soles of my shoes on the concrete pavers as if trying to slow myself down.

Charlotte stirs in the carrier on my chest. I smooth her hair, whisper gentle words to her, catching a faint waft of cinnamon – I've used Billy's soap – as I kiss her forehead.

'She's doing well.' It's Natalia, walking alongside me. 'I can see how happy she is.'

A simple statement, but from Natalia, it means a lot.

I lock my elbow with hers. 'I'm glad you're here.'

'Wouldn't miss it for the world.' She gives a kind smile and I am reminded how fortunate I am to have someone like Natalia on my side. As soon as I told her everything, she began to berate herself.

'I *knew* there was something off when Alex was saying all those things about you. How could I have been so bloody gullible? It's like, when you've been immersed in it yourself, the narrative is so believable that you just take it on face value. I was obsessed with the idea that I'd got it wrong last time – at least, that's what he was telling me. I couldn't bear the idea of anything happening to Charlotte, particularly not given what you'd had to go through with Billy. God, I'm so, so sorry. I should have believed you.'

'You tried to support me.' She had thought she was doing the right thing. In a way, it's a relief to know that Alex was convincing enough to fool someone as experienced in coercive control as Natalia. With the stress of her forthcoming coroner's case, she'd been particularly vulnerable to his manipulation. Although both of us have now emerged from our respective challenges relatively unscathed, back then neither of us had stood a chance.

Elspeth apologised also. Alex had been ringing her daily, she told me, spouting thinly veiled criticisms of me in long-winded monologues. It was hard for her to think, she said, and he had been so convincing, so seemingly concerned for my wellbeing that she had naively believed his words, had assumed she would be helping me by speaking up at work. He had invited her round for coffee several times, had attempted to befriend her, even as she had steadfastly declined his repeated proposals to catch up in person, apart from the one day she had visited our house – the day Karla had first accosted me as I returned home from work. Elspeth hadn't realised Alex was manipulating her and using her in his plot to cast me as an unfit mother. When she found out the full story, she was horrified. I forgave her; I, of all people, knew how convincing he could be.

Leaves flutter at my ankles as we trek further down the path, to a far corner of the cemetery. I pull my coat tighter to keep out the wind.

'It'll never go away,' I say.

'No.' Natalia's face is grim. 'But maybe it will start to get easier in time.'

We're here now, under the small tree casting shade on Billy's gravestone. There's a photo – my favourite one of him; Alex had let me choose that, at least. Billy, his face lit up with his infectious grin, meeting my eyes with love. I know now that although I hadn't been able to feel a bond with him for the longest time, my deep love for him was always there inside me – and I trust he felt it too.

'Charlotte, it's your brother,' I say, lifting her from the carrier and cradling her in the nook of one elbow, so she can face his image. I wish more than anything that they had had the opportunity to know each other, to play together. But she *will* know him still – I'll make sure of that.

I place the small bouquet of buttercups at the base of Billy's gravestone. His favourite flower. I had held it under his chin many times, telling him he liked butter because of the yellow reflection on his skin. A memory from my childhood, my mother doing the same to me.

She is here, my mum. She might not have a gravestone, but she is with me in my own mothering, just as she was with me in those final moments with Karla, gifting me the strength I needed to fight back.

'They're looking into Mum's death,' I say. 'They'll be using ground-penetrating radar to examine the block of land my parents had up in the highlands, to try to find her.' Even as

I say it, I am aware how unlikely it is that her body will ever be recovered.

'Hello, my dears! How are you?'

It's Aunty Sal, rugged up in woollens, bearing a large bouquet of daffodils. She hugs me with the same ferocity I remember from childhood, almost winding me with her embrace.

'I was just telling Natalia about the police investigation for Mum.'

'Thank goodness. Finally.'

I can see regret on Sal's face as she places the daffodils on Billy's grave. 'If only she could be here,' she says. 'But in lieu of your mum, I suppose we can be at least a little thankful for Magdala.'

'Thank god for Magdala, indeed.' Natalia's face is solemn as she regards Billy's gravestone.

It was Magdala who had called the police. Despite her drowsy state, she had been watching the scene unfold in Karla's faux nursery via the concealed baby monitor I had alerted her to several days earlier, and which she had hidden in some sort of misguided attempt to protect her son. She hadn't been aware that Alex and Karla had been using it to communicate – Karla in her house breastfeeding Charlotte, Alex in his study while I was at work.

At the inquests into Karla's and Alex's deaths, Magdala had testified about what she had 'witnessed' on the video monitor that evening: that Karla was an obsessed stalker who had murdered Alex. That she had then heard Karla trip and fall down the stairs. She didn't mention any of the truth about Alex, including her son's threats against me.

I was shocked to read her police statement, where she painted me as mentally unwell, presumably in an attempt to gain custody of her only remaining grandchild. Even as I was furious she was so willing to conceal the truth in order to get what she wanted, I understood. Charlotte was all she had left of her precious son – I got it.

I saw Magdala outside the coroner's court, her skirt pushed tight against her knees by the wind, her face set in a frown. She knew I knew the truth, what I could reveal about her son, destroying his reputation.

But she didn't know the whole truth of what had happened that night on the stairs. Neither did the police. Thank god Magdala had access to only the one camera, its vision limited to Karla's nursery.

She fell, I said as the police and ambos entered. *I had just come to after being knocked out. Karla was standing at the top of the stairs and she tripped as she ran down.*

The police weren't convinced until they interviewed Magdala. Whatever she said must have been enough to corroborate my story. And then there was the evidence Karla herself had left behind. Pages and pages of notes detailing her every plan. After poring through them and finding details of how she'd killed Billy and planned to seize custody of Charlotte, then finding Billy's dinosaur bathers and the lock of his hair that she'd stolen, which did indeed contain traces of her DNA just as she'd worried about, the police discussed the possibility of opening another inquest into Billy's death. I declined, citing fatigue. It was enough to know I had done nothing wrong. It finally allowed me to release any belief that I had contributed, even in some small way, to Billy's death.

Karla had been responsible for lacing my coffee milk with mirtazapine on the morning she killed Billy. She had planned everything in meticulous detail, for years. She had played Alex as well as she had played me, mixing mirtazapine into our coffee machine water in order to drug us both and Magdala on that final day. Her well-timed comments about Charlotte crying and her maroon notebook filled with red herrings had diverted my suspicion away from her and made me question Alex's trustworthiness. Though I'd called him out on his connection with Elspeth, just as Karla had planned, by then she was already fed up with waiting for Alex to leave our marriage. Her desperation led her to orchestrate a speedier, more concrete way to have Charlotte all to herself: legal guardianship – with me, Magdala and Alex dead. No matter how much she had once cared for Alex, Charlotte had become her end game.

'Do you ever worry how Charlotte will turn out?' Natalia asked me some months back. It was only then that I contemplated the possible impact of Karla's and Alex's genetics on her. How could I possibly tell my daughter what her biological parents had done, let alone my role in the whole affair? One day I will, when she's old enough to understand – honesty and transparency are at the core of my values. I trust in my connection with her, believe I have the courage and discernment to know when and how much to tell her when the time is right.

I give Charlotte another squeeze, inhaling her delicious cinnamon scent. I'll never tire of that smell – both my babies rolled into one.

'He could be such a little rascal,' Natalia says, pointing at the photo of Billy on his headstone. 'So cheeky. So much fun.'

'I wish I'd met him.' Aunty Sal smiles.

'I miss him,' I say simply.

My grief from Billy's death is deep. It can still wipe me off my feet at times. But the grief sits in my heart alongside overwhelming love. As every part of me longs to hold him in my arms again and kiss his sweet face, I often wonder how his life might have turned out had he been allowed the opportunity to grow up and experience the love my over-protective walls had kept me from giving him for too long. Thank goodness I am finally learning how to love every part of myself and give this love to Charlotte, exactly as she deserves. Exactly as I deserve. It was what my mother had attempted to provide. It wasn't fair that her life was taken, nor that she was taken from me. But I know that while she was with me, she did her very best.

'I'm sorry you didn't get to meet your grandma,' I whisper to Charlotte, 'but I'm going to keep searching for her.'

Charlotte gives a soft murmur and I hug her, feeling her body relax against my chest. 'Everything is going to be all right,' I say, and as the warmth of her body radiates into mine, I am reminded of a simple and pure truth: I can trust in myself. I can trust in love.

Acknowledgements

This book would not be possible without the help of so many people to whom I am deeply grateful.

Cathy Corbett, Adam Fry, Amanda Furber, Yolanda Sztarr, Jim Trauer, and Mum – your honest and thoughtful insights, suggestions and feedback have been profoundly helpful. I deeply appreciate the time, effort and care you so generously gave. Enormous thanks.

Alice Savona – your regular encouragement and creative enthusiasm have meant so much. Thank you.

Helen Koehne – thank you for being there for me on the hardest day, and for your kind, level-headed advice.

Kent Mallinson and Jeta Chan – sincere thanks for your plot-point expertise.

Christine Nagel – your careful and insightful editing is truly appreciated. Thank you for your precision and care.

Julian – thank you for the care and effort you've invested throughout this journey. I am deeply grateful for your support.

Milly and Seba – thank you for your patience with my writing over all the years, and for your perfect plot suggestions. I still don't know where two twelve-year-olds came up with that twist – but I loved it!

Grace Heifetz – your belief in me from the very beginning, your boundless optimism and your steadfast support have meant so much. I am eternally indebted to you.

Beverley Cousins and Charle Malycon – thank you for your patience, wisdom and thoughtful guidance through every stage of the novel. Your support has been indispensable. I cannot thank you both enough.